*To my grandchildren, Ethan, Ben and Amber.*
*May they always be happy and never know poverty.*
*Also, to all the women of Wednesbury, past and present, who will*
*always welcome you with a cup of tea!*

# 1

Dora Parsons screwed her eyes shut tightly at the pain from the slapping on the backs of her legs. She would not cry; she would not give her grandmother the pleasure of seeing her tears.

'You stupid little bugger! Do you know how much that milk costs? And you spill it all over the place!'

Stifling the sobs, ten-year-old Dora breathed a sigh of relief as the blows finally ceased and she was swung round to face the woman who had delivered them. Clamping her teeth together, she glared her defiance – there would be time for tears later when she was alone.

'Clean it up!' Edith Pitt snarled, jabbing a finger in the direction of the spillage.

'I'll tell Mum when she gets back from the market,' Dora mumbled and instantly knew it was a mistake.

Edith grabbed hold of Dora's blonde hair and pulled her head back. Looking into the girl's blue-green eyes, she growled, 'You tell her what you like but remember – this is my house and you both live here because I allow it!' Throwing Dora away from her, she pointed again to the spilled milk on the table.

Dora went to the kitchen to fetch a cloth to mop up the mess. Her grandmother was right; if she chose to, she could evict Dora and her mother. Then they would be homeless and penniless. Dora couldn't risk that, even at only ten years old she knew she would carry the guilt for the rest of her life. Hurt and anger threatened to overwhelm her, but she bit back her feelings.

'Wash that cloth well, otherwise it will stink the place out!' Edith snapped as Dora cleaned up the spill and retrieved the tray.

Dora nodded and did as she was bid. Back in the kitchen, she scrubbed the material in the sink and went out of the back door to hang it on the washing line in the garden. Looking around her, she knew she was lucky to live in a big house like this, when so many others were caught in the stranglehold of poverty. The residence stood in its own gardens at Spring Head, a well-to-do area of Wednesbury in the Black Country. It was away from the grime of the town centre, where the buildings were covered in fine black dust carried on the wind from the coal mines. Smoke from household and factory chimneys and forges hung in a grey pall over the people and their homes.

Dora turned her gaze to the house with its six bedrooms, indoor bathroom, kitchen, scullery, hallway, sitting room, parlour, music room and study. There were servants' quarters up the back stairs too, but these lay empty as Edith refused to spend money on hiring a cook or maid. Why would she when her daughter, Mary, did all the cooking and cleaning?

Dora wasn't allowed in any of these rooms, having been told they weren't for little girls to play in. The sitting room caught the sun in the mornings and her grandmother had a table in front of the window, her armchair placed next to it. She liked to look out and ensure no one was sneaking up the drive onto her property.

With a snort, Dora went indoors to await her mum's return, hoping to steer clear of her bad-tempered grandmother. She had been trying to help by fetching the milk jug from the cold slab, and as she'd placed it on the table she had tilted it, causing drops to plop onto the surface. It was enough to send Edith into one of her rages, the ones she reserved for Dora when Mary was out.

As she walked quietly up the back stairs, Dora thought her grandmother was a spiteful old woman.

Through another door and up a few more steps, she came to the attic. She looked through the small round window onto the driveway, her eyes searching for sight of her mother.

Dora was so very lonely. She had no friends of her own age to play with, and because she didn't go to school she would never find any playmates. Edith Pitt held the purse strings and would not pay the fees for Dora to attend. But there was more to it than that. Dora felt as though there was a part of her missing. She couldn't put her finger on it, but she didn't feel quite whole.

With a sigh, Dora turned away and climbed onto a dusty old rocking horse. She found some comfort as she rocked the dappled horse back and forth, stroking its long pale mane.

After a while, she got down and sat on the well-worn carpet with an atlas on her lap. She studied the maps intently, trying to imagine what the other countries of the world were like.

Presently, she put the book aside and moved to a large chest and lifted the lid. She pulled out a black organza dress, then held it up to look at it before she slipped it on. It swamped her and smelled musty, but she grabbed its hem and twirled around. Humming a little tune to herself, Dora imagined herself to be at a ball as she danced a few steps in the cramped space. Delving into the chest again, she withdrew a straw hat covered with faded silk roses. Blowing away the dust, she plonked it on her head with a smile before looking in the box again. Taking out old newspapers, she scanned them quickly, then put them to one side to read properly at another time.

Dora had been in the attic before but there were lots of boxes to explore, and this one was new to her.

Dora found baby clothes wrapped in tissue paper, a box of costume jewellery and a pile of books. After a while, Dora ensured each item removed was replaced carefully, including all of the garments, and Dora left the attic as she had found it.

Downstairs once more, she heard her grandmother call out to her.

'Dora! Put the kettle to boil and make some more tea. Dora, do you hear me?'

'Yes, Gran,' Dora replied. Going to the kitchen, she set the kettle on the range and arranged a tea tray, being extra careful with the milk this time.

'Bring me some biscuits as well!' Edith yelled.

Carrying the tray of freshly-made tea and a plate of homemade biscuits to the sitting room, Dora placed it on the table next to Edith. She looked on longingly as Edith snatched up a confection and shoved it into her mouth greedily.

'Pour the tea!'

Dora did so, carefully, still hoping to be offered a sweet treat but knowing it would not happen.

'What have you been up to?'

'Nothing,' Dora answered quietly.

Edith harrumphed, her grey-green eyes narrowing as she glared at her granddaughter. 'Nothing usually means something,' she said sharply.

'I haven't done anything wrong,' Dora replied.

Edith was out of her chair in a flash and landed a slap on Dora's cheek. 'Don't you back-chat me, my girl!'

Returning to her seat, Edith picked up her cup and saucer, her eyes burning into the girl in front of her.

Dora's hand went to her stinging face, anger and hatred making her tremble.

Edith smiled nastily, delighting in thinking that the child shook with fear. 'You're getting too big for your boots, young lady, and I won't have it. Do you hear? Not in my house, so you mark my words.'

Dora nodded, not trusting herself to answer for fear of incurring Edith's wrath once more.

'Get out of my sight, you foul little wretch!'

Dora fled the room, running out into the garden where the sun shone down fiercely. She walked to the gate and waited for her mother to come home, finally allowing her tears to fall.

It was an hour later when she at last saw her mum walking towards her, laden down with bags. Dora ran to help carry the shopping back to the house.

'Hello, sweetheart, have you been waiting for me?'

'Yes, I thought you'd never come,' Dora answered.

'Have you been good for your gran?'

'Yes, I made her some tea.'

'Good girl, that's just what I could do with. My feet are killing me.'

'You should rest more, Mum,' Dora said as they entered the kitchen.

Mary Parsons smiled down at her young daughter, then gave her a wink. 'There's something for you in that bag.'

Dora excitedly searched and found a paper cone filled with sweets from Teddy Gray's shop.

'Thanks, Mum!' Dora hugged her mother before popping a boiled sweet into her mouth.

'Don't tell your gran – remember she pays for everything and she would think it wasteful. Go and hide them in your room.'

Dora nodded and skipped away.

Mary watched her go, feeling sad that they had to conspire for the girl to enjoy a little treat.

'Is that you, our Mary?'

Edith's voice carried from the sitting room and Mary sighed. 'Yes, Mum.'

'Good. I could do with a cup of tea. I haven't had one since you went out,' Edith lied. Whilst Dora had been waiting at the gate, Edith had tidied away all evidence of the refreshments her granddaughter had provided.

'I'll get the kettle on, then put the shopping away,' Mary returned, knowing full well the old woman was lying.

Mary knew exactly what had turned her mother bitter, and why she could be so nasty at times, but what she didn't know was whether Edith even realised she was doing it. Mary hated that Dora bore the brunt of it at times, but there was little she could do to prevent it. They were living in Edith's house, the place where Mary had grown up, and the home she loved. Edith held the purse strings, which kept Mary and Dora tied to her.

They could, of course, pack up their few belongings and leave – but where would they go? Mary had no money of her own; she had no training to help her find work and she had Dora to think of. No, for the foreseeable future they were trapped.

Mary took the tea tray in to her mother.

'Thank God! I'm dying of thirst here!' Edith said as she shuffled forward in her seat to pour the tea.

'Dora said she made you a drink earlier,' Mary said.

'She's a liar,' Edith spat. 'You need to curb that girl's bad behaviour now before it gets out of hand.'

Mary took up the pot and poured herself a drink, Edith having only seen to her own.

'Dora's a good girl, Mum,' Mary said.

'She lies through her back teeth!' Edith snapped.

'She may exaggerate a little sometimes...' Mary said, trying her best to keep the peace.

'Is that what you call it? I beg to differ. I'm hungry, what's to eat?'

'I managed to get some belly pork cheap. I thought with some new potatoes and green beans...'

Edith nodded. 'That will do for this evening, but what about now?'

'Fresh bread and cheese?' Mary asked.

'Yes, and plenty of it. I'll waste away to nothing at this rate.' Edith patted her ample stomach beneath her full-length skirt.

Mary went to prepare enough for all three of them, although she and Dora would have theirs in the kitchen.

'Why doesn't Gran like me?' Dora asked as she and her mother sat at the table to eat.

Mary frowned. 'What makes you think that?'

'She shouts at me and smacks me when you go out.'

Mary drew in a breath through her nostrils. 'Dora, she's an old lady now and quick with a temper. She gets frustrated because she can't get about like she used to.'

Dora almost smiled at that. The old bat could jump out of her chair quick enough when it suited her.

'Just try to stay out of her way, sweetheart,' Mary went on.

'It's difficult when I'm supposed to look after her while you go to the shops.'

Mary sighed. 'I know, but we have to remember that this is her house and she feeds and clothes us.'

Dora nodded, having been taught not to speak with her mouth full, but she thought to herself, *It's the same old argument; Gran's the boss!*

'We'll do some more lessons this afternoon, if you would like,' Mary said in an effort to change the subject.

'Why can't I go to school like other children?'

'Oh, Dora, for goodness' sake! You know why, because I have no money to send you, and your gran won't pay.'

'That's just spiteful,' Dora muttered.

'Stop it! Let's have no more of this animosity between you two because I'm sick of it. Never mind the lessons; go outside and enjoy the sunshine.'

Dora slid from her chair and slunk out through the back door. She wandered around for a while, moping over her situation, then headed for the gateway at the front of the house.

It was there she saw a boy leaning against one of the brick-built pillars flanking the end of the drive. His warm smile intrigued Dora. Who was he and what did he want?

## 2

Dora looked the boy up and down as she approached him. The shirt beneath the waistcoat had a frayed collar and the trousers, with hands hanging loosely in the pockets, stopped just above the ankle bone. His brown boots, scuffed and dirty, looked too big for him, but the boy didn't seem to mind. His brown hair was curly and his amber eyes held a twinkle of mischief.

'Hello,' Dora said as she stood the other side of the gateway.

'How do,' the boy replied as he took in Dora's appearance. Her white smock dress was clean and her blonde hair combed and plaited neatly, tied at the ends with pretty pink ribbons.

Dora smiled at the old-fashioned way he had greeted her.

'What are you doing here?' Dora asked.

'Nuthin',' the boy said, as he crossed one foot over the other, resting his toes on the cobbles.

'What do you want?'

'Nuthin'.'

'What's your name?'

'John Skinner, but everybody calls me Skinny.'

Dora thought the sobriquet suited him very well as he was rather thin and gangly.

'I'm Dora Parsons.'

'Do you live there?' Skinny asked as he tilted his head towards the house.

'Yes, but it's my gran's house. I live there with my mum.'

'Three women under one roof, I bet that causes trouble,' he said with a cheeky grin.

'Sometimes.'

'Where's your dad?'

'He died when I was a baby,' Dora said, then asked, 'Where do you live?'

'Over at Doe Bank.'

'You're a long way from home.' Dora was surprised; she had surmised he resided more locally.

'It's a nice day so I thought to take a walk,' he answered simply.

'And you ended up here,' Dora said.

Skinny nodded.

'Why here?'

'Why not? It's as good a place as any.'

It was Dora's turn to nod.

In the pause that followed, Dora heard the birds singing in the trees in the garden, and insects buzzed past her ears. A dog barked somewhere in the distance, and the bell of St John's church chimed twice, calling out the hour.

'Shouldn't you be at school?' Skinny asked.

'Shouldn't you?'

'Nah, I ain't got the money,' Skinny said.

'What about your parents?' Dora asked.

'I ain't got any of them neither.'

Dora itched to correct his grammar but kept her counsel for fear of offending him.

'I'm sorry to hear that – so who do you live with?'

'My mates. We all share an old abandid place near the railway line.'

Dora could barely hide the smile at his mispronunciation as she asked, 'How do you manage for food and things?'

'I can't tell you – it's secret.'

Dora raised her eyebrows, telling him she guessed it was by stealing, but she said nothing.

'You got any brothers or sisters?' Skinny asked.

'No, there's just me,' Dora answered wistfully.

'Me an' all, I've only got my pals.'

'Where are your folks?'

'Gone. They took off years back and left me to fend for meself.'

'That's terrible! Why did they leave you behind?'

'I ain't got a clue. Prob'ly cos they couldn't afford to look after me.' Skinny shrugged as he spoke, as though it was no great hardship. Changing his position, he leaned his back against the gate pillar.

'Aren't you angry about it?' Dora asked.

'Why should I be? I don't know where they are and getting mad don't solve anythin'.'

'I suppose that's true,' Dora said.

'Have you 'ad your dinner?' Skinny asked.

Dora nodded. 'Have you?'

Skinny shook his head.

'Wait there,' Dora said before rushing back to the house and in through the back door.

'Mum, can I have some bread and cheese, please?'

'You've only just had your lunch,' Mary said, pausing in her preparation of the evening meal.

'Oh, it's not for me, it's for my friend, John Skinner.'

Mary frowned. Dora had no friends as far as she knew, and it was something that caused her grief.

Dora's next words came out in a rush for fear Skinny would have disappeared by the time she returned to the gate.

'John is my new friend; he's hungry because he's had no lunch. He lives with his friends over at Doe Bank because his parents abandoned him!'

'Take a breath, Dora. All right, take John to sit on the little bench beneath the old oak tree where your gran won't see you. I'll make up some lunch for him.' Mary smiled as Dora raced off, suspecting that John Skinner was a figment of Dora's imagination. It didn't matter to her, as long as her daughter was happy.

Placing a plate of bread and cheese on a tray, she added a glass of milk and a few biscuits.

Dora had been teaching herself to whistle and was glad of an excuse to try it out as she stood at the front of the house. As Skinny turned at the shrill sound, Dora hooked an arm, calling him to her.

Skinny ran up the driveway and followed Dora to the bench she was pointing to.

A moment later, Mary arrived with the tray, her surprise evident that John was in fact a real boy.

'Mum, this is John Skinner, Skinny to his friends. John, this is my mum, Mary Parsons.'

'Pleased to meet you, Mrs Parsons.'

'Likewise, John. Dora said you missed lunch, so I've brought you this.'

'Ooh, ta, Mrs Parsons,' Skinny said as he eyed the tray.

'Thanks, Mum,' Dora said with a beaming smile.

'I'll leave you to it,' Mary muttered before returning to the kitchen. As she worked, she kept an eye on Dora and her new play-mate from the window.

She saw them laughing together and could only guess at their conversation, but she was happy her daughter had found someone of her own age to converse with.

The afternoon wore on and as the sun lowered, Skinny carried the tray back to the kitchen, Dora alongside him.

'Ta, Mrs Parsons, that were bostin'!'

'You are very welcome, John,' Mary replied.

After saying her farewell, she hoped the boy would visit again – not just for food, but to spend time with Dora.

Once she had walked Skinny to the gateway, Dora returned, humming a little tune.

'He seems like a nice boy,' Mary said as Dora sat at the table.

'He is, Mum.'

'I'm glad you've found a friend.'

'Me too.'

'How did you come to meet him?'

'He was hanging about by the gateway and we just got to chatting.'

'Well, I'm pleased you did.'

'Skinny said he'll come again, if you don't mind, that is.'

'I think that would be grand. Dora, just be careful of your gran, though, she might not like having a stranger coming to the house.'

'I will, Mum. Shall I set the table?'

'Yes, please, love.'

Neither were aware of Edith standing behind the door, eavesdropping on their conversation. Returning to her chair in the sitting room, she scowled. Mary was right in what she said, Edith didn't want strangers coming to her house. As she stared out of the window, Edith planned to put a stop to that boy's visits. She smiled cruelly as she thought about how it would upset that brat Dora.

She pondered over her granddaughter. She was a clumsy kid at times, always spilling things, like the milk earlier that day. Edith didn't like the child and probably never would, for she had no intention of ever trying to. She saw Dora as a nuisance and a drain on her resources. Dora made a noise and a mess, things which only served to incense Edith. Now she was in her dotage, Edith felt she should be cared for by Mary with no interruptions – like the annoying demands of a young child.

All she wanted was for Mary to be at her beck and call so she could spend her remaining years in relative peace and quiet.

Just then, Dora came through with a tray of tea and biscuits, which she placed on the table close to her grandmother.

Edith glared and saw the fear cross Dora's face. 'You can't fool me, madam, I know what you're up to.' The old woman's voice was barely more than a whisper but the menace it held was clear. 'I think it's high time you were gone from my home.'

Dora shivered and fled the room.

Edith grinned as she snatched up a biscuit, her false teeth clacking together as she chewed. With luck, Dora would get so scared she would run away, which would please Edith immensely.

Pouring her tea, she gave a little cackle at the thought of being the instrument of the girl's disappearance, and no one would be any the wiser.

But then she began to cough, at first a tickle and then a gasp. Edith was choking on her biscuit.

## 3

Dora heard the coughing from where she hid behind the door. She knew her years of torment could end right then and there if she did nothing. Chastising herself for wishing the old bat would choke to death, she ran for her mother.

Watching as the biscuit piece was dislodged with a banging on Edith's back and with a glass of water to follow, Dora could not rid herself of her wish. Her grandmother still lived, and Dora felt wretched. She knew she'd done the right thing in fetching her mother, but she couldn't help her feelings in wanting the old woman gone.

'I'm all right!' Edith snapped as Mary continued to fuss.

*Ungrateful wretch!*

'Dora, put the kettle to boil and make your gran a fresh cup of tea, please,' Mary instructed.

Doing as she was told, Dora was glad to be out of the room.

It was Mary who took the hot beverage through to Edith before returning to the kitchen.

'Well done, Dora, if not for your quick thinking...' Mary let the sentence hang in the quiet kitchen. 'Go and play for a while, I'll call you when it's time to eat.'

Dora went up to the attic again to rummage through the countless boxes and chests stored there. Although it was dusty with very little light, this was her favourite place to be. Here she could be anyone she wanted to be, she could pretend she was in another country like those shown on an atlas, or she could be a person from history. The attic was her safe place, where no one could hurt her; she felt secure and happy here. At the very bottom of one of the boxes, she found a battered tin box that she'd never seen before, and inside were handfuls of photographs of people she didn't know. Then she pulled one out and caught her breath. It was her parents on their wedding day. Dora stared at the man in the picture – her dad. Tracing a finger over the image, she felt the sadness creep over her. Although she had never known him, she felt sure he would have loved and protected her. He would never have allowed Edith to treat her so badly – at least, it gave Dora some comfort to think so.

Putting the photograph aside, she delved further into the tin, finding another with Edith and a man she supposed was her grandfather.

Replacing the pictures, Dora searched in another box, which was filled with baby clothes. Some must have been hers, but she was perplexed to find blue ones amongst the pink. Who had those belonged to? Maybe they had been purchased before she was born and had been stored when the newborn had turned out to be a girl. Were her parents secretly hoping for a boy? That would explain the blue, but had they been disappointed when Dora came along? Had they had to rush to replace the garments with pink ones? She didn't think that was the case because she felt so loved by her mum, but it was certainly a conundrum. Carefully repacking the clothes, she moved on to discover a stack of books covered in a thick layer of dust.

Hearing her name being called, Dora left the attic reluctantly; it was her refuge – a place of safety where she could lose herself in fantasies of another life.

'Oh, there you are. Sit down and eat your dinner while I take this to your gran,' Mary said.

Dinner was what they called the evening meal but Skinny had used the word in place of lunch. Dora smiled at the thought, before wondering what her new friend would be having to eat at this time.

Dora said nothing to her mother about the photographs she'd found for fear of upsetting her. She didn't want to open old wounds, so she kept the discovery to herself. Besides, she didn't want to be banned from going up into the attic. This way, her hiding place could stay her secret and she could go and look at her dad any time she felt the need.

After they'd eaten, Mary asked Dora to fetch her gran's tray so she could wash the dishes.

As Dora lifted the tray, Edith spoke. 'Who was that boy in my garden?'

'John Skinner – he's my friend,' Dora answered warily.

'Well, I don't want him here again. It's bad enough that you are under my roof, but I won't have kids running all over the place!'

'We only sat in the garden and we didn't make a mess or any noise.'

'I don't give a bugger! It's my house and I don't want him here! If you want to be with your *friend*, you can leave. The sooner the better, as far as I'm concerned.'

Dora scowled and rushed from the room. In the kitchen, she banged the tray on the table.

Mary turned at the sound and saw her daughter's eyes brimming with tears. 'What's wrong, sweetheart?'

'Gran said Skinny can't come here again!'

Mary sighed as she dried her hands on her apron. 'I was hoping she hadn't noticed so you could have someone to play with. She must have seen him come up the drive. I'm sorry, love.'

'Gran's being unfair, Mum!'

'I know, but there's not much we can do about it. I'll have a word and see if I can change her mind, but I warn you – don't get your hopes up.'

Dora nodded, trying desperately to hold back her tears, then went quietly to her room.

Mary made tea and took a cup to Edith. 'Dora has a new friend,' she said, placing the cup and saucer on the small table by Edith's chair.

'I saw him, scruffy little urchin.'

'John is very polite, Mum, but looks a bit down on his luck.'

'I've told your daughter I'll not have kids here, no matter who they are. I can't cope with the noise, not with my health.'

'The doctor said there's nothing wrong with you, you're as strong as an ox,' Mary returned as she sat opposite Edith and picked up her knitting.

'What does he know, he's just a quack! I'm not well, Mary, and probably not long for this world.'

'There you go again, you'll outlive us all. What would it hurt to let Dora have a playmate if they stay quiet and outside?'

'I'll not have it, Mary! Once I've gone, you can do as you like, but until then my word is law in this house.'

Mary sighed, her needles clacking together as the jumper she was knitting grew in size. As she had expected, she had tried but failed to change Edith's mind regarding the young visitor, and now Dora would be alone once more. Hearing a snore, she looked up. Edith was asleep with her head back and her mouth wide open, her upper false teeth having slid downward.

*How can you be so spiteful?* Mary asked in the silence of her mind. *Dora is just a child, a young girl who strives constantly to please you. And what do you do? You berate her at every given opportunity! We know this is your house because you remind us every day, but I wish you would be kinder to Dora.*

Laying her knitting aside, she woke Edith gently. 'Come on, Mum, let's get you to bed.'

* * *

The following morning, after breakfast, Dora ran down the drive to wait at the gateway, hoping Skinny would come. She would have to tell him what her gran had said about not having people up at the house, but there was no reason they couldn't chat on the roadway.

The minutes turned to hours and the hot sun drove Dora to sit on the lawn, her legs too tired to hold her up any longer. She picked at the grass as her hopes of seeing Skinny fell. She wondered where he was and what he was doing. She watched a bumblebee skim across the lawn as though it was too heavy to fly high, but found no pleasure in the sight today. All she could think about was whether Skinny would visit.

Called inside for her lunch, Dora ate sparingly. She had no appetite. Given permission to leave the table, Dora rushed once more to the gateway to await her friend's arrival.

Mary sat at the table and watched her go. She sighed with sadness that Dora, up until now, had had no friends. Then her mind took her back to how they came to be here in the first place.

Eleven years ago, she had met Jim Parsons in the market one day. The most handsome man in the town, the one all the girls had their eyes on. Jim, however, had set his cap at Mary Pitt. She had agreed to walk out with him and soon their affection for each other turned to love. But that love had got away from them, and Mary discovered she was pregnant. A rushed marriage was arranged, and Mary was ecstatically happy. Finally, they could be a real family. Jim was a miner and they were lucky enough to be given a house to rent, which was tied to the pit.

Then the twins had arrived. Joseph and Dora were very small, and Joseph struggled from the outset. Within a fortnight of coming into the world, the little boy passed away.

Without realising what she was doing, Mary sat as she had that fateful day, her arms held as if cradling the tiny form of her dead son. She rocked back and forth on the chair, silent tears rolling down her cheeks as she relived once again that dreadful time in her life.

The doctor had told them their son's lungs had not fully formed and his little heart would never have been strong enough to carry him through life. It was a blessing in disguise, he said, for the child would have suffered pain for whatever life he had left.

Mary had buried her son in the cemetery at St John's church and had not set foot in the place since that day. She had clawed her way out of her depression to take care of her daughter and husband, but Joseph was never far from her thoughts.

She sat now looking down on the invisible child in her arms. She kissed his forehead and laid him in the little white coffin that was not there, as if moving in a dream.

Retaking her seat, Mary's mind moved forward three months. It was then that tragedy had struck again.

# 4

Having settled Dora to sleep, Mary had prepared Jim's bath for when he returned from the pit. She had eaten her meal and placed his in the range to keep warm.

Jim arrived home and took his bath. Then he ate his meal before going upstairs. There he packed a bag, which he brought down with him.

'What are you doing?' Mary asked.

'I'm leaving.'

'What? Why?'

'Because I can't stand your mother interfering in our lives any more! Because she blames Dora for Joseph's death! She comes here every day and derides me for everything I do. If I put coal on the fire, she says it's upside down! She's constantly telling you how to look after Dora without a care for your feelings or mine!'

'She's only trying to help, Jim.'

'But she's not, Mary! She can't keep her nose out of anything. I swear if she berates me for not getting promoted one more time...'

'I'll tell her not to come so often...'

'I've tried that and it's made no difference. I just can't go on like this, Mary. Your mother will see us parted one way or another in time. She hated me from the beginning and I can't see it getting any better in the future.'

'Jim, please, let's discuss this,' Mary begged.

'No. Mary, don't make this any harder than it already is.'

'Jim!'

'No, Mary! I've had enough and I'm leaving.'

'Then don't ever come back! And don't even think to see Dora because I won't allow it!' Mary had used her daughter as a threat in the hope her husband would not leave her. But it didn't work; he went anyway, leaving Mary in floods of tears. He had turned on his heel and walked out, leaving his wife in a world of pain she thought would never end.

Scores of questions rolled through her mind now, as they had then. What was happening? Why had he not said something before? Had he been missing work to find other accommodation? Where had he gone to live?

Staring into her cup, the tea having gone cold, Mary recalled how she had cried herself to sleep that night and many more since. The following day, she had had to suffer the humiliation of telling the pit boss her husband had left her. The man had shaken his head sadly when he informed her that she had to vacate the property, since Jim had absconded from both his home and job.

The pictures flitted through her memory of packing her few belongings before having to walk across town to her mother's house, Dora bundled in a shawl bound to her chest. Again, she remembered the embarrassment of telling Edith that Jim had gone and that she had to leave the house they had shared together.

'I never liked the lad anyway,' Edith had said. 'I always said he was no good. You shouldn't have married him, but you didn't have much choice, did you? Well, my girl, you're in a right mess now!'

Mary winced as the words came back to her.

'I suppose you want to move in here with me, do you? You can, provided you keep that child quiet, I can't stand too much noise. You won't be able to work, so you'll have to look after me to earn your keep.'

Mary had agreed and within the week had settled herself and Dora into the house in which she'd grown up. And she'd been there ever since. That was ten years ago and Mary had regretted it every day. She'd had no choice, of course, it was that or the workhouse, for she had no money of her own and with a young baby could not have gone out to work.

Edith had made her life a misery for all of those years. Having her daughter at her beck and call night and day, Edith had run Mary ragged. Without realising, Mary dragged in a painful dry sob, but it didn't break her train of thought. Her mind moved on with the images that, even after all these years, continued to torture her.

It was one morning that Mary knew the fates had not finished with her yet. Dora's cries were echoing through the house from her day cot in the sitting room. Mary rushed through, having just prepared the child's bottle. Mary's milk had dried up and so she was unable to continue to breastfeed her daughter, much to her chagrin. Picking Dora up, she pushed the teat into the tiny mouth and Dora sucked greedily. Turning her eyes to Edith, wondering why her mother hadn't picked up the sobbing baby, Mary saw her answer. Edith sat in her chair by the window with her fingers in her ears.

'Why didn't you pick her up?' Mary had asked.

'I'm not touching that child, she's evil!'

Mary couldn't believe what she was hearing as Edith ranted on.

'She's a thief! She stole that little boy's life from him. She took all the goodness when she was in the womb and that lad had no chance of life because of her! She's the devil's spawn!'

Mary had retaliated of course, telling Edith she was a stupid woman to think such things. Joseph had died because he wasn't properly formed, and it was no one's fault, but Edith would have none of it. The argument had raged for what seemed an eternity before Mary removed the rickety old day cot and placed it between the range and the table in the kitchen. The kitchen was a place Edith almost never ventured into, so Dora would be safe under Mary's watchful eye.

Days had turned into weeks and on into months and years, and still Edith had no time for Dora. She spoke to her only when necessary, otherwise the girl was ignored, at least, until Mary went out that was.

Mary had tutored Dora at home, having no money to send her to school, and Dora was a willing student. She learned quickly and was very intelligent; an old head on young shoulders.

Her tears now having ceased, Mary gave a little smile at how well her daughter was turning out. It was just a shame she had spent so many hours alone, without company of her own age. Now Dora had met John Skinner, and Edith was all set to spoil that for her.

With a long sigh, Mary set her mind to finding a solution which would allow Dora and John to become firm friends without Edith's spiteful interference.

In the meantime, Dora sat waiting for Skinny. She felt her skin prickle where the sun had turned it to a golden brown. She counted the chimes of the church clock in the distance. Five. Dora got to her feet and turned towards the house. Skinny wouldn't come now, it was too late in the day.

Taking slow steps, she began to walk up the drive and it was then she heard the pounding of boots on the cobbles. Spinning round, she ran back to the gateway, where she saw her friend skid to a halt.

'I'm... sorry... I'm... late,' he puffed. 'I... got... held up.' Skinny leaned forward, resting his hands on his knees in an effort to catch his breath.

'It doesn't matter – you came,' Dora said with a beaming smile.

'What did you do today?' he asked, breathing easier now.

'I waited for you.'

'What, all day?'

Dora nodded and smiled shyly.

'I'm honoured.'

'And so you should be,' Dora replied with mock indignation, which caused them both to laugh. 'I need to tell you something,' she went on and Skinny noted the change in her demeanour. 'My gran says I'm not to have anyone in the house or garden.'

'That ain't very nice.'

'I know, but because it's her house I have to obey.'

'Fair enough, but she can't stop us meeting here, can she?' Skinny tapped his boot on the road a couple of times.

'No, that's true.' Dora's mood lifted at his words, for it proved he wanted to continue to visit. 'What was it that made you late?'

'I was – at work.'

'Oh, what work do you do?'

'I used to go on the rob, but now I scavenge instead.'

Dora's mouth dropped open at the revelation. 'You used to steal?'

Skinny nodded. 'Not any more, but I was good at it.'

'Stealing is wrong.'

'I know, but how else was I to live?'

Dora thought about his question as she looked him up and down.

'Nobody will give me a job 'cos I'm too young. The only way to eat was to pinch the food.'

Dora didn't feel so bad about his 'work' when she heard that.

Not wanting to think he stole money or other people's things, she changed the subject. 'Do you want a drink?'

'Ar, I'll 'ave a pint of porter.'

'You will not! You'll have some lemonade, the same as me. Wait there.' Dora ran to the house and a short while later returned with a little basket containing ham sandwiches, chunks of cheese, cake and a bottle of homemade lemonade. The two sat on the cobbles and enjoyed their picnic.

Indoors, Mary smiled. Her little girl was happy again, and Mary intended for her to stay that way, no matter what Edith said. She prayed the fates were busy elsewhere and would leave her in peace for a while. The niggle at the back of her brain, however, told her that peace would not last long. She knew deep down that her steps through life were never meant to be easy, that she would have to fight to attain things and fight even harder to keep them.

As she prepared the evening meal, Mary mentally challenged those fates. She had made up her mind – whatever they put in her path, she would overcome. It was time Mary Parsons grew a backbone.

## 5

The following morning, Dora was up bright and early and was astonished to find Skinny waiting for her.

'You're early!'

'I thought you might like to come and meet my mates,' he said with a grin.

'I'll have to ask my mum.'

'Go on, then.'

Running back to the kitchen, Dora asked her question.

'Sweetheart, I'm not sure that's very wise.' Seeing her daughter's face fall, Mary sat on a kitchen chair and held Dora's hands. 'We've only known John for a couple of days...'

'But Mum...'

'Listen to me. We know next to nothing about him, Dora. Look, I tell you what, you can go only if I come with you.'

'I'm not sure how Skinny will feel about that,' Dora answered.

'It's your choice. Either I come along or you don't go.'

'All right. Shall I tell him?'

'Yes, then if he agrees, we can take a basket of food to share for lunch.'

Dora's face brightened and she scampered away to deliver her message. A moment later she was back. 'Skinny agrees, Mum.'

'Very good. Fetch the big basket from the scullery for me and we'll pack it to take with us.'

Bread, butter, ham, cheese, pickles, cake and biscuits were placed into the carrier and covered with a tea cloth.

Mary went through to the sitting room and spoke to Edith. 'I'm going out for a couple of hours.'

'Where? What about my lunch? What time will you be back?'

Mary sighed. 'I won't be too long. I'm sure you can manage to make yourself a cup of tea.' With that, Mary returned to the kitchen, Edith's voice ringing in her ears.

'You can't just go off and leave me on my own! What if something happens?'

'Come on,' Mary said to Dora, who was grinning broadly. 'Let your gran look after herself for a while.'

Mary grabbed the basket and they left the house, closing the door behind them.

At the gate, Mary greeted John then said, 'I hope you understand why it's necessary for me to come.'

'I do, Mrs Parsons, and I ain't taking any offence. It makes prefect sense, you wanting to keep Dora safe.'

Mary and Dora exchanged a quick glance at John's misuse of the English language, but neither wished to embarrass him by correcting him.

They meandered through the busy streets, dodging dray carts carrying barrels of beer to the many public houses. Small children ran around laughing and squealing as their mothers gossiped outside their front doors.

Traversing Lea Brook Road, they passed beneath the railway line. They stopped on Lea Brook Bridge and gazed down onto the Walsall Canal. They waved to the people on a narrowboat chugging along beneath the bridge, and Dora walked to the other side to watch the boat emerge into the sunshine once more. Passing a smithy's shop, Dora heard the banging of hammer on iron coming from within.

Leaving the road, they came to a few buildings a little way onto the heath. The scrub was dry and brown, scorched by the sun, and it crackled beneath their feet as they walked. There were two sets of semi-detached houses badly in need of repair. Windows were cracked and dusty, and the roof of one was missing a few tiles.

So this was the area known as Doe Bank.

John led them towards the first building they came to and let out a shrill whistle, making Mary and Dora wince.

'That's our call sign,' he said by way of explanation as he led them inside.

A moment later, five youngsters poured in through the back door: two girls and three boys.

'This is Dora and her mum, Mrs Parsons,' John announced.

All five of the children said hello, with big welcoming smiles. Mary was shown to a kitchen chair next to an old table in the living room, where she placed the basket. She took in the details of each child as they were introduced by John.

'This is Queenie, we call her that 'cos her name is Victoria Spittle, Victoria after our queen, see?'

Mary smiled as she looked at the brown eyes and dark hair of the pretty girl. Her clothes had seen far better days, but they were clean, as were her hands and face.

'She's twelve, ain't yer Queenie?' The girl nodded and John continued with, 'This is Owl, Jenny Baker, Owl on account of...'

'Her big beautiful green eyes,' Mary said. Again, the girl was clean but dressed in rags.

'Persactly! She's eleven. Carrot is eleven as well; his name is Paul Montague.'

Mary took in the flaming red hair and eyebrows, as well as his twinkling blue eyes.

'Lofty is fourteen, Albert Cooke,' John went on.

Mary smiled kindly at the boy she guessed was no more than four foot ten inches tall with light brown hair and blue eyes.

'And this is Fingers, Terence Bluck, and he's fourteen an' all.' He had fair hair and the brightest blue eyes Mary had ever seen. As he held out his hand for Mary to shake, she saw the reason for his nickname – long slender fingers.

'Welcome,' Fingers said as she shook Mary's hand, and it was obvious he was the leader of this merry little band. 'Queenie, I'm sure Mrs Parsons would appreciate a cup of tea, if you'd be so kind.'

Mary was surprised at the boy's way of speaking. Clearly, he had been well educated, and she wondered what had brought the little coterie together in the first place.

'Thank you, that would be lovely. I hope you don't mind my coming here with Dora to visit you all.'

'Not at all, Mrs Parsons, you are welcome any time,' Fingers replied.

'May I ask why you don't use your Christian names?' Mary asked.

''Cos having nickersnames is more fun!' Skinny jumped in and frowned when the others fell about laughing. 'What?' he asked.

'Skinny tends to get words confused sometimes, but it's one of the things we love about him,' Fingers explained.

Mary was surprised at the open show of affection. It was rare for boys to show their feelings, with most having it drummed into them that to cry was to be seen as weak. Even as men, they were guarded about declaring their love to their sweethearts. Therefore, Fingers allowing his feelings to be seen came as a bit of a shock to her.

Queenie produced a cup of weak tea in a chipped cup balanced on a cracked saucer. Mary thanked her and, pointing to the basket, she said, 'I've brought lunch for everyone.'

'Thank you, that's very kind. Owl, would you mind finding some plates, please?' Fingers asked.

Quick as a wink, a selection of mismatched crockery was brought out from what Mary assumed was the kitchen. She removed the basket from the table and the plates were laid out.

Dora unpacked the food and Mary watched eyes light up and smiles form at the thought of a good feed. She sipped her tea as the food was shared equally between them all.

Mary might not have known what had happened for this little group to come together, but she was confident she would find out in the fullness of time. One thing she did know was that they seemed to fit together better than any blood family. From the little she'd seen, there was obviously love and trust, each of the children accepting Fingers as their leader. His manner was kind, polite and intelligent, and he quietly demanded they respect each other.

She listened as they chatted, drawing Dora into their conversation as though she was already one of them. Mary's initial concerns melted away upon seeing her daughter's happiness at finding yet more new friends. She felt in her heart that Dora would be safe here any time she wished to visit.

Sitting quietly, Mary took in her surroundings. There were patches on the walls which spoke of damp in the winter months. The fireplace, she guessed, did not see much use, even when the weather turned colder. How could these children afford to buy coal when they could barely feed themselves? There was a rickety table and a kitchen chair. The peg rug on the floor was old but clean, which told her it was shaken outside every day.

These kids didn't have two ha'pennies to rub together, but they had love and friendship in abundance. As she glanced around, she saw Fingers watching her, and Mary gave a bashful smile.

'Would you care to see where Queenie and Owl live?' Fingers asked.

'Oh, erm – yes.' Mary was taken aback, having assumed they all resided in this one house.

Everyone trooped to the building next door, which was in no better shape, but evidently the girls had tried to make it into a home. There were net curtains at the windows, clean but with holes in them. A scrap of carpet lay on the floor, brushed so hard it was almost down to the knots. Their table and single chair sat in the kitchen, which was spotless.

'It's very nice, ladies,' Mary said, receiving beaming smiles at the praise.

'It's easy to keep clean 'cos we don't have much,' Owl said.

'We don't complain, though. We have what we need,' Queenie put in.

'So you live here – just the two of you?' Mary asked, trying to be subtle with her questions.

'Yes, the boys live next door. We get together in the evenings, but come bedtime we go home,' Queenie answered.

'I'm sorry, I shouldn't have asked.' Mary flushed, feeling her toes curl in embarrassment at appearing to pry into their private business.

'It's all right, we don't mind, do we, Queenie?' Owl said, her big green eyes holding a warm smile.

'Of course not,' Queenie agreed.

Fingers watched the exchange with interest and wondered if Mary Parsons would report them to the authorities. Although they were breaking no laws by living here, it was possible they could be forced into the workhouse. Somehow, Fingers doubted Mary would do such a thing. He felt her to be a kind lady, for hadn't she brought them all a grand lunch?

Returning to her seat in the boys' house, Mary decided to ask no more questions for fear of offending someone and risking making Dora and herself unwelcome in the future.

'Mrs Parsons, I'm sure there's a lot you wish to know but would prefer not to ask outright. May I assure you, Dora and yourself are most welcome to visit any time we are at home. Eventually you will hopefully get to know us very well, should that be your desire.'

'I... thank you. I shouldn't have...'

'It's only natural you would want to know about the people your daughter associates with. We really don't mind. If you have a question, please ask.'

'I will, but for now I think it's time for us to be on our way. Thank you for the tea. I'm sure we'll meet again.' Mary gathered up the now empty basket and ushered Dora to the door.

'Thank you, everybody,' Dora called as she was pushed along in front of her mother.

The whole gang stood in the sunshine and waved, and it was Skinny who spoke first once mother and daughter had disappeared down the path.

'I don't think Mrs Parsons was very happy with us.'

'Why do you say that?' Fingers asked.

'Because she rushed off. Did we do something to befriend her?' Skinny asked innocently.

Fingers put an arm around Skinny's shoulder and said, 'I don't think we offended her, Skinny. It's my contention that Mrs Parsons is unhappy, and has been for a long time, but I don't think it has anything to do with us or her visit here.'

'I wonder what it is, then.'

'All will come to light in the fullness of time, my friend,' Fingers said.

'Do you think so?'

'I do indeed. I think we'll see a lot more of Dora Parsons.'

'I like her, do you?'

'I do, Skinny, she's a little smasher. I'm not sure what she'll think of us when she finds out how we've provided for each other, though.'

'Oh, she knows, Fingers. I told her I used to be on the rob.'

Fingers burst out laughing at his friend's innocence.

'What?'

'Nothing,' Fingers said, then added, 'I love you, brother.'

'I ain't your brother, not really.'

'No, Skinny, sadly I'm not, but we can all of us here think of the others as brothers and sisters, can't we?'

'Yer, I s'pose so.'

'Then come, brother, and let's go and annoy the girls.' Fingers grinned and they ran into the house. It wasn't long before squeals could be heard as everyone ran from house to house, playing Tag.

* * *

Mary and Dora wound their way home, the streets still as busy as ever.

Dora was chattering away but Mary wasn't really listening; her mind was on Fingers. For a fourteen-year-old he was very astute, and Mary was intrigued about his background. He appeared to be a very capable leader and it was clear he was adored by the others.

The only way she would find out about any of them would be to hear their stories. She had been told they could visit again, but would it be seen as interfering? Would they think she was spying on them? Would they be concerned she would inform the police or the workhouse? Mary would never do such a thing and made up her mind to say so on her next trip to Doe Bank. She felt they would all be better off with a little plain speaking.

'So can we, Mum?'

'What, sweetheart?'

Dora sighed. 'Can we go again tomorrow?'

'We'll see.'

Dora smiled. When her mum said that, it usually meant yes.

Entering the house, Mary called out to Edith that they were home. Receiving no reply, she went to the sitting room.

And there she found the old woman on the floor.

## 6

'Mum! Oh, my God! What's happened? Dora, come quickly!' Mary yelled as she rushed over to the prone woman.

As Dora ran in, Mary said, 'Help me get your gran up and into the chair.'

Placing their arms beneath Edith's, they hauled her to her feet and into her armchair. Mary dropped to her knees, asking again what had happened.

'I was going to make a cup of tea, but when I stood up, I went dizzy and fell. I couldn't get up on my own,' Edith explained, her hand moving to her head.

'Are you hurt?' Mary asked.

'No, just shaken.'

'I should never have left you alone. I'm sorry, Mum. Dora, make some tea, please, there's a good girl,' Mary said, getting to her feet.

As Dora turned, she could have sworn she saw the ghost of a smile on Edith's face. *So that's your game, you old bat!* Dora thought as she went to put the kettle to boil. In her heart, Dora knew her grandmother had not fallen at all, but was only doing this to make them feel guilty about going out without her. Dora felt sure today was the first and last time she and her mum would be visiting Doe Bank together. Mary would not want to leave Edith alone again now.

Making the tea, Dora wondered if she would ever see her new friends again. Taking the tray through to the sitting room, she caught bits of the conversation.

'You took a basket, I saw you!' Edith snapped.

'We were looking for mushrooms,' Mary lied.

'I'll bet you didn't find any.'

'No, we didn't,' Mary answered. 'Drink your tea while I get you something to eat.'

Edith sniffed and glared at Dora.

Dora returned the look and saw something in her grandmother's eyes. Was it fear? Was Edith worried that Dora was on to her? Dora gave a smile that only lifted the corners of her mouth, her way of confirming the old woman's thoughts.

Edith scowled as Dora skipped away to the kitchen.

Alone now, Edith did indeed think that child was aware of her ploy to keep Mary at home. She had watched them leave the house and, after making herself a hot drink and a sandwich, she had ruminated a plan. Being careful to clear away all evidence of having had refreshments, Edith had watched the gateway carefully. The moment she had seen Mary and Dora returning, she had placed herself strategically on the floor.

She smiled to herself, knowing her little ruse had worked. Whatever those two had been up to would not happen again. Mary would not risk Edith being alone and be accused of being neglectful. However, Dora was the one to watch; the child was far too clever and could catch Edith out if she was not careful. Then again, she could always use the threat of eviction as she had so many times before. That decided, she relaxed and waited for her food to be brought to her.

* * *

Whilst Dora and Mary were seeing to Edith, back at Doe Bank, Fingers had called everyone together.

'It's time to replenish the larder,' he said.

'I'll get off up the market, shall I?' Skinny asked.

'Only to scavenge, mind,' Fingers warned.

'I get better stuff when I'm on the rob,' Skinny moaned.

'I know, my friend, but consider this: where would we be if you were caught and arrested?'

'I wouldn't get appended,' Skinny replied.

Fingers smiled warmly and ignored the mispronunciation. 'Scavenge only, please. We don't want Mrs Parsons to stop Dora coming to visit because she thinks we are thieves, do we?'

'No, that would be terrible,' Skinny replied, feeling suddenly fearful.

Turning his attention to the girls, Fingers asked, 'Would you take some of those dolly pegs we made and try to sell them in the town?'

'Yes,' they chorused.

'And don't get arsey if they take you for gypsies,' Carrot put in, which earned him a cuff across the head from Queenie.

'Carrot, Lofty and I will go to the wharf by Wiggins Mill Pool and see if we can score a job loading or unloading.'

'Why do I 'ave to scavenge?' Skinny asked, clearly unhappy with the notion.

'The idea is that you get known by the stall holders in the market. They will see you collecting the fruit and vegetables they can't sell and eventually they will give you some of the better produce,' Fingers explained patiently. 'Would you rather go with Carrot and Lofty?'

'No, it's all right. I understand now,' Skinny said.

'Well done. If not for you, we wouldn't eat,' Fingers said, clapping Skinny on the back, 'so you have the most important role.'

Skinny grinned. 'Right, girls, grab your pegs and I'll walk with you to the town.'

Soon enough, the old house lay empty as the gang left and went their separate ways.

At the wharf, the three young lads watched a horse and cart draw up. The cart was loaded with crates of apples and the carter jumped down to speak with a man on a small barge. They appeared to be arguing, and Fingers guessed the heated exchange concerned the transference of produce from cart to boat. As the boys walked closer, his summation was proved correct.

'I was paid to bring 'em only!' the carter said.

'An' I am paid to ferry 'em!' the boatman retorted.

'Excuse me,' Fingers interrupted as he drew close, 'do you need help with loading? We can do it – for a price.'

'That's all well and good, but who's gonna pay that price?' the carter asked.

'I can,' the bargee called. 'I can get the money back from the boss. How much, lad?'

'A shilling,' Fingers said.

'Do a good job and I'll make it two.'

Fingers grinned. 'Thank you, sir.'

Between them, Fingers, Carrot and Lofty unloaded the cart and stacked the crates neatly on the barge. Paid their two shillings, they were given an apple apiece to help slake their thirst.

The bargee waved his thanks as the boat chugged away. The carter tipped his cap and, climbing onto the driving seat, he clucked to the horse to walk on.

Sitting on the wharf between the two basins, the boys pocketed their fruit, while hoping to find more work before nightfall.

Whilst they were lifting and carrying in the hot sun, Skinny was strolling the market looking for discarded fruit and vegetables. Fingers had said to get himself known there, but in truth he already was, for he patrolled there often looking for a handout.

'Back again, Skinny?' a lady shouted.

'How do, Mrs O'Connell,' he called back with a nod.

The plight of the youngsters was well known by the stall holders in the marketplace, and they helped where they could. The summer months saw produce spoil if it was not sold quickly enough, so often Skinny acquired a bumper harvest. The winter, however, was a different matter, there being little left to rot on the market area when the stall holders went home.

'Here, sweet'eart, have these,' Mrs O'Connell said as she put four apples in a paper bag, then did the same with potatoes.

'Ta, Mrs O'Connell, you ain't half kind,' Skinny said as he took the gift.

'Old man Hollingsworth is up at the top, try your luck there,' she answered.

Skinny nodded then threaded his way between the stalls, his eyes on the floor in search of a dropped coin or a wayward vegetable. Coming to the top of the market, he heard the resonant tones of Mr Hollingsworth the butcher. A crowd of women were gathered around his stall, the noise of their laughter loud even in the racket of the market.

Standing amid the women, Skinny could hear other sellers calling out their wares. He caught the occasional whiff of wet fish, and as he was jostled aside, he smelled the aroma of fresh bread. His mouth watered and he was tempted to gnaw on an apple from the bag, but he resisted. Whatever he collected was to be shared by the group, and it was his job to provide as much as he could.

Skinny smiled at the banter taking place between the butcher and his customers.

'You'm a robbing bugger, Holly,' a woman yelled, much to the amusement of the others.

'Sausages and bercon for one and six? I'm doing you a favour. I tell you what, I'll slap this on the top for two bob.' Holding up a piece of tripe, he wiggled it before dropping it onto his scales.

'Go on, then,' the woman relented and dug into her purse for her money.

The afternoon wore on into early evening and the crowd began to melt away, but Skinny remained. His legs ached from standing so long, but it was worth it when the butcher wrapped half a dozen sausages and tossed them to the patient boy.

'Thanks ever so, Mr Hollingsworth,' Skinny called out before wending his way back through the market. Spotting an empty box by a stall, he grabbed it for his 'shopping'. Still searching the ground, he glanced up occasionally to see the vendors packing up for the day.

Hearing someone call his name, Skinny turned in the direction of the shout. The lady on the bread stall beckoned him with a crooked finger.

'There you go, bab,' she said as she placed a loaf in his box.

'Ta muchly, Mrs Jones,' he answered gratefully.

Further along, he found a cabbage, its outer leaves beginning to turn black. Into the box it went. He moved on, and before long a couple of withered carrots joined it.

Skinny was happy with his haul and smiled to himself. Seeing something twinkle in the dying sun, he dived to pick it up. His smiled turned to a grin when he saw it was a sixpence. He whistled a little tune as he strode home, knowing they would have a feast that night.

Arriving back at the house, he placed the box on the table. The girls came rushing in from next door, having heard his whistle, and rifled through the box.

'We'll need some wood for the fire to cook this lot,' Queenie said as she emptied the box of its contents.

'I'll go,' Owl volunteered as she grabbed the box.

'I'll come with you,' Skinny said.

So the pair set off to search the heath for sticks to light a fire in the range on which to cook their meal.

Fingers, Carrot and Lofty were home by the time they returned with a box full of kindling. Queenie had scrubbed the potatoes and chopped them into a pan of water, which she'd fetched from the standpipe in the back garden. A few good cabbage leaves and the carrots were added, along with a shrivelled onion she found in the cupboard. The sausages were pricked and lying in a small frying pan ready to be cooked.

The chatter was loud as Fingers lit the range, feeding the sticks in along with the little coal they had left.

Carrot set the table with plates and cutlery and Lofty found some salt and pepper in the girls' kitchen next door.

Queenie sliced the bread while Owl kept an eye on the sausages, turning them to prevent them burning. The aroma had everyone's mouth beginning to water, and before long there was silence as they all tucked into a hearty meal.

They had no idea that over in Spring Head, Dora was feeling thoroughly wretched.

## 7

'I can't just go off and leave your gran alone again, Dora, look what happened earlier,' Mary said as she watched her daughter's blue-green eyes brim with tears.

Dora pushed her plate away; she was no longer hungry. Her mum had explained that one of them needed to be with Edith at all times now. Dora was horrified with the idea, for it meant that they could not visit her friends at Doe Bank.

'Please try to understand, sweetheart,' Mary continued.

Dora clamped her teeth together in an effort not to cry, but it didn't work, and her tears spilled down her cheeks.

Jumping up from the table, Dora ran from the kitchen.

Mary sighed. She didn't want to disappoint Dora, but on the other hand she would never forgive herself if anything happened to Edith whilst she was out. She was reluctant to allow Dora to go to Doe Bank alone; she was only ten years old, after all. Then again, Dora was very grown-up in a lot of ways. Having been around adults all her life, it was a wonder she could interact with her peers as well as she did.

Mary wondered whether she could let Dora go if John Skinner

collected her and brought her home. That would certainly be a solution to the problem, but what about when they needed to find food or try to earn a copper? They would have to take Dora along or leave her alone in that run-down house. Mary shuddered at the thought. No, Dora was better off at home, with an occasional visit from Master Skinner.

Whilst Mary was weighing up the pros and cons, Dora had dashed into the attic. She had pulled out the photograph of her parents' wedding and was staring at the man she thought was her father.

'Why did you have to die? You wouldn't have let Gran treat us so badly, would you?' she whispered. Replacing the picture, she moved to the little round window and stared out. She longed to be old enough to come and go without having to ask permission first.

Dora had felt lonely before she had met Skinny, but now she had met the others too, the loneliness imposed on her by her grandmother threatened to suffocate her. The sadness it brought with it weighed heavily on her, and she thought she might never be happy again. She had one hope left – which was that Skinny would continue to call on her when he could. Dora knew she had to be content with that for now, because she could see no other solution.

As she stared out of the window, she quietly cursed her gran for being so wicked. Dora determined she wouldn't be cruel like her gran when she grew up. She would be kind and patient with her children, like her own mum was with her.

The sun began to lower towards the western horizon and shadows formed in the dusty attic. Dora checked the photograph was safely back in its place before leaving the space she always felt comfortable in, and made her way downstairs.

Hearing raised voices, Dora went to the sitting room.

'I can't manage on my own, Mary!' Edith yelled.

'I don't think you're as bad as you sometimes make out,' Mary retaliated.

Edith slapped a hand on her chest dramatically. 'Oh, my poor heart! I'm not long for this world and once I've gone you'll regret being so selfish.'

'There's nothing wrong with your heart, Mum! The doctor told you so. And you're the one being selfish. You won't even try to do anything for yourself!'

Dora stood in the doorway with her mouth open in surprise at the argument raging before her. What had sparked this off? Was it something to do with their outing? Or was it Edith's so-called fall?

'I can't, Mary! I need help to do things, as well you know.'

'Then I think it's high time you employed a nurse!'

'I can't afford a nurse! Besides, I have you.'

'Mother, Dora and I feel like prisoners in this house, don't you understand?'

'I understand that you eat my food, burn my coal and gas, and live under my roof!' Edith spat nastily.

'Well, that can change! What would you do then, eh? How would you manage living on your own if we weren't here to pander to your every wish?' Mary was trying her best to stand up to her mother, despite the ring of truth in Edith's words.

Dora waited with bated breath for the answer. Would her gran fight on? Or would she back down? She had never seen her mum so angry before, and certainly never heard her stand up to Edith so forcefully.

As Dora watched, Edith dissolved in a paroxysm of crying. That was it then, Edith had won. Dora knew her mum would not continue to argue now; the feeling of guilt would force her to concede.

Edith wailed and rubbed her eyes on a handkerchief pulled from her cardigan pocket.

Dora watched all this through the mirror on the wall opposite Edith's chair, and although the sobbing was loud, Dora didn't see a single tear.

Mary harrumphed and marched from the room, and it was then that Edith raised her head and smiled widely.

Dora returned to the kitchen quietly, knowing Edith was unaware she had been seen exulting in her triumph. Dora watched her mother plate up salad for their evening meal.

'Dora, love, take this through to your gran, please,' Mary said.

Carrying the tray into the sitting room, she placed it on the table next to Edith.

'What are you staring at?' Edith asked sharply.

'Nothing,' Dora replied, taking a step backwards.

Edith was unaware that Dora had witnessed the explosion of tempers as she snarled at the young girl. She lifted her walking stick and swung it at Dora, but Dora deftly moved out of the way.

'You are a nasty old woman,' Dora hissed.

'And you are a child of the devil!' came the reply.

'I don't like you.' Dora's lip curled as she spoke.

'That's fine, because I hate you!'

Dora pushed her nose in the air and sniffed, then she walked out, leaving Edith seething at having missed the girl with her cane.

Sitting at the table, Dora wanted to ask about what had started the contretemps but didn't dare. She could see her mum was still angry, so she tucked into her food with relish. Salad with ham and boiled potatoes along with pickled beetroot and cheese was her favourite, and Dora ate hungrily. She noted, however, that Mary only picked at the food on her plate.

'I told your gran you should be allowed out to visit your friends and that I would have to go with you – to start with, anyway.'

So the whole thing was about her, which made Dora feel guilty.

'I could go on my own, Mum, I'm big enough now.'

'You may think so, lovey, but there are a lot of bad people out there, you wouldn't be safe.'

*I'm not safe here*, Dora thought, but said nothing.

'What would you do if someone tried to take off with you?' Mary asked.

'I'd scream my head off,' Dora replied.

'It's too dangerous, sweetheart.'

'But Mum...'

'Finish your food and leave it with me. We'll find a way for you to be with your friends.'

Dora smiled and continue to eat. 'I don't like Gran.'

'There are times I don't like her either,' Mary concurred.

Then there was a knock at the back door. Mary opened it and there stood John Skinner, panting hard.

## 8

'Mrs Parsons,' Skinny gasped, 'I'm sorry to come, but...'

'Calm down, John, catch your breath,' Mary said as she invited him in.

The boy nodded but rushed on. 'It's Owl, she's proper poorly!'

'What are her symptoms?'

'What?'

'Tell me what you think is wrong with her.'

'She's hot, sweaty, saying daft things.'

'Sounds like a fever. Have you had the doctor call?'

'Can't afford it!'

Mary looked at Dora, who was standing next to her. 'I'll have to go with John and see to Owl. I need you to stay here with your gran.'

Dora nodded as Mary grabbed her shawl and bag. She watched them walk swiftly away before closing the door.

'Who's that making all that racket?' Edith called.

'Nobody, Gran.'

'You're a little liar!' Edith yelled as she, too, watched Mary and the young boy disappear down the drive.

Dora ignored her grandmother, then the shout came again.

'Dora! Get in here!'

With a big sigh, Dora walked through to the sitting room.

'Who was that at the door?'

'It was my friend.'

'What did he want?'

'Some help. One of the other children has been taken ill,' Dora answered.

'So Mary drops everything and rushes off? What about me? Who's going to help me?'

'What do you need, Gran? I can get it for you,' Dora said.

'I don't want anything from you! What I want is for you to leave my house! Pack a bag and bugger off!'

'Why?'

'Because I've told you before, I don't want you here! Why don't you listen? I want you out so Mary and I can live in peace!'

'What's brought this on?' Dora asked quietly.

'You and your little pal making Mary leave me all alone, that's what!'

'But you're not on your own, I'm here.'

'Yes, and I wish you weren't. Now, I'll tell you one last time – get out of my house!'

'Where would I go?'

'I don't care, but I want you gone before your mother gets back.'

'And if I don't go?' Dora asked, feeling tears sting her eyes.

'I'll throw you both out! Your mother would have to go to the workhouse. Would you have that on your conscience?' Edith grinned wickedly. Dora shook her head. 'I thought not, so I suggest you get going.'

Dora dashed from the room and took the stairs two at a time, making her way to the attic first. Grabbing a small old Gladstone bag, she shook off the dust. Putting her parents' wedding photo in the bottom, she ran down to her room. A change of clothes, under-wear, a spare pair of boots, woollen stockings, coat and hat were all pushed into the bag before Dora hauled it downstairs. She left the house via the back door, her heart hammering in her chest.

Edith stood by the window and watched Dora go, then the old woman did a little jig as she cackled with delight.

Dora had no idea where she was going, but knew she couldn't go to Doe Bank, otherwise she would have to explain to her mother why she had left Edith alone. Coming to the marketplace, Dora paused, not knowing which way to go. Although the sun had gone down, it would be a while yet before darkness fell. Putting her bag down, she sat on it and allowed her tears to fall at last. She didn't know how long she sat there as people passed her by.

* * *

In the meantime, Mary had rushed to Doe Bank with Skinny. In the girls' house, she was shown upstairs by Queenie, while the boys stayed in their own house to keep out of the way.

Mary was shocked when she saw how the children were living upstairs. A mattress on the floor with a couple of old blankets were all that was in the room.

Owl lay on the makeshift bed, her breath wheezing and sweat oozing from her pores. Mary touched the girl's forehead and felt the heat.

'I need a cloth and cold water,' she said.

'Right,' Queenie acknowledged, and disappeared through the door.

Mary checked Owl's young body for any signs of a rash, but thankfully there was none.

Owl's large green eyes smiled up at the woman who had come to help.

'Don't worry, lovey, it's just a summer cold and we'll have you feeling better in no time,' Mary said, by way of comfort, but first she had to get Owl's temperature down.

Queenie arrived with a clean rag and a bowl of cold water.

Mary bathed Owl's forehead, making the girl shiver as the cold cloth touched her burning skin. 'We need to mix some honey and lemon to help with her sore throat,' Mary said, and saw by the look Queenie gave her that they had none. Nor were they in a position to acquire any. 'Don't worry, I'll send you some and you can administer it.'

'Ta, Mrs Parsons, we ain't half grateful,' Queenie answered quietly. Her tattered clothes hung on her thin frame and she'd found an old, battered hat from somewhere.

'Can you keep bathing her down until she doesn't feel so hot to the touch?'

Queenie nodded as she took over.

'Good girl. I'm going home now, but I'll get Skinny to come later for the cough syrup.'

'Thank you for coming, Mrs Parsons, and for helping my friend.'

'You're welcome,' Mary said with a smile.

Outside, Mary explained to the boys about the illness and asked Skinny to come to collect some medicine later.

'Ta ever so,' he replied.

'We are grateful for your coming, Mrs Parsons,' Fingers said. 'In all truth we were at a loss as to what to do.'

Again, Mary was surprised at the boy's well-educated voice, which didn't fit at all with the rags he stood up in.

'Don't you have any money at all?' Mary asked.

'The odd few pennies, which is spent on food,' Fingers replied.

'You should try to put some aside for a doctor's visit.' Even as she said it, she knew it could never happen. These children were living hand to mouth, in rags, in a couple of abandoned houses. How could they possibly afford to save money?

Fingers saw the look on her face and smiled. 'Would that we could, but alas, it's not possible.'

'I'm sorry, I should think before I speak,' Mary said, feeling sorry she couldn't help more. 'I'll get off home and give Skinny some syrup for Owl's throat if it becomes sore and she develops a cough.'

'Again, you have our thanks,' Fingers said.

Mary waved goodbye and set off home. The light was beginning to fade, but as she eventually came to Lower High Street she glanced up into the marketplace. She saw a child sitting there, all alone and crying, and as she got closer she was alarmed to recognise the young girl as her own daughter.

'Dora? Sweetheart, what on earth are you doing out here?'

Dora looked up into her mother's eyes. 'Mum, I... Gran threw me out!'

'What?' Mary snapped as she wrapped her arms around her sobbing daughter.

'She said if I didn't leave, she'd make you go to the workhouse!'

'Oh, for God's sake! That woman is a menace!' she snapped. Then Mary harrumphed loudly before she went on, 'Come on, let's go home, where I'll sort everything out.' Taking Dora's hand and picking up the bag, Mary led her daughter back to the house.

'Is that you, our Mary?' Edith called.

'Yes, Mother,' the reply came as Mary set the kettle to boil.

'Mary, I don't know where that girl of yours has got to, I've been calling and calling.'

'Give me a minute, I'm making tea,' Mary shouted back. 'Fetch the biscuits, will you, Dora?' she said more quietly.

'Mum, how was Owl?'

'She's fine, lovey, she had a temperature because of a summer cold, but she'll be all right. I left instructions for the others to follow, so by the morning she'll be much better.'

'Thanks, Mum.'

'Right, let's take this through to your gran and get all this nonsense straightened out,' Mary said as she grasped the tray.

Dora stood in the doorway and watched her gran's face in the mirror. Her grey hair was drawn severely back and into a knot at the nape of her neck. The lines on her face deepened as she scowled.

'You oughtn't leave me alone, Mary. I've had one fall, what would I do if I had another? Where have you been?'

'I had to go out. Now, what's all this I hear about you throwing Dora out?'

'I would never!'

'Well, she tells me you threatened her with the workhouse.'

'She's a bloody liar!' Edith snapped.

'Look, Mum, I know this isn't ideal, but we have to all get along. I can't referee every time you two disagree.'

'She shouldn't be here, she should have died alongside the other one!'

Mary closed her eyes tightly for a moment as the memory of her dead son rose strong in her. 'Why do you have to keep bringing that up? Don't you realise how painful it is for me?'

'You're not the only one to lose a child, there's plenty out there that have. You have more important things to worry about now.'

'Like taking care of you, you mean?'

Edith nodded as she poured her tea.

Dora wondered what other one Edith was talking about. Had there been another child who had passed away? When was that? Was it before Dora was born? Then Dora recalled the blue baby clothes she'd found in the attic, which now made sense.

'If you and Dora can't be civil, then stay away from each other,' Mary growled.

'That suits me. Keep that brat away from me, otherwise I won't be responsible for my actions. And while we're at it, I don't want any more urchins at my door!'

'It was an emergency,' Mary began.

'I don't care what it was, just send them away!'

It was just at that moment that Skinny came knocking once more.

## 9

Mary answered the knock and asked the boy to wait while she went to the highest shelf in the pantry. Standing on the cracket, she reached down the ridged bottle with a cork stopper, which she shoved into Skinny's hands.

'One teaspoon, only if Owl starts to cough, understand?' The boy nodded. Mary asked him to repeat the instructions.

Skinny obeyed, then said, 'Ta, Mrs Parsons.'

'I'll be along early in the morning to check on her. Now, off you go and don't drop it,' Mary said kindly.

'Who was that? Have they gone?' Edith called.

'Yes, Mother,' Mary replied with a roll of her eyes, making Dora giggle. 'Dora, off to bed so I can get your gran into hers. Maybe then I will have a bit of peace.'

Kissing her mum goodnight, Dora did as she was asked.

'Right, Mum, let's get you upstairs and settled,' Mary said, helping Edith to her feet. Walking behind the old woman in case she fell, and dousing the lights behind her, Mary listened to the groans and grumbles. Once in Edith's room, Mary helped her into her nightclothes and into bed. Then, with a goodnight, Mary went to her own bedroom. Pouring cold water from the jug into the large bowl, Mary had a quick wash, combed her hair and after changing clothes she collapsed into bed, feeling exhausted.

Darkness had fallen without her even noticing, and with a yawn Mary wondered how much longer she could go on like this. Edith alone was wearing her out and now she found herself worrying about the children from Doe Bank.

The bright moon cast a silvery glow through the window and passing clouds sent shadows to disappear into the dark corners of the room, but Mary didn't see them, she was already fast asleep.

Early the following morning, after dressing in a white cotton blouse and a long fawn skirt, and getting Edith to her chair in the sitting room, Mary prepared breakfast.

'I'm going to the market today, but I'll not be too long.'

'You're always off out somewhere,' Edith grumbled.

'If you want to eat, I have to go. Dora will be here if you need anything.'

Returning to the kitchen, Mary whispered, 'I'm going to check on Owl, then I'll call at the market on my way back.'

'Can I come?' Dora asked.

'No, sweetheart. I need you to look after your gran.'

'But Mum...'

'I tell you what, I'll ask Skinny to come back with me and take you to Doe Bank for the day if it's all right with the others, how's that?'

Dora threw her arms around her mum. 'Thank you!'

Gathering her purse, basket and shawl, Mary left quietly.

Dora watched her go, feeling the excitement build inside her. A whole day with her friends; she couldn't wait.

'Where's my cup of tea?' Edith yelled, her voice breaking Dora's reverie.

'Coming, Gran.' Setting the tray, Dora carried it to the sitting room.

'About time! I could die of thirst here!' Edith snapped.

*I wish!* Dora quickly dismissed the thought and as she turned to leave, there was a gushing sound from the chimney before a great pile of soot plopped down into the grate. Tiny black motes flew around, before slowly coming to rest on the tiled hearth.

'Get that cleaned up, child,' Edith instructed as she sipped her tea.

Dora took the small brush and shovel from the companion set and began sweeping up the soot.

'Not like that, you idiot! It's going all over the place!'

Dora sighed, and it was as she turned her head to look at her grandmother, who was now standing, that she saw the walking stick come slashing down. Quick as a flash, she brought her arm up to cover her head and crouched down. She screamed as the stick cracked across her back, shooting pain down her spine to all four limbs.

Jumping to her feet, Dora turned to the old woman, hate burning in her blue-green eyes. A small brush in one hand and little shovel in the other, she pushed them upwards towards Edith's face as the stick rose again. 'Don't you *ever* do that to me again!' Dora's voice was like a rasp on metal.

'You cheeky young bugger!'

In an instant, Dora dropped the implements and pushed her grandmother hard in the stomach. It was as if Edith folded across her middle in slow motion before she landed hard in her armchair.

'Oh – oh, my heart!' Edith gasped as her hand flew to her chest. Her head lolled to the side, her eyes closed and her mouth open.

Dora stared, horrified at what she'd done. She'd killed her grandmother!

'Gran, Gran!' she called but Edith didn't move.

Terrified now, Dora ran from the room. Instinctively, she grabbed her coat from the hook on the back door before fleeing for her life.

Edith heard the back door bang shut and opened one eye to see Dora racing down the drive. With a cackle, she said aloud, 'That's it, you little swine, you run and don't come back!' Picking up her cup, she enjoyed the rest of her drink more than she could ever remember enjoying a cup of tea.

Whilst Edith was goading Dora, Mary had arrived at Doe Bank and was greeted warmly. Owl was feeling a little better, her high temperature having lowered during the night. The ridged bottle, she noted, was a quarter empty of the honey, lemon and brandy syrup. She guessed they had all had a taste, which brought a smile to her face. Next to the bottle and spoon on the bare floorboards was a cracked saucer with its half candle. Not having thought of it before, Mary realised there was no gas to the old properties.

Downstairs, Mary accepted a cup of weak black tea from Queenie.

'We can't thank you enough, Mrs Parsons,' Fingers began.

'Call me Mary, all of you, please.'

Fingers inclined his head. 'It was most kind of you to send the medicine for Owl.'

'It's for a cough and to ease a sore throat, but it tastes nice, doesn't it?' Mary smiled, to say she was fine with them all having tasted her homemade mixture. She watched as Carrot and Lofty left to find work at the wharf, before asking, 'Would you mind if Dora came to spend the day with you?'

'I don't see why not. Queenie will be here to keep an eye on Owl, but Skinny and I have to try to find a job which will pay a few pennies,' Fingers replied, then added, 'Are you not concerned Dora might contract whatever ails Owl?'

'No, it's only a summer cold, after all, and no one else appears to be affected. I was hoping Skinny would collect and return Dora, but...'

'Course I will!' Skinny interrupted enthusiastically. 'Won't I, Fingers?'

'Yes, if you wouldn't mind,' the other boy said.

'Can't 'ave Dora walking all by her own,' Skinny added.

'Thank you. It's difficult for me as I have my aged mother to take care of, but Dora will be thrilled to visit.'

'Mrs... Mary, Dora can come at any time – provided we're not out earning, that is. If we're here, I'm sure Skinny wouldn't mind escorting Dora from and to her home,' Fingers replied.

'It would be my pleasure,' Skinny said, full of his own importance.

'That's agreed, then. Right, I should be getting back because I have to call into the market on the way home.'

'I'm ready – I'll escort you, Mary,' Skinny said eagerly as he snatched up her basket.

'Thank you, everyone,' Mary said with a smile.

The two chatted as they walked and Skinny gave Mary an insight into their lives and how they had come to be living as they were.

'My mum died having me and my dad d'aint want me, so I was dragged up by a neighbour. When they moved to Wolver'ampton they couldn't tek me with them, so I was left behind. They d'aint say persactly where they were going in case I tried to foller 'em, so I went wandering. Fingers found me in a shop doorway and took me back to Doe Bank.'

Mary's heart went out to the boy, who had evidently never had any schooling.

'Fingers's step-dad chucked him out cos he d'aint like kids and wouldn't pay the fees the fancy school charged. Fingers found the houses where we live now and tried to mek them nice.'

Skinny paused while Mary bought some vegetables and dropped them into the basket he still carried.

'Owl's mum died when she was little, then last year her dad went an' all. He was a miner and had coal dust in his lungs. The pit master threw Owl out of the house 'cos it was his property. Then he tried to put her in the workhouse, so she legged it.' The statement brought back memories of her own eviction, and Mary gave a little shiver.

Another pause came as potatoes went into the basket.

'Carrot left 'cos there was ten kids younger than him in the family.'

'So to relieve the pressure on his parents, he moved out?'

'Ar,' Skinny nodded.

'That was a very grown-up decision to make,' Mary said.

'They was gonna sell him anyway, so he decided to run. Lofty was sold to a chimney sweep 'cos he's little and thin. He said his knees and elbows got skinned a lot and used to bleed, then they were bathed in salt water to harden 'em up. So one night he hot-footed it out of there.'

Mary purchased some pork chops, then Skinny continued.

'Queenie's mum died, and her dad thought as the oldest of four she should take over as being mum to the others. Then he tried to—'

'I understand,' Mary jumped in quickly, 'so in order to keep herself safe from his unwanted attentions, she left.'

'That's about it,' Skinny said. 'Somehow, Fingers seemed to find us all and now we'm a family.'

'How do you manage for food and clothes, coal and candles, and personal items for the girls?'

'We scavenge when there ain't any work. I used to go on the rob, but Fingers won't allow it no more. He sez we have to stay on the right side of the law. It's hard, I can't deny, specially in the winter when it gets really cold.'

As they walked up Spring Head, Mary asked, 'How long can you go on like this before one of you is seriously ill, though?'

'Dunno, but it's all we've got.'

Going in through the back door, Mary put a finger to her lips. When Skinny nodded his understanding, he placed the basket on the table.

'I'm back. Dora?' Mary called out.

'She's run off!' Edith yelled. 'She tried to kill me then she took to her heels!'

Mary and Skinny stared at each other, horrified looks on their faces.

## 10

Mary pointed to a kitchen chair with a quiet, 'Shush,' and as Skinny sat down, she rushed into the sitting room.

'What's happened?' she asked, glancing at the mess on the hearth rug.

'Your *daughter* attacked me with those!' Edith stabbed a bony finger at the fire irons.

'Why?'

'Because she's evil! That soot fell and I asked if she'd mind cleaning it up and – she went for me! She hit me in the belly, it's lucky the chair was behind me to break my fall!'

'Where's Dora now?'

'How the hell should I know?'

'I'll have to go and look for her.'

'What about me?'

'Mother, you are perfectly capable of making yourself a drink and something to eat. I'm going to search for Dora. I'll be back when I find her.' With that, Mary dashed back into the kitchen.

Skinny followed her out of the back door, having heard every word.

'I must tell the police that Dora is missing,' Mary said as she looked this way and that in the hope of spotting her daughter.

'They won't do nothin',' Skinny said. 'You'd do better to let us find her.'

'Where can she have gone? Which way would she choose? Oh, Dora, where are you?' Mary's anguish was evident as her hands went to her face.

'Mary, come on, let's tell the others and then we can make a plan,' Skinny said, clutching her elbow. 'Fingers will know what to do.'

Standing on the corner between Spring Head and Ridding Lane, Mary looked around frantically. The noise spilling out from the public house was lost on her as her eyes strained to see down Lower High Street. Turning, she stood on tiptoe to see across the marketplace.

'Mary, come on!' Skinny urged again.

His voice snapped Mary out of her trance-like state, and she nodded. They began to run, oblivious to the stares of people they passed.

Arriving back at Doe Bank out of breath and sweating, Skinny called out for Fingers.

'He's gone across the Coppice,' Queenie said as she came through from the kitchen. 'He said he was going to try his luck at the canal at Gospel Oak.' Seeing Mary's troubled face, she asked, 'Mary, Skinny, what's happened?'

'Dora's gone missing – I have to find Fingers!'

'Oh, bugger! Mary, sit down and I'll make you a brew,' Queenie said as Skinny ran off to find his friend.

'Thank you but no, I can't stop. I have to find Dora!'

'Where will you look? Which direction? You could go down one street as she goes up another. You could wander all day and not see her. Sit and wait for Fingers and try not to panic.'

Mary sat and then her tears fell. Her whole body rocked as she cried like her heart was breaking.

Queenie made the tea and listened to the woman sobbing. *She's so kind, she doesn't deserve this*, she thought.

'I'm sorry,' Mary said with a sniff, accepting the weak tea.

'Don't be, you either care or you don't. Dora's lucky to have you as her mum.'

Just then, Owl came in.

'How are you feeling now?' Mary asked, suddenly remembering the girl had been poorly.

'Stacks better, thanks,' Owl answered and looked at Queenie, questions written all over her face.

Mary explained what Edith had said about Dora's supposed attack and her daughter subsequently running away.

'Dora would never!' Owl said in astonishment, her big green eyes opening even wider. 'She's far too nice to do such a thing.'

'My mother can be a spiteful woman sometimes. If Dora did attack her, I believe she would have been provoked into it. Girls, I'm sorry, I can't wait any longer, I have to go and look for her.'

The sound of pounding boots on the hard packed earth of the heath had all three turn to the door.

'I finded him, Mary!' Skinny said, panting hard, 'I told him... what's... happened.'

'I'm sorry to hear this, Mary, but don't worry, we'll find her,' Fingers said after snatching a breath.

'How? She could be anywhere by now!' Mary wrung her hands, becoming anxious once more.

'If she's still in Wednesbury, we'll find her,' Fingers assured her.

'Skinny, go and fetch Carrot and Lofty, please, they're on the towpath at Lea Brook Bridge, you probably passed them on your way here.'

'Righto,' Skinny said with a nod and took to his heels yet again.

'We need to get a network set up,' Fingers continued, 'so I'll need all the help I can get.' He looked to Owl as he spoke.

'I'm in,' she replied.

'Me an' all,' Queenie added.

'And me,' Mary said.

'Right, Queenie, where's that old map of the town?'

Queenie shot next door and returned a moment later with a dog-eared folded piece of paper.

'Thank you,' Fingers said as he carefully unfolded the map and laid it on the table. He stared at it, thinking hard, while they waited for the others to return. From the corner of his eye, he could see Mary shuffling her feet in frustration.

'Mary, does Dora know the town well?' Fingers asked at last, not taking his eyes from the map.

'The marketplace, certainly.'

'Then you take that area,' Fingers said, and Mary nodded eagerly.

Skinny, Carrot and Lofty came rushing in, puffing and blowing from their exertions.

'Skinny told us,' Lofty said.

'Good. Mary is doing the market. Lofty, you take the pubs in Meeting Street and Dudley Street. Carrot, Holyhead Road and Albert Street. Queenie, New Street. Owl, High Street and Union Street. Skinny, Portway Road, and I'll do Camp Street and Russel Street. Mary, what is Dora wearing today?'

'Oh, erm...'

'Take your time, think,' Fingers instructed gently.

'A white dress and lemon cardigan,' Mary said.

'All right, pass the word, everyone. We need to find Dora before nightfall.'

'Why the public houses? Dora wouldn't go into one of those,' Mary said.

'Every pub in the town has one or more kids helping out, so we'll ask them to join our search. They'll tell the draymen who will keep an eye out and spread the word to the next tavern they visit. Youngsters working in shops, tea rooms, on the canals, in the wharves, round the railway station – they are all part of our network.'

Mary was astounded, and at last a smile formed on her lips. 'Thank you,' she whispered. Surely, with help such as this, they were bound to find her missing daughter.

'Let's get to it, then, we have a lot of ground to cover,' Fingers said, then to Mary he added, 'We'll find her.'

Each child set off in the direction allocated to them, all praying Fingers was right and they would find their new friend.

* * *

Dora wasn't sure where she was going when she ran from the house. All she could think of was that she had killed her grandmother. She charged up Church Street into Ethelfleda Terrace and into the grounds of St Bart's Church. Sitting on her coat on the grass in the lea side of the building to catch her breath, Dora was petrified the police would be searching for her. If she was caught, would they put her in jail? She was only ten years old, after all. What would happen to her? Would her mum ever forgive her? Where would she end up? Would she be sent to the asylum?

Feeling wretched beyond belief, Dora sobbed quietly, the tears coursing down her cheeks and dripping off her chin into her lap. She had nowhere to go and no one to turn to. She knew she couldn't go to her friends at Doe Bank, she didn't want to get them involved. She was alone and had to stay in hiding somehow. She must find somewhere to spend the night, where she would be safe and sheltered. Then there was food and water to find. How she was supposed to do this all on her own, she had no idea, but she had to try. She would be an outcast now, an outlaw in fact, on the run for committing murder.

Picking at the grass, Dora tried to think what to do as the late summer warmth wrapped her in its comforting embrace. Lying down on her coat, she gazed up at the azure sky, watching the birds performing their aerobatic dance. Exhausted by crying and the adrenaline finally leaving her, Dora felt her eyelids begin to droop and, lulled by the music of the insects, Dora allowed herself to drift into the sanctuary of sleep.

Whilst Dora slept, her friends were busy, calling their message to carters, passing it to children playing in the streets, and the web of searchers quickly widened. Youngsters helping in the yards of ale houses dashed to the next one to stretch the thread of the missing girl in the hope of finding her. Railway porters and canal boats were asked to keep an eye out for their friend.

All day, the search went on and as the sun lowered gently to the horizon, hope waned. No one recalled seeing a young girl dressed in lemon and white who was called Dora Parsons.

Everyone gathered back at Doe Bank as the sun set, leaving a scarlet sky in its wake.

Mary was distraught, pacing the room as Queenie lit the candles against the oncoming darkness.

'I asked at every stall in the market. I spoke to complete strangers and no one had seen her! Where on earth could she be?'

'She'll be holed up somewhere out of the chill of the night. We'll start looking again early tomorrow. It won't take long now the network is in force,' Fingers said, trying his best to console Mary.

'I'll go home. Maybe she'll come back when it gets really dark,' Mary said. 'Thank you, everyone, I appreciate your efforts.'

Bidding them farewell, Mary trudged home, feeling weary to the bone.

'Is that you, our Mary?' she heard the call as she stepped into the house.

'Yes,' she replied tiredly. Her legs ached from walking the streets all day and she felt wrung out like an old dishcloth.

'I've had no food and I'm starving!' Edith yelled.

'Would it hurt you to ask after your granddaughter?' Mary mumbled as she put the kettle to boil and lit the gas lamps.

Going through to the sitting room, she noted the mess of soot still on the hearth, but the lamps were lit. With a sigh, she began to clean up, but her emotions spilled over as she realised this was the cause of all the upset. On her hands and knees, Mary burst into tears.

'Crying won't help!' Edith snapped. 'The best thing to do is to keep busy. Making us something to eat will take your mind off it.'

Turning to face Edith, Mary ground out, 'My girl is missing! She's out there in the dark on her own and it's all because of you!' Mary's arm shot out towards the window and she was gratified to see Edith flinch.

'Don't be so dramatic. She'll be back when her belly grumbles loud enough.'

'She could be hauled away and sold on! She could be snatched and forced into a brothel! She could be drawn into the underworld of theft and murder!' Mary was on her feet now, her anger boiling to the surface.

'For God's sake, Mary, get a grip on yourself!'

Throwing down the little brush and shovel, Mary stomped from the room.

Making tea in the kitchen, she muttered, 'Whatever happened

here, I can see why Dora took off. I'm seriously thinking of doing the same, and to hell with you, Edith Pitt!'

'Where's my cup of tea?' the call came.

Mary ignored it as she sipped her hot drink.

A moment later, Edith appeared in the doorway.

Mary stared at the table as Edith sat down with a groan. Her tea finished, Mary put the cup and saucer in the sink and left the room.

Edith heard her climbing the stairs and called out, 'What about me?' No answer was the stern reply.

## 11

Dora had no idea her friends were searching for her, and as night fell, she donned her coat and tried the door to the church. It was locked. She shivered as she glanced around her, not from cold but from fear. The sky had turned inky black, and the stars glittered into life one by one. An owl hooted and she shivered again.

Walking back out onto the street, she thought about the woman for whom the street was named. Ethelfleda, the Lady of Mercia, who had protected the land from invading Norsemen. Dora didn't feel as brave as that lady, who must have lived so very long ago. In fact, Dora felt more and more afraid with each step she took.

Walking the route of Church Steps towards Trouse Lane, she was surprised to see an old man standing on the corner. He held out his pannikin as she approached, and Dora dug into the pocket of her coat. Pulling out a halfpenny, she dropped it into the metal cup, the sound ringing clear in the quiet night.

'I'm afraid it's all I have,' she said softly.

'Thank you, miss,' the old man said as he fished out the coin and shoved it in his pocket. 'It's a bit late for you to be out alone, I'm thinking.'

Dora nodded as she took in the beggar's ragged clothes, visible in the pool of yellow light from the street gas lamp. His tattered attire didn't fit at all with his elegant speaking voice, Dora thought.

'Might you be on your way home?'

Dora shook her head, not wishing to give her reason for not being tucked up in bed.

'I see. It's not safe out here on the streets at night, you know. May I ask your name?'

Dora looked up and down the road for any signs of danger, and seeing none, she returned her attention to the beggar. 'Dora Parsons.'

'My name is Elijah. Whatever drove you out here must have been quite dire. But you know, if you don't go home, you won't sort it out, Dora.'

'I can't.' Dora's voice was hardly more than a whisper.

'Hmm, that bad, eh?'

'Worse.'

'Oh, dear. You feel like telling me about it?'

Dora shook her head again. 'It's too awful!' she said, a sob catching in her throat.

'Nothing is ever as bad as it first appears, and sometimes sharing a woe helps.'

'I've done something terrible!'

'So much so that you can't right it?'

'Yes,' Dora admitted with a nod.

'If you tell me, it may be we can find a solution between us.'

Dora's next words came out in a rush. 'I killed my Gran – I think!'

The beggar gave a soft whistle, then said, 'You think? Are you not sure?'

'Well, no – I pushed her and she fell into her chair. Her eyes were closed and she wouldn't answer when I spoke to her.'

'Did she bang her head on anything?'

'No, she just plopped into her armchair.'

'Well, that doesn't sound like something that could hurt some-one. Consider this, could she have been playing dead to teach you a lesson? Do you think that's possible?'

After a moment, Dora replied, 'Yes, now you mention it, that could be a possibility. She doesn't like me, you see. She hits me all the time when my mum isn't around.'

The beggar nodded. 'And what does your dad say about that?'

'He died, so there's only Gran, Mum and me.'

'If I may offer an opinion?'

'Yes.'

'It's my thinking your gran isn't dead at all. It's most unlikely she could pass from this world from a push from you, unless her heart gave out, which would not be your fault.'

'Really?'

'Most certainly. Now, the only way to find out for sure is to go home.'

'Maybe you're right. But what about you?'

'Me?'

'Yes, have you a home to go to?'

'Yes, my dear, I have and I shall go there once I'm sure you are safely back with your mother. So, young lady, lead the way.'

The two chatted quietly as they walked along the streets and up into Spring Head, the words her mother had drummed into her about not speaking to strangers having gone completely out of her head.

'I live here,' Dora said.

'Very well – in you go.'

'Will you come in with me? Please say you will, my mum won't mind, I'm sure. She'll probably make us some tea.'

The beggar glanced up the drive at the welcoming lights in the windows.

'Thank you. Well, if you're sure, then I accept your kind invitation.'

Walking up the drive together, they reached the back door, but when Dora tried the handle, she found it locked. Calling out, she banged hard and in not even a moment the door was open and she was wrapped in her mother's arms.

'Mum, Mum, you're squeezing me too tight!' Dora croaked.

'Oh, sweetheart! You've had us all so worried!' Mary sobbed.

'Mum, this is Elijah, he brought me back safely so I invited him for a cup of tea.'

'Please come in,' Mary said and set the kettle to boil. She looked at the old man, whose hair and long beard were silver-white, but surprisingly clean and combed. His clothes were tattered and he held a stick like a shepherd's crook. His boots had seen better days but held a shine on the toecaps, and Mary wondered if he had been a military man at one time.

Cutting bread and cheese for Dora and her visitor, Mary made a huge pot of tea as she listened to Dora explaining why she had run away.

'Darling, your gran is fine!' Mary gushed.

Dora looked at Elijah, and he nodded as she said, 'You were right.'

'About what?' Mary asked.

'Elijah said Gran might have been trying to teach me a lesson.'

'Not a very good one, either, if you don't mind my saying,' Elijah added.

Again, Mary was surprised by his speaking voice, with no trace of a Black Country accent.

'Dora and her gran don't get on, I'm afraid,' Mary said.

'So I gathered,' Elijah said without recrimination.

'Skinny and the others have been out searching for you all day and I was going to the police station in the morning to report you missing!'

'I'm sorry, Mum,' Dora said miserably, then more sternly she added, 'but if Gran hits me with her stick again I'll go – and never come back!'

'Mary! Mary, what's going on?' a voice screeched from upstairs.

Elijah quickly got to his feet, saying, 'I must be away.'

'Thank you for bringing Dora back safely. Can I make recompense?' Mary asked, reaching for her purse.

'No, dear lady, the food and drink were recompense enough.' Elijah touched the halfpenny in his pocket, a coin he would treasure, for it had been given selflessly. Bidding them goodnight, Elijah left via the back door.

Hearing groans and puffing and blowing, Mary rolled her eyes. *Now the truth will out*, thought Dora. *And if Gran tries to put the blame on me, I'll just tell her straight, and to blazes with the consequences!*

## 12

Edith clumped down the stairs as Elijah left, and saw Dora and Mary sitting at the table.

'You're back, then,' she said scathingly.

'Don't start, Mum, please,' Mary said in answer.

Ignoring the comment, Edith went on. 'You've had your mother worried sick, young lady!'

'I've apologised to Mum already,' Dora replied.

'Where's my apology?' Edith asked.

'I'm not sorry I did what I did. You shouldn't have hit me with that stick!' Dora jabbed a finger at Edith's walking cane.

'Don't be impudent!'

'Stop trying to blame me all the time! You struck me, remember!' Dora yelled.

'Stop it, both of you!' Mary interjected. 'I'm sick to death of you falling out all the time!'

'I knew it would be my fault,' Edith said as she took a seat and eyed the extra cup on the table.

'A kind old man brought me home,' Dora said as she noted the look. She was not about to say more because she wanted Elijah to be between her mum and herself.

Edith harrumphed. 'Any more tea in that pot?'

Mary fetched a cup and saucer and poured the tea for Edith.

'So where have you been?' Edith asked pointedly.

'None of your business,' Dora replied.

Mary sighed loudly. No matter what she said or did, these two would never see eye to eye. 'We're all tired. Why don't we drink up and let's all get to bed.'

\* \* \*

It was very early the following morning when Mary and Dora rushed along to Doe Bank to let everyone know Dora was home and safe.

The gang were up and eating a meagre breakfast in the boys' house when they arrived, and it was Skinny who ran to hug Dora.

'We came to thank you all very much for your help yesterday,' Mary said.

'We're just glad you are back,' Fingers said to Dora, but with a smile directed at Mary, who looked exhausted but happy.

Skinny let go of his friend and returned to his piece of toast. Mary was given tea, while Dora explained why she had run away in the first place.

'Why didn't you come here to us?' Queenie asked.

'I didn't want to impose on your good nature, and I was frightened about getting anyone in trouble,' Dora answered.

'You can suppose all you like, can't she, Fingers?' Skinny said.

'Indeed,' Fingers replied. 'In fact, if you would like to stay for the day, you are quite welcome.'

'Can I, Mum?' Dora was excited at the prospect of spending a whole day with her friends.

'Of course you can, but be home before dark,' Mary instructed.

'I will.'

Mary watched as Queenie, Owl and Dora went next door, chatting excitedly. Then she took her leave.

As she walked home, Mary considered the events of the previous day. Because of a fall-out with Edith, Dora could have been lost to her forever. If not for that old beggar, she might never have been found. Due to the swift action taken by the children of Doe Bank, the message of a missing girl was passed around the town quickly and efficiently. Now another message would travel the same route saying Dora Parsons had been found and was safely home with her family.

Mary thought again about Elijah the beggar, the kind old man who had brought her daughter home. She couldn't remember having seen him on the streets before, but Wednesbury sprawled out across a fair distance, so it could be they hadn't crossed paths previously. She hoped he knew how grateful they were, and that they might see him again.

The shrill voice greeted her as she entered the back door, and Mary sighed.

'Where have you been? I've had no breakfast yet and I had to negotiate the stairs on my own!'

'Clearly you managed well enough,' Mary said under her breath.

'Did you hear me?'

*The whole world heard you!* Mary thought but said instead, 'Yes, Mother! I'm making you some breakfast now.'

'About time, too!'

Mary put the kettle to boil and reached for bacon and eggs to cook for Edith. As she worked, she couldn't help but wish that she'd stayed at Doe Bank with the children instead.

* * *

Elijah, too, was breaking his fast with a mug of hot tea, bacon and eggs, and toast and jam. He sat in the tea rooms, having paid with the money he'd collected begging on the streets. The owner of the café did not object to him eating there for he was clean and tidy and didn't smell bad, and Elijah was grateful for a place to sit down. As he ate, he recalled the flurry of activity of the day before.

It had still been morning as he was walking past the Joiners' Arms in Camp Street, when he had called to a young boy who dashed from the back yard of the building, nearly running into Elijah.

'Why the hurry, lad?' Elijah had asked.

'A little wench has gone missing, run away from home, Mister, and I'm passing the word.'

'Who is she, do you know?'

'Girl by the name of Dora Parsons and she's dressed in lemon and white.'

Elijah had given the boy a penny, which he fished from his coat pocket, and sent him on his way. Then the old man had taken some time to consider – where would he go if he had run away? He put himself in the little girl's shoes and tried to imagine her feelings. She would be scared and want to hide somewhere she could feel safe. A church, maybe?

Elijah had spent all day looking in all the churches of Wednesbury. Walking from St John's then to St Mary's chapel, he had at last seen young Dora as she left St Bart's as the night was drawing in. The question then had been which way would she go? Ethelfleda Terrace, Church Hill or Church Steps? Once he was sure of her direction, he made his way through the back yards of the houses along Wellcroft Street to Trouse Lane, where he stood in wait.

He certainly hadn't wanted to follow her, for she might have feared she was being preyed upon and taken to her heels. Had that have happened, he would have lost her, for she could run much faster than him. He recalled again how he prayed she would not be frightened by him as he shook his pannikin, and God be praised she had stopped to talk to him.

Elijah smiled at the waitress who presented him with another mug of tea. Then his mind returned to the place where Dora lived. He knew the street and the house; he had passed it many times over the years.

Sipping his tea, Elijah allowed himself to be drawn back into time gone by, when his life had been very different to the one he lived now.

\* \* \*

Whilst Elijah was reminiscing, Mary was being run ragged by Edith. Trying to clear the breakfast dishes, Mary was interrupted by being told to fetch Edith's knitting. The old woman wanted to finish the cardigan she was making for herself. Then she wanted fresh tea, and a visit to the privy before she finally settled, allowing Mary to get on with her chores.

Mary's mind, however, was on her daughter. She had been so relieved to see Dora home, and realised how lucky she was that the old beggar had found her. Dora could so easily have been picked up by an unscrupulous type and sold on. She could have been on a ship to distant lands by now. Mary shivered at the thought. Thank God Dora was safe.

Snapping her mind back to the task in hand, Mary rolled out the pastry for the pie she was making. Then she wondered what Dora and the others would have for lunch. She would pack a basket and run it down to them once she had cleared away her baking.

With cheese, bread, fruit, cake, tea, sugar and milk neatly

packed, Mary called through that she was popping to the market. She set off for Doe Bank instead. Hurrying down the street, she hoped Dora would not see the visit as her mother checking up on her. Mary was concerned only that the children should have something to eat.

It was a long walk and there were many ways to get to her destination. Joining Lea Brook Road, Mary walked quickly through the tunnel beneath the railway line. Passing the chapel and the pottery works, she crossed Lea Brook Bridge. The rows of houses either side of the tramway told her she was almost there.

When she arrived, she sang out Dora's name and all three girls came outside to greet her.

'Mum?' Dora asked.

'I can't stop, sweetheart, I just brought you all some lunch,' Mary said breathlessly as they went indoors.

'Ta,' Queenie said as she took the food passed to her by Dora.

'Thanks, Mum,' Dora said giving the cake to Owl.

'Enjoy your day, lovey, I'll see you later. Bye, girls,' Mary said and turned to leave.

'Thanks,' the three chorused before Queenie put some aside for the boys when they returned.

Mary rushed home, stopping only to buy some flour in case her outing was questioned by Edith.

At five o'clock, Dora arrived home, escorted by Skinny.

'Thank you for seeing Dora home safely,' Mary said to the boy.

'S'all right, can't have a lady walk by herself,' Skinny said with a grin.

'Will you be going again tomorrow, Dora?'

'No, Mum...' Dora began but Skinny cut across her words, eager to pass the message he'd been given.

'Fingers said to say we won't be in tomorra, Mary, cos we all 'ave to go out to earn a few pennies.'

'All right, Skinny.' Mary still felt awkward calling him by his nickname but knew he was more used to it than his given name of John.

'I'll see you in a couple of days, then,' Skinny said before waving and disappearing down the drive.

'I'll take a cup of tea to your gran, then you can tell me all about your day,' Mary said.

'I'll do it,' Dora offered.

'I'm trying to keep you two apart, Dora, so I don't want you going in there on your own.'

'I know, Mum, but look at you, you're tired out.'

'I am, I can't deny that.'

'Right then,' Dora nodded and carried the tray through to the sitting room, having no idea at that moment what awaited her. She knew her gran would make some smart remark or other, but she could just ignore that. What scared her, however, was that Edith was sitting and playing with her knitting scissors in a worryingly threatening way.

## 13

'Where have you been all day?' Edith asked angrily as she watched Dora place the tray on the table.

'I spent the day with my friends,' Dora replied haughtily.

'Friends! You don't have any friends, just a filthy urchin boy!'

'I do so have friends!' Dora retorted as she picked up the ribbon that had slipped from her hair to the floor. Re-plaiting her long blonde hair, she tied the ribbon in place.

'You've made a right mess of that. Come here.'

Dora eyed the old woman suspiciously. What was her grandmother up to? It was strange that she suddenly wanted to give Dora a hand with her hair when she had never done so before.

'Come here, I said!' Edith growled.

Dora stood with her back to Edith so she could have her two plaits adjusted, but then she felt the tug and heard the snip, snip. Edith whirled her around and presented Dora with her plaits, an evil grin on her face. Dora's hand shot to her head and slid down her hair, which was now only shoulder length. She looked in horror at the plaited hair in her other hand, then up at the smiling woman who had chopped off her lovely locks with the scissors kept in her knitting bag.

Unable to say a word, Dora walked slowly from the room to her mum in the kitchen.

'What the...?' Mary began as she saw the look on her girl's face.

'Gran did it!' Dora croaked before bursting into tears.

Mary gathered her sobbing daughter in her arms. She closed her eyes tight as she fought the anger building inside her. 'It's not the end of the world, sweetheart, it will grow again.' Mary tried her best to console Dora but it was no use, Dora was grieving the loss of her beautiful long hair and suffering once more the cruelty of her grandmother.

'Let me see,' Mary said. Finding a comb in her bag, she slid it through Dora's hair, and with each stroke her frown deepened. 'I think tomorrow we will have to go and see the hairdresser in the town. She can tidy it up for you.'

Dora faced her mother, a look of thunder on her countenance. 'I hate Gran! I'll never forgive her for this!'

'Dora, we can put this right...'

'How? Can you re-join this' – she held out the plaits and grabbed the hair on her head – 'to this?'

'No, but...'

'No, nobody can! Gran's gone too far this time!'

'I'll talk to her...'

'Mum, don't bother, because you know she'll twist it so it's my fault, though quite how that could be I don't know.'

'I'm sorry, love.'

'Stop apologising for her, Mum!' Dora's temper broke its barrier.

'I know I shouldn't.'

'No, you shouldn't! She's a spiteful old woman and I'm sick of it! I'd rather live out at Doe Bank with nothing than here with her!'

'Dora, you can't mean that.'

'I can and I do, Mum! Look what she did to me!' Dora's tears came again, her anger having subsided and turned to despair.

'We'll go to the hairdresser first thing in the morning,' Mary said before she stormed into the sitting room, having snatched the plaits from Dora. Following along, Dora stayed in the doorway.

Holding out the hair, its ribbon bows still attached to the ends, Mary growled, 'Why, Mother?'

'She's forever playing with it, and it gets on my nerves.'

'It's not your place, Mother! Dora is *my* daughter!'

'Don't take on so, it's only a haircut.'

'She's sobbing her heart out! Why must you be so vile to her all the time? I'll have to take her to town tomorrow and see if the hairdresser can salvage anything from the mess you've made!'

'You'll not be using my money.'

'I will. You should have thought about that before you got scissor-happy!'

'Don't you yell at me, you ingrate!'

'You're lucky we don't move out and leave you to fend for yourself. This splenetic behaviour has to stop, Mother, because I refuse to put up with it any longer!'

'You don't have much of a choice, really, do you? You could always go to the workhouse, I suppose.' Edith showed no remorse for what she'd done and raised her eyebrows as if in challenge.

'I'll tell you again, keep away from my daughter,' Mary said, her voice like a rasp on metal.

'Or what?'

'Or we'll leave you here to die alone and unloved.' Mary saw her words had the desired effect as Edith frowned. 'Nobody wants to be on their own when they take their last breath, but you will be. You can rot in that chair for all I care.'

'That's a terrible thing to say to an old person whose time is almost up!'

'This was a terrible thing to do to a youngster who has only tried to help you! A child who has never warranted the spite you show her!'

'Well, it's done now, so stop your wailing about it.'

'I can see now,' Mary said in a quieter voice.

'See what?' Edith asked.

'Why my father left you all those years ago!'

\* \* \*

Whilst the argument at Spring Head had been raging, the Doe Bank gang had spread the word that the missing girl had been found and was home again safe and well. Now, as they all sat in the boys' house, they discussed Dora Parsons and her mum.

'Mary brought that food you just ate for your supper,' Owl said, 'she's ever so kind.'

'I agree,' Carrot mumbled, his mouth full of bread and cheese.

'But Dora has a sadness about her,' Fingers said as he cut some apples to share.

'It's 'cos of her gran; the old woman is spikle to her all the time,' Skinny put in.

'Why is her gran spiteful? That's the question,' Fingers asked.

'I dunno,' Skinny replied, not realising Fingers' words were not aimed at him specifically, ''cepting her gran owns the house so Mary and Dora have to do as they'm told.'

'Ah, well, that does make a bit more sense of why Mary and Dora put up with her behaviour. The grandmother has a hold over them,' Fingers said.

'How do you mean?' Lofty asked.

'The grandmother rules the roost. If Mary and Dora don't conform, she could threaten to throw them out onto the streets.'

'They could come and live here with us,' Skinny said enthusiastically.

Fingers smiled.

'There's plenty of room in our house,' Queenie added and looked to Owl who nodded in confirmation.

'Thank you, ladies, but I'm hoping it won't come to that. It's my belief they will remain where they are, for the foreseeable future, anyway. I can't imagine them giving up living in a nice big house with plenty of food and nice beds unless they absolutely *have* to,' Fingers replied.

Skinny pushed his empty plate away, with thanks to the girls, who had saved the boys some of their lunch.

'How did we do today?' Fingers asked as he laid a shilling and sixpence on the table.

'I got a bag of logs for the fire,' Skinny said.

'Well done, we'll need those come the winter,' Fingers praised the boy.

'I didn't do so well today,' Carrot said sadly as he added his threepenny bit to the other money.

'It's more than we had yesterday, Carrot, so good on you.' Fingers always ensured he gave praise where it was warranted, and encouragement when times were lean. 'Any luck, Lofty?'

'A tanner.' The sixpence was placed with the rest and the whole pile pushed towards Queenie.

'That's good,' Fingers said to Lofty, then to Queenie he asked, 'If you would be so kind as to see what food you can get with that, please.'

As the sun dipped behind the horizon and darkness fell, Fingers lit the candles and Queenie and Owl told them all about the lovely day she'd had with Dora, picking wild flowers and playing games.

'Dora really enjoyed herself,' Owl said.

'Good. Then it was a day she will remember after her terrible fright yesterday,' Fingers replied.

They said their goodnights and retired to their respective mattresses, knowing the following day would be busy trying to earn some more money.

Over at Spring Head, Dora too went to her bed, her mind whirling with what she'd overheard.

Her grandfather had left her grandmother! Dora was not really surprised, if Edith had been as vitriolic to him as she was to her. She wondered if he was still alive, and if so where he was now. Could she ever find him? Where would she look? How could she go about it? Would her mum help?

Dora slipped into sleep, with no answers to the questions filling her head.

## 14

After breakfast the following morning, Dora and Mary set off for the hairdresser on Holyhead Road. Mrs Beckett worked from her parlour and was well known for doing a good job for a decent price.

The market stalls were being set up as they passed, and Dora heard the vendors calling cheery greetings to one another. The sound of metal poles clanging as they were put together was loud, and horses' hooves clattered on the cobblestones as produce was being delivered by cart. Boys were wheeling their wooden barrows, carrying heaps of dirt-laden potatoes, whistling as they went. Awnings were being erected to shade the stalls and vendors from the fierce sun, and fruit and vegetables were being piled up neatly to tempt potential customers. Having to run every so often to keep up with her mum, Dora kept her eyes down. She didn't want to see the looks of pity from people when they spied her hair.

Before long, they arrived at a soot-blackened house and Mary rapped the knocker. Presently the door was opened by a middle-aged woman.

'Can I help you?'

'Yes, I hope so,' Mary said, pushing Dora in front of her.

'Oh dear, what have you been doing?' Mrs Beckett asked.

'I didn't do it, my gran did!' Dora answered indignantly.

'I'm sorry, my mistake. Please come in, you poor girl,' the woman answered sheepishly.

Mary and Dora followed the woman into her work room and Dora was shown to a kitchen chair.

'What would you like me to do?' Mrs Beckett asked.

'The best you can with what's left,' Mary answered.

'What's your name, sweetheart?'

'Dora Parsons.'

'Well, Dora, for you to have a nice style it will mean me cutting a little more off.'

'No! I don't want you to!' Dora wailed.

'I'm afraid it's necessary. You don't want to leave it as it is, do you?'

Dora shook her head miserably.

'All right, then. I'll take as little off as possible but I promise you'll like it when I've finished.'

Dora sat quietly, grimacing as she heard the scissors snipping away. She prayed she wouldn't end up looking like a boy.

After an hour, Dora was given a mirror to see her new hairstyle and she beamed with pleasure. A neat fringe sat above her eyebrows, and the sides and back fell to rest on her shoulders. As she turned her head this way and that, she felt the swish of soft hair around her face.

'There you go, what do you think?' Mrs Beckett asked.

'I love it! It's very grown-up, thank you, Mrs Beckett!'

Mary sighed with relief as she paid her money, adding her own thanks to those of her daughter.

Walking home, Dora held her head high and smiled as the warm wind lifted her fair locks.

'Dora, try to stay away from your gran if you can. I know it's difficult, but I think that really is the only way,' Mary said as they walked up Spring Head.

'I will, but it's impossible when I have to take her tray in.'

'I understand, so I can do that from now on.'

'Mum, you do enough for her. It's not as though she can't walk, because she goes to the privy.'

'I know, but we can't antagonise her or we'll be out on our ears.'

'I wish we could leave and live somewhere else.'

'I know, but that's not possible, I'm afraid, Dora. I don't have any money of my own, so we'll have to be patient. There will come a time when your gran won't be around any more, but we just have to grin and bear it for now.'

*That time can't come quick enough!* Dora thought, but instantly chastised herself. She simply wanted to be with her mum, just the two of them. Dora and Mary walked home, hand in hand, both lost in their own thoughts.

The call came as expected when they entered through the back door.

'You're back, then?'

'Yes, Mum, we're home. I'll make some tea.'

'I'll take it through,' Dora said.

'I don't think that's a good idea, love, she'll only start her ranting again,' Mary answered.

'I don't mind, Mum, you can't do everything.'

'All right, sweetheart, if you're sure, but when you take the tray in, put it down and come straight out.' Mary considered going in with her, but she didn't want Dora to think she wasn't trusted. Listening out for any argument that might begin, Mary knew it wasn't fair that her daughter had to wait hand and foot on Edith, but what could she do? She was exhausted from all the running around so just had to pray Dora would heed her words.

Dora nodded. She wanted to help her mum as much as she

could and if it meant seeing to her gran, then so be it.

Carrying the tray through, Dora laid it down and turned to walk away.

'You've had your hair done, then.'

'Yes.'

'It looks awful. Far too grown-up for you!'

'I like it.'

'You would. I suppose Mary paid for it with my money?'

Dora shrugged, then, with a flick of her head, she left the room.

'How is she?' Mary asked as Dora sat at the table.

'Nasty as ever,' Dora replied as she took a homemade biscuit from the plate.

'You two will never get along, will you?'

'No, Mum, I don't think we will. She's so rotten to me all the time. Was it Granddad leaving that made her so bitter?'

Mary's sharp intake of breath made Dora wish she'd never asked.

'Sorry, Mum, but I overheard what you said.'

'Your granddad left home when I was about your age. They used to argue all the time and I suppose he had enough.'

'Is he still alive, do you think?'

'I've no idea, lovey. I wouldn't know him if I fell over him.'

'We could try and find him!'

'Why would we do that, Dora? He'd be a stranger to us!'

'But maybe we could go and live with him?'

'It's not a good idea, pet. He may have passed away, and if not, he might not want us. It could be he has a new family now. If he wanted us, he would have come back to see me. Besides, we don't know where he went, he could have gone abroad, even.'

Dora looked downcast and, to cheer her up, Mary said, 'How about we take a walk to Doe Bank before bedtime? I'm sure we'll be made welcome there.'

'Ooh, yes, please!' Dora beamed her delight.

'Go up the garden and collect some windfall apples and we can take them with us. The basket is in the scullery, but mind the wasps.'

Dora was gone in an instant and Mary smiled as she watched her daughter run across the lawn. She thought about what Dora had said a few moments before, and how strange it was that history had repeated itself. Her father had left, as had Dora's, and now there were three females under one roof – never a good combination. Mary said a silent prayer that if and when Dora married, the same thing would not happen to her.

After giving Edith her evening meal, Mary said she and Dora were going out for a walk.

'Oh, well, do enjoy yourselves, don't worry about me being left on my own, again,' Edith said sarcastically.

'You'll be all right for a couple of hours,' Mary said.

'I'll have to be, won't I?'

Desperate to keep the peace, rather than pursue the matter, Mary left Edith to her foul mood.

Dora had listened to the exchange and fretted that her mum might change her mind and bow to the pressure exerted by her gran, but for once Mary remained stalwart.

The sun lowered as they walked, painting the sky a brilliant crimson. Children's shrieks and laughter filled the streets where they played. Birds chirped as they fought over the best night-time roosts. A dog barked somewhere in the distance and the church bell pealed the hour. The warm wind carried aromas of cooking, and Dora tried to guess what people were having as the zephyr kissed her skin.

Mary was right when she said they would be welcomed. They were invited enthusiastically into the boys' house, and everyone complimented Dora on her new hair style.

'My gran cut off my plaits, so I had to go to the hairdresser. Mum took me, and the lady was really nice.'

'Why did your gran cut your hair?' Skinny asked.

Dora looked to Mary for an answer and, when none came, she shrugged her shoulders. 'I don't know, but I do like it better this way. It's a bit more grown-up.'

'Well, your new style suits you, Dora, you look very pretty,' Fingers said.

Dora gave her thanks with a beaming smile.

Queenie made them tea, and the children accepted the apples gratefully. Then everyone told their visitors about their day.

Dora listened as Lofty and Carrot argued good-naturedly about who had done the most work that day. Mary and Dora laughed as their words turned into gentle shoves.

Skinny explained there was not much to be had at the market and Owl quickly said he was not to fret as they had enough for a meal. What she didn't say was it would only be potatoes and cabbage and, once that had gone, the cupboards would be almost bare once more.

'We did find some kindling, but it's getting harder, so we have to move further afield,' Queenie said. 'We thought we could try the slag heaps and see if there are any coal nuggets left after the pit bank wenches have gone.'

Mary listened quietly until eventually she said it was time they left.

'I'm staying home tomorrow to bake a pie with these apples before they spoil, so if you want to come, Dora, you're welcome,' Queenie said.

'Can I, Mum, pleeeease?'

Mary nodded and Dora gave a little squeal of joy.

'I'll come for you, Dora,' Skinny said, 'and I'll take you home when I get back from work.'

'Thank you,' Mary and Dora chorused together.

Saying farewell, mother and daughter set off for home. Dora chatted incessantly but Mary's mind was elsewhere. She was still thinking about whether her father, Dora's granddad, could still be in the area. She pondered the idea of trying to find him, if only to see if he was still living. She had thought about it a lot over the years, but taking care of Dora and Edith took up all of her time. Could she find the time now to search? Did she really want to? How would he react if she managed to discover his whereabouts? Would he welcome her or shun her? The questions weighed heavily as Dora prattled on the periphery of her hearing.

Arriving home, Dora went straight to bed, leaving Mary to deal with Edith.

The old woman was asleep in her chair and Mary looked at her, anger and hurt mingling in her heart. *You drove my dad away, my husband, too, and now you're trying to do the same to my daughter.*

Edith opened her eyes as if she knew she was being watched. 'It's about time! I'm ready for bed.'

'There's no reason you can't do that by yourself!' Mary said sharply, her thoughts of earlier fuelling her anger.

'I can't manage the stairs, Mary, you know that!'

'What I know is you are not an invalid. I've seen you use the stairs on your own, and Dora tells me you can walk about when you choose to.'

'That child is a born liar! She wants a bloody good hiding!'

Mary ignored the comment as she dragged Edith out of her chair. Following Edith to the stairs proved her point about the old woman managing perfectly well on her own.

After getting Edith into her nightgown and settled into bed, Mary spoke quietly and with menace. 'You touch my girl again and I won't be responsible for my actions.' Without waiting for an answer to her statement, Mary walked from the room.

## 15

True to his word, Skinny arrived early to collect Dora. Mary had packed a basket with food for their lunch. A large meat and potato pie, a wedge of cheese, a fresh loaf, buttered scones with a little pot of jam, fruit cake and lemonade.

'Have a lovely day,' Mary said, passing the basket into Skinny's outstretched hands.

'We will. See you later, Mum,' Dora said, clearly eager to be gone.

'Don't be late back.'

'I'll bring her back, Mary,' Skinny assured her.

'Off you go, then.' Mary watched them go and she smiled. She was so very glad Dora had at last found some friends.

'Are we eating today or what?' the screech sounded from the other room.

'One thing at a time!' Mary yelled back, before cutting some bread for toasting on the fire in the range. The tray ready with a plate of buttered toast and a pot of tea, she carried it through to Edith.

Opening her mouth to berate Mary, Edith thought better of it when she saw her daughter's glare.

Mary returned to the kitchen to have a cup of tea in peace.

The morning at Doe Bank was no different from any other as the children ate what food they had and went off to work. Queenie and Owl stayed home to welcome Dora and bake a pie with the windfall apples.

Leaving Dora with the other girls, Skinny raced off to the market for a day's scavenging.

While they worked, peeling and coring the apples, Dora shared what she'd overheard about her grandfather running away.

'Is that what makes your gran so spiteful, do you think?' Owl asked.

'Owl!' Queenie said sharply.

'What? It's true, ain't it?' Owl answered the reprimand.

'I don't know, but I suspect so,' Dora said. Then she confided that she had found the blue baby clothes in the attic and her gran's comments about being the child left alive.

'That woman is wicked! Fancy saying those horrible things to a kid!' Owl remonstrated.

'I try to ignore her,' Dora replied.

'It must hurt, though,' Queenie said as she packed the pastry full of apple slices.

Dora nodded and changed the subject so that she didn't get too upset. 'I wonder how the boys are getting on.'

'Good, hopefully,' Queenie replied.

Skinny, at least, was faring well in the market. An old box in hand, he'd collected some fruit from Mrs O'Connell, and a few potatoes which he'd found rolling around on the floor by the vegetable stall. The clatter of horseshoes on the cobbles was loud as carts were drawn up and down the streets. The calls of the vendors were a verbal exchange as each tried to outdo the others. Women wrapped in shawls pushed and shoved their way through the throng, looking for a bargain, and Skinny joined the melee.

Threading his way between the stalls, he saw old clothes for sale, boots, pots and pans, fruit and vegetables, flowers which gave off a heady perfume. Moving on, he smelled fish, then heard the clink of crockery as a stallholder piled cups into a high tower. Skinny watched the man's hand move from side to side, making the cups undulate like a snake before they were placed back on the barrow. Saucers were placed on the length of the man's arm up to the shoulder, then Skinny gasped as he tilted his arm and the crockery slid down into a neat pile in his hand.

Skinny could have watched the man's antics all day, but he dragged himself away and plodded on, his eyes always searching for discarded food. He was given a fresh loaf and a chunk of cheese, and he found a couple of onions before he got to the butcher's stall. Placing the box on the floor between his feet, he steeled himself for a long wait. Mr Hollingsworth might give him something for free if he waited until the crowds thinned out.

Watching a woman dig in her purse, Skinny saw her drop a coin. 'Hey, missus, you dropped summat,' he called out.

The woman retrieved the coin, giving her thanks, and Skinny smiled at the warm feeling of doing a good deed. Before she walked away, the woman gave him a penny and he tipped his cap in thanks.

Eventually, there were only a few women around the stall, and the butcher threw a small package to Skinny, who caught it deftly. Dropping the faggots into his box, Skinny called his thanks. Time to move on.

As he passed yet another vegetable stall, he saw a cauliflower on the floor, its florets beginning to brown. Adding it to his box, his mouth watered at the thought of cauliflower cheese for tea. The vendor spotted him and crooked a finger. Skinny went sheepishly, thinking he was in trouble, but the woman smiled.

'Here you go, lad,' she said kindly and gave him two large carrots and a small bag of green peas. 'Cook the pods an' all,' she advised.

'Ta, missus,' Skinny beamed.

Wending his way down the market, Skinny decided it was time to go. The girls would be delighted with today's haul, and he wanted to spend some time with Dora before he had to take her home.

The aroma of baking greeted him as he entered the boys' house and the girls jostled around him, glad to see him as well as what was in his box.

'That pie smells bloody lovely!' he said, making them all smile.

Sharing out the food Mary had prepared, a plate was put aside for the others for when they returned.

Skinny's penny went into the coffers in the table drawer, and they chatted as they ate. Before long, Fingers arrived back, quickly followed by Lofty and Carrot. More coins joined Skinny's penny before they enjoyed the lunch kept for them by Queenie. The apple pie was left to cool and would be their pudding that evening.

Before she knew it, the day was drawing to a close and Dora was giving her thanks and saying her goodbyes. Carrying the empty basket, Skinny walked her home.

'Everybody sez ta for the dinner, Mary,' Skinny said as he handed over the basket.

'You're welcome.'

Once Skinny had gone, Mary listened to Dora chatter as she peeled and chopped potatoes.

'Mary! Where's my tea? I'm spitting feathers here!' the yell came from the other room.

Mary sighed loudly, then set the kettle to boil.

'I'll take it through, Mum,' Dora said, seeing the tiredness on her mother's face.

'I thought we agreed you wouldn't be doing this any more,' Mary said.

'Mum, it's madness for you to have to do everything. You'll make yourself ill, then where will we be? I'd have to see to Gran all the time, then. Please let me help,' Dora pleaded.

Mary's heart melted at her daughter's concern. 'Thanks, sweetheart, then you come right back. Don't get drawn into an argument.' Mary hated herself for having no energy and being unable to keep Dora out of Edith's way. With cooking, cleaning, washing, ironing, shopping and looking out for the children at Doe Bank, as well as taking care of Edith, Mary was worn to a frazzle.

Dora nodded but knew it would be difficult not to disagree with her gran. Balancing the tea tray, Dora walked carefully into the sitting room and placed it down.

'Where've you been all day?' Edith growled.

'Out.'

'I know that much! But where?'

'I visited my friends,' Dora answered.

'Friends! Hah! You won't have any friends when I tell them what you are!'

'What do you mean?' Dora asked with a frown.

'You're a murderer! You killed your brother!'

'I didn't! I don't have a brother!'

'Not any more you don't, because you stole his life before he was born!'

Dora fled the room in floods of tears and Edith cackled, loving her power to make the girl cry.

'Oh, Dora! What's happened now?' Mary asked as the crying child ran into the kitchen.

Dora explained between sobs what Edith had said and, as Mary tried to comfort her daughter, she wondered if the wheel of fortune would ever turn in her direction.

For now, however, she had some explaining to do

## 16

The following morning was bright and warm, typical of August, and Dora was up early.

'Happy birthday, sweetheart,' Mary said as she gave her daughter a big squeeze. 'Eleven years old today! I don't know where the time goes.'

'Thanks, Mum,' Dora said as she spied the gift on her breakfast plate.

'Go on, open it.'

Dora tore off the brown paper and was delighted to see it was a story book: *Twenty Thousand Leagues Under the Sea* by Jules Verne.

'We're having another of your favourites for tea – corned beef, onion and potato pie,' Mary went on.

'Thank you. I love my present,' Dora said as she clasped the book to her chest.

'We can read it together if you want to,' Mary said, relieved Dora was happy with her gift.

'Shall I take Gran a cup of tea?' Dora asked, concerned that her mother was looking peaky. She was sure also that Mary had lost some more weight, so she had determined to try to help her mum more around the house in an effort to relieve some of the burden on Mary's shoulders. If just taking tea through to her gran would help, then Dora would do it and put up with the snide remarks.

'I'll do it, love.'

Dora nodded and placed her book on the table. Then, before Mary realised, Dora picked up the tray and wandered through to where Edith sat staring out of the window.

'It's about time! What took you so long?'

'I was opening my birthday present.'

'Oh, your birthday, is it?'

Dora nodded as she laid the tray on the table.

'How old are you?'

'Eleven.' Dora thought any self-respecting grandmother would know the age of her grandchild, but not Edith. She didn't give two hoots.

'At your age, you should be out working!' Edith snapped.

'I'm still too young.'

'Nonsense! You could be sweeping chimneys. I'll have a word with Mary and see if we can't get you a job. You could go into service as a scullion, maybe.'

'I don't want a job! I'd rather go to school!' Dora bit back her anger. She refused to let the old woman rile her today.

'It ain't a matter of what you want, girl! You should be bringing in money to pay for what you eat!'

*Just drink your tea, you old bat!* Dora thought as she went back to the kitchen.

'I told you not to go in there. What was all that about?' Mary asked, having heard the voices but not the conversation.

'Gran thinks I should be working. She wants to put me into service as a scullion.'

'Oh, Lord, when will she stop interfering?'

'Not until I'm gone, Mum. She really believes it's my fault that my twin died.'

'I explained all that to you yesterday, sweetheart. It's not your fault at all. The baby wasn't strong enough to survive; you have to understand that and not dwell on it. Your gran is just being unkind. Take no notice of her and enjoy your birthday.'

Dora's lips drew into a tight line, but her gran's words always stung, especially as they were delivered with such venom.

'Now you're a big girl, I think you should run an errand for me,' Mary said in an effort to make Dora feel a little better.

'By myself?' Dora asked excitedly.

'Yes. I need some odds and ends from the market, so I'll give you a list and some money. Count your change, mind.'

'I will.' Dora ran to collect the basket and, once she had the list from her mother, set off, full of her own importance. At last she was old enough to be out on her own and she revelled in it. Hearing children laughing and shouting, Dora stopped outside the railings of the school. She watched the boys and girls racing around and she wished she was part of the happy scene. With a sigh, she moved on and again she thought of the talk she'd had with her mum the night before.

Mary had explained all about Dora's twin brother Joseph and how he had died. Dora had asked, 'Is that why I always feel a part of me is missing?'

'Probably,' her mum had answered. 'People say that twins have a special bond. But whatever your grandmother says, Joseph's death was not down to you, and I don't ever want you thinking it was.'

The sun beat down as Dora ambled along and she heard the birds singing and bees buzzing past.

Entering the marketplace, she went directly to the stall she needed to buy from. She checked her list: tomatoes, lettuce, radishes, cucumber, spring onions and beetroot were tucked safely in her basket, and after checking her change, she thanked the stall holder and turned to walk away.

'Hello, young Dora Parsons. How are you this fine day?'

'Elijah! I'm well, thank you. It's so nice to see you again.'

The old man smiled and inclined his head. 'Likewise, my dear. Out shopping, I see.'

'Yes, it's my birthday, so I'm allowed out on my own today.'

'Well, now, happy birthday to you.'

'Thank you,' Dora said with a smile.

The two walked back through the market, chatting as they went. Dora told the man all about her friends at Doe Bank and how she hoped her mum would allow her to visit alone later that day.

Elijah listened as the young girl spoke confidently about her playmates and how she loved being with them.

Halfway up Spring Head, Elijah bid her farewell and watched as she skipped along home. Dora turned and waved before turning into the driveway. The old man sighed and ambled away.

'Ah, there you are. Did you get everything?' Mary asked when Dora placed the basket on the table.

'Yes, and I checked my change.'

'Good girl.'

'Oh, and I met Elijah in the market and he walked me home,' Dora said as she unpacked the basket.

'That was very kind of him,' Mary said.

'Mum, I was wondering – can I go to Doe Bank this afternoon?'

'I don't see why not, as it's your birthday,' Mary agreed, somewhat reluctantly. It was a fair trek for her daughter to make alone, but she realised it was time to begin letting go of the reins.

'Yippee! Thanks, Mum.'

'However, if no one is home you come straight back – agreed? And I want you home for your tea.'

'Agreed.'

Whilst Mary busied herself in the kitchen, Dora sat with her new book.

Once she had finished her lunch, Dora set off for a visit with her friends and hoped someone would be in when she got there.

After she had left, Mary sat alone in the kitchen with a cup of tea. Her daughter was growing up fast and she knew there would come a time when Dora would meet a nice young man and go courting. That time was a way off yet, though, and Mary must keep Dora safe in the meantime.

Edith, it seemed, was making noises about Dora going out to work, even though she was still so young. It would be up to Mary to talk Edith out of the ludicrous idea, and Mary was certain it would cause more arguments than ever. However, Mary was adamant that her daughter would only go out to work when Dora was ready, no matter how much Edith raged.

'I don't suppose there's a chance of tea and a bite?' Edith called out.

Mary sighed and set the kettle on the range. Placing homemade scones, jam and cream on a plate on a tray, she carried it through. 'Tea's coming.'

'Hurry up, I'm parched!' Edith snapped.

Mary bridled as she strode back to the kitchen and, as she made tea, she wondered if Edith had wished Dora a happy birthday. She doubted it.

Taking the tea through she said, 'It's Dora's birthday today, you know.'

'Hmm,' Edith mumbled, her mouth full of scone.

'Did you wish her a happy birthday?'

Edith shook her head.

'Why not?'

Edith swallowed then said, 'Because I wouldn't mean it.'

'Why can't you just—'

'I can't like her, Mary! Why do we have to keep going over this?'

'She's your granddaughter!'

'I know and I wish she wasn't! I can't stand that child around me, Mary! There's something evil about her. You should take her to a priest and get her exorcised!'

'Don't be so stupid, Mother!' Mary was incensed at the remark. 'Why are you being so horrible?'

'I'm telling the truth! That girl will bring trouble to this door, you mark my words!'

Mary stomped out of the room and, as she sat at the kitchen table, tears of anger and frustration, sadness and loss ran down her cheeks. She was furious with Edith for her harsh words, and frustrated that the old woman wouldn't see sense. She was sad that Dora had to bear the brunt of Edith's hatred, and she felt keenly the loss of her husband, still harbouring feelings of regret that she could not have prevented his leaving. Her own father had left them when she was a girl and Mary wondered if that was when Edith had begun to turn nasty.

The silent tears dripped into her lap. Would her life change for the better when Edith was no longer around? She shouldn't wish her mother ill but couldn't help wondering what it would be like with just Dora and herself in the house.

Swiping away her tears, Mary pulled the pie out of the range for her girl's birthday tea, and hoped she was having a lovely time with her friends on her special day.

Just then, Dora walked in through the back door. 'No one was home,' she said gloomily.

'Oh, darling, what a shame. Never mind, you can go again after tea,' Mary said, and laughed as Dora danced around the kitchen with joy written all over her face.

## 17

Dora ate her evening meal quickly, eager to visit her friends. After a wash and change into a clean smock dress, she was ready to go.

'Don't speak to anyone,' Mary warned, 'and home before dark.'

'I'll be fine, Mum, don't worry.'

'Take this.' Mary handed over a small basket. In it was a large meat and potato pie, a few tomatoes, a lettuce, a jar of chutney, some ham and cheese.

'Thanks, Mum.'

'Off you go and enjoy yourself.'

Mary watched Dora leave by the back door. She was anxious about allowing her daughter to go out alone again, but knew Dora needed some freedom and trust, and Dora had kept her word so far today. With a sigh, she went to the other room.

'Where's she off to?' Edith asked.

'She's gone to see her friends.'

'What's in the basket?'

'I told her to look out for mushrooms,' Mary lied.

'I'll bet you did,' Edith said, not believing a word of it.

Ignoring the jibe, Mary picked up her knitting. The white cardigan for Dora was growing as her needles clacked together.

'That girl needs to be at work,' Edith said.

'What *Dora* needs is to be in school. She's not old enough to work, Mother,' Mary countered.

'Most girls are in service at that age.'

'Let's not go over this again.'

'I'm only saying...'

'Yes, and you keep telling me! I won't change my mind, no matter how many times you say it.'

Edith slurped her tea as she watched Mary deftly knitting.

'You should teach her how to do that, at least then she'd be doing something useful.'

'Mother, Dora is my daughter and I'll decide what she will and won't learn. Her numbers and letters are more important.'

'Won't do her any good. 'Sides, she ain't clever enough.'

Mary sighed and clamped her teeth together, refusing to rise to the bait.

Edith, however, was not about to give up. 'I can't keep her forever; she needs to pay her way.'

'She will, all in good time,' Mary responded.

'Sooner rather than later.'

'Leave it, Mum, please.'

Edith sniffed. Pulling out a handkerchief from her cardigan sleeve, she dabbed her eyes.

Mary closed her own eyes tight for a moment, then laid her knitting aside. Rising, she walked from the room, her anger mounting at Edith's pretence of being upset.

In the kitchen, she looked out of the window. The sun was still shining, so she went into the garden to enjoy the last of its rays. Sitting on the bench beneath the oak tree, she began to relax in the heat of the late afternoon. The birds twittered as Mary rested her head against the tree trunk and her eyelids slowly closed. She heard a horse's hooves on the cobbled street and a cart's wheels rattle along. A fly landed on her hand and she flicked it away. Insects buzzed and the sun warmed her skin. Finally, she felt at peace.

\* \* \*

In the meantime, Dora had hurried over to Doe Bank and was welcomed by her friends. They shared the food and Dora watched as they ate with relish.

'I got stacks of things from the market today too,' Skinny told her.

'And we collected bundles of kindling ready to sell tomorrow,' Queenie added.

'That makes sense. I came to visit earlier but you were all out,' Dora explained.

'Did you come by your own self?' Skinny asked.

'Yes, Mum agreed it was time,' Dora said proudly.

'That's great, but I'll take you back when you'm ready,' Skinny said and blushed at Dora's smile of thanks.

Lofty dug Carrot in the ribs and they giggled. Fingers shot them a look that said not to embarrass their friend.

'May I ask why your mum allowed you to travel all this way alone, twice in one day?' Fingers asked.

'Because it's my birthday, I'm eleven today.'

A chorus of happy birthdays sounded, and Dora beamed with pleasure.

'You'm an old lady now,' Carrot joked.

'Nah, she's only middle-aged yet,' Lofty said with a cheeky grin.

Dora laughed along with her friends. She was the happiest she could ever remember being and knew she would remember this day for the rest of her life.

Suddenly Fingers asked, 'Skinny, where did you put that hoop and stick?'

Skinny jumped up and ran outside, the others following along behind. Producing the items, he passed them to Dora. Seeing her blank expression, he explained, 'You have to roll the hoop then keep it going with the stick.'

Dora tried and tried but to no avail; the hoop wouldn't roll on the heath.

Skinny showed her how it was done and everyone applauded his efforts.

Lofty found some sticks, giving one each to the boys to be used as hobby horses. The girls were the maidens in distress and the boys were the knights who came to save them.

Once the ladies had been rescued, Owl pulled out a length of rope from under the kitchen sink and everyone had a turn at skipping.

Dora was taken by surprise when Lofty tapped her on the shoulder, shouting 'Tag!' before taking to his heels. Dora chased around, finally tagging Skinny. The game went on for ages until, out of breath, they all trooped back indoors for a drink of water.

Eventually, Skinny said, 'It's getting late.'

'I'd better get off home. Thank you for making my day so special.'

Skinny grabbed the basket and he and Dora left amid shouts of, 'Tarrar, birthday girl!'

On the way home, Dora saw Elijah walking into the marketplace and she called out to him. Elijah turned and waved when he recognised who it was. They walked towards each other and said hello, and Dora introduced her friend Skinny.

'It's nice to meet you, young sir,' Elijah said as they shook hands.

'Elijah was the one who found me when I ran away. He took me home,' Dora explained.

Skinny nodded.

'Skinny is walking me home today.'

'That's very gallant of you,' Elijah answered with a smile.

'Can't let her go without a shaparoon,' Skinny said proudly.

'Indeed, a chaperone in these times is very important.'

Dora was gratified the old man had not pointed out Skinny's pronunciation error.

'We need to be getting along, otherwise Mary will have my guts for garters,' Skinny added.

'It was lovely to see you both. Farewell.' Elijah waved as they parted company.

'Who is he?' Skinny asked as they walked on.

'I don't really know anything about him other than his name and that he's a beggar.'

'He's very clean for a beggar. And he speaks very well.'

'I know. It's strange, isn't it?'

Eventually they reached Dora's home and Skinny escorted her to the back door. Handing the basket to Mary, he gave his thanks for the food and Mary gave hers for his accompanying Dora home.

'See yer later,' Skinny said briskly and then he was gone.

'How was your visit?' Mary asked.

'It was marvellous. We played Tag, and I tried to roll a hoop with a stick but I couldn't do it very well. Owl lent me her skipping rope, oh, and the boys were knights who rescued us poor maidens!' Dora leaned backwards with the back of her hand to her brow in a dramatic pose. 'Thank you for trusting me to go by myself.'

Mary and Dora shared a loving hug, then a screeching voice was heard.

'Mary! What did I say about having scruffy urchins in my house?'

'Sorry, Mum,' Dora said quietly.

'Don't you worry about your gran, I'll deal with her. You just enjoy the rest of your birthday.'

Dora nodded and, as Mary went to speak with Edith, she felt the old woman was trying to spoil everything. Hearing raised voices, Dora went to her bedroom where she could read her new book in peace, but even up here she could hear her mother and grandmother going at it hammer and tongs. Clamping her hands over her ears, Dora again wished she and her mum could live somewhere else, anywhere else...

## 18

'The boy walked her home! We should be grateful to him, not angry,' Mary snapped.

'He could have left her at the gateway. He didn't need to trespass on my property!'

'He didn't...'

'He did! I saw him!' Edith growled.

'Stop it! I'm heartily sick of your whining! Push me no further, Mother, for if you do I swear you'll never see me again!' With that, Mary stalked out in high dudgeon.

Edith sat, pondering Mary's outburst. She was fighting back more often of late, and Edith realised she would have to curb her tongue if she was not to drive Mary away. The child she could do without, but Mary took good care of her. Edith knew she would struggle with chores and shopping if she was alone and the top and bottom of it all was that she needed Mary. Not that she'd admit that, of course. With the realisation that she had better watch out if she didn't want Mary walking away, Edith determined to be more careful with her snide comments and threats.

In the kitchen, Mary sat at the table and stared at an empty cup.

Edith was sending her mad and it was all she could do not to take Dora and leave. The same old argument raged in her mind; she had nowhere else to go. She was desperately unhappy but could do nothing to make life any better for herself or Dora. She just had to grin and bear it until such time as Edith shuffled off her mortal coil. But Edith could live for years yet – years of misery for Mary and Dora. They were trapped in a cage, a gilded one but a cage nevertheless.

'Mary, love, could you light the lamps so I can see to knit?'

Mary sighed as she buttered scones. At least Edith had asked rather than demanded.

Setting the kettle to boil, she spooned some jam onto the plate next to the scones. Her anger had subsided now, melting away, leaving her feeling like the worn-out unhappy woman she was. Taking the food through, she lit the gas lamps before returning to the kitchen.

* * *

Whilst Mary and Edith had been fighting, Elijah had strolled back to Church Hill House where he lived. Once indoors, he stripped off his beggar's clothes and after a wash he dressed in silk pyjamas and a dressing gown. In the kitchen, he fed the range and put the kettle on the top plate to boil. On another hot plate, he placed a pan of stew to heat through. As he worked, he thought about young Dora Parsons. She had told him about her grandmother Edith and how cruel the woman could be, driving poor Dora to run away.

Elijah learned a lot as he walked the streets in the guise of a beggar. He liked the fact that no one knew his true identity as he held out his pannikin for any change folk could spare.

Elijah led two lives, which he was careful to keep separate. His time as a beggar had taught him to listen to everything and to be observant. These lessons helped with his other life as a business-man. Owner of a fleet of narrowboats and barges, Elijah was lucky enough to be able to choose which life to lead on any given day.

With a plate of hot stew and a cup of tea, his mind was still on the unfortunate Dora and her mother. His thoughts then turned to Edith Pitt, a woman he had known for many years.

He recalled how he and George had grown up side by side from being small children. They had sat next to each other in class at school and had chased girls together as youngsters. Even as young men about to embark on a life in business, Elijah and George had kept in touch, regularly meeting for drinks and the occasional meal out.

Then George had met Edith.

They had married against his advice. Edith had taken a dislike to Elijah from the outset. Over time, the two friends had become distant, with Elijah left in the dark as to why he didn't see much of his old pal any more. Then, one day, Elijah had been delighted when George had sought out his friend once more. George had finally left Edith for another woman, and so their old friendship had sprung into new life. George explained that he'd been under Edith's spell and that when she'd told him of Elijah having designs on her, he'd allowed the distance between him and his friend to widen. He apologised and once again, Elijah and George enjoyed each other's company on the odd evening out. Elijah often shared a meal with George and his lady friend, Constance.

Elijah knew Mary had been born and he had watched her grow, marry and have a daughter of her own – all from afar. It was his promise to George on his deathbed that he would watch over Mary and her child. He had kept true to his word, without ever giving himself away, and never having met either until that day Dora had absconded.

Many times, Elijah had wondered about divulging his secret,

but he worried it would cause tremendous upset if Edith found out. So he had kept his counsel and his promise to George.

* * *

The following morning, the sun was out early and, as it looked set to be another fine day, Mary decided to wash the bed linen.

Heating pots and pans of water for the tub, she asked Dora to strip the sheets from Edith's bed.

'Give me a hand with the laundry, then you can go across to Doe Bank.'

Dora ran up the stairs and into her grandmother's room. Looking around her, Dora saw the floral patterned wallpaper with the heavy brocade curtains at the window. A wardrobe and tallboy stood along one wall, with a marble-topped stand holding a water jug and bowl. On the bedside cabinet sat a small glass water decanter with a drinking glass upside down on top of it. The whole room smelled musty and old. Dragging the eiderdown and blankets off the bed, she laid them on the ottoman before pulling off the sheets. Tugging hard, she saw the mattress move slightly and something slide to the floor. Seeing it was a document, she picked it up and read the title page.

*Last Will and Testament of Edith Pitt.*

Desperately wanting to read it but knowing it was private, Dora glanced at the door standing ajar. Should she just peek? She knew there would be ructions if she was caught snooping, but her curiosity got the better of her. Opening the document, she read the words quickly before her breath caught in her throat.

Replacing the will in its place beneath the mattress, she gathered up the linen and went downstairs, her heart hammering in her chest.

Now she had another dilemma. Should she tell her mother what she knew or should she keep her lips sealed?

Dora watched as Mary cut a sliver of soap and dropped it into the half-full tub of hot water. Shoving the sheets in, Mary pounded them with the dolly, which Dora always thought looked like a small three-legged stool attached to a long handle.

'Thanks, lovey, would you start to fill the rinsing tub, please?'

Dora nodded and went outside with a pail from the scullery. From the standpipe in the garden, she filled bucket after bucket of cold water, which she poured into the old tin bath that Mary had dragged outside earlier.

Going back indoors, she watched Mary lift a sheet from the hot soapy water with a set of wooden tongs. The sheet was dropped into another pail and was then carried outdoors, where it was tipped into the cold water to be thoroughly rinsed. Mary and Dora then folded the sheet lengthways and Mary fed it between the rollers of the mangle while Dora turned the handle. The sheet fell in a rippled heap into a large wicker basket, then it was pegged onto the washing line to dry.

All morning, mother and daughter toiled, Dora still saying nothing about having seen Edith's will, but it played on her mind nevertheless. Deciding not to say anything to her mother, but needing to share the burden, Dora concluded that the best person to speak to would be Fingers. He'd know what to do for the best, she was sure.

Carrying a lunch tray through to Edith, Dora scowled at the woman she hated.

'About time an' all!' Edith snapped.

'I was helping Mum with the laundry.'

'And so you should. You need to earn your keep.'

Dora glared as Edith looked over the food on her plate. Cold meat and potato pie, pickles, cheese, ham and fresh bread and butter. Edith nodded then demanded, 'Cup of tea!'

Dora shot off to obey the order, after which she would have her own lunch, then she'd be free to visit her friends.

Whilst they ate, Mary asked, 'Would you help me empty the wash tubs before you go out, please?'

Dora nodded and swallowed her food. 'If no one is in, I'll come straight home.'

'Good girl. While you're gone, I'll make up your gran's bed and find something nice for our tea.'

The mention of Edith's bed brought Dora's mind once more to the will. As she chewed, she considered again whether to reveal what she had read. How would her mum react? Would Mary be angry that Dora had pried into things that didn't concern her? As Dora saw it, it did concern her, for wasn't she family? She was only a child, yes, but she was old enough to know what was going on.

Afraid of the repercussions, Dora maintained that keeping her tongue behind her teeth was the safest option – for now, at least.

## 19

'I think I'll go to Doe Bank a bit later today, Mum, when everyone will be home,' Dora said.

'That's sensible. It will save you a wasted journey. I'll tell you what, let's make a cake you can take with you.'

Dora beamed with pleasure.

'You get everything ready and I'll wash these plates,' Mary said.

Dora fetched the butter from the cold slab and the flour, eggs and sugar from the pantry. Pulling out the mixing bowl from a cupboard and a wooden spoon from the drawer, she set to making the cake under Mary's watchful eye. When the mixture was ready, she threw in a handful of currants Mary provided, then, after greasing a tin, Dora filled it with the mixture. 'Can I?' she asked, holding up the spoon.

Mary nodded and Dora licked it clean.

The cake was placed in the range by Mary, and Dora washed up the spoon and bowl before putting the rest of the ingredients back in their respective places.

'I'm going upstairs to read my book for a while,' Dora announced when the kitchen was clean and tidy once more.

'I'll give you a shout when the cake is ready.'

'Thanks, Mum.' With that, Dora went to her room.

Lying on her bed, her book open on her belly, Dora pondered again Edith's will. She wished the time would pass quicker so she might seek the counsel of her friends. The aroma of baking drifted up the stairs and Dora smiled. It wouldn't be long now and she could make her visit to Doe Bank. Going back to her book, she read on, but finding herself unable to concentrate, she put it aside. Her mind whirled with questions about what she'd read in her grandmother's will. She felt guilty at having looked at it, but the temptation had been too great and she had succumbed.

Going to the window, she looked out onto the garden, the sunshine lighting up the lawns to a bright emerald green. The contrast between this and the darker patches beneath the canopy of the apple trees was stark.

Her excitement mounted and, unable to contain it any longer, she ran down the stairs to the kitchen.

'Your cake is almost done,' Mary said as she set Edith's tray with cup and saucer.

'I smell cake,' Edith yelled.

*I'm not surprised, with a nose that big*, Dora thought, then her stomach lurched. Her gran would be wanting her share, something Dora hadn't reckoned on.

'Cut me a large slice,' Edith called out.

Dora said nothing, she just glared down at the table in front of her.

'There you go, look at that!' Mary said as she placed the cake tin straight from the range onto a wooden board on the table.

'Gran wants a large slice,' Dora said solemnly.

'Well, she'll have to carry on wanting because this is going with you to Doe Bank just as soon as it's cooled,' Mary answered.

Dora grinned. 'She'll be angry, though, Mum.'

'Nothing new there, then. Don't you worry about your gran, I'll deal with her. Now, let's get this out of the tin and wrapped up so you can go on your visit.'

The cake, fresh bread, cheese, ham and apples all packed into a basket, Mary said, 'Remember, straight there and don't—'

'Speak to anyone,' Dora finished the warning with a smile. Grabbing the basket, she gave her thanks and set off.

'Where's my cake?' Edith yelled.

With a sigh, Mary went to inform the old woman there would be no cake as it had gone with Dora. It was scones and jam or nothing.

'You did what? I'm not a bloody charity, Mary! You have no right to be giving my food away!'

'Well, it's done now, so stop your carping. Do you want scones or not?' Mary asked, dragging her hands down her apron.

'Yes, I suppose I'll have to if that's all there is!'

Mary stamped back to the kitchen and prepared the snack.

'I'm surprised at you, Mary!' Edith began again as Mary passed the plate to her.

'Don't go on about it.'

'Money doesn't grow on trees, you know. We've little enough as it is without you giving it away!'

'Mother, for God's sake, quit your moaning!' Mary fired back.

'I'm just reminding you...'

'Well, please don't. I'm fed up to the back teeth with all your *reminding*!' Mary exploded.

Edith sniffed and reached for her handkerchief and Mary muttered, 'Here we go again,' as she returned to the kitchen.

While mother and daughter were yelling at each other, Dora walked swiftly to Doe Bank, swapping the basket from one hand to the other when it began to make her arm ache.

Crossing from Union Street into Dudley Street, she heard men talking and laughing as she passed an inn on the corner. A moment later, she turned to see a man come flying through the door to land heavily on the cobbles. 'And don't come back!' Dora heard the words before the inn door swung closed. The man got up, brushed himself down and with a crooked smile he wove his way down the street unsteadily.

Dora hurried on through the tunnel beneath the railway line and out onto Lea Brook Road. Striding over Lea Brook Bridge which spanned the canal, Dora smiled. She was almost there.

About halfway down a ginnel between some houses which led onto the heath, she heard a voice and stopped as a man confronted her from the other end of the alley.

'Hello, little lady, you're in a hurry, ain't yer? What have you got there?'

Dora paled as she realised he was blocking her way. *Don't speak to strangers.* The words her mum had drummed into her came quickly to mind.

'Cat got yer tongue?' the man went on as he took a step towards her. Dora moved backwards as she kept her eyes on the man. He looked undernourished, his thin frame evident beneath his dirty old clothes. His hair was long and uncombed and his teeth were yellow as he pulled his mouth into a wide grin. The skin was stretched over his face and his eyes had a dead look about them.

'Give me a look in yer basket.'

Dora shook her head, still backing away.

'I only want a look.'

*You want to steal my food is what you want!* Dora thought as she continued to retreat step by step. What could she do? She couldn't fight off a grown man. He would overpower her in an instant and take off with her basket, and he might hurt her in the process. Dora's heart pounded in her chest as her mind whirled.

Then, in a flash of inspiration, Dora looped her arm through the basket handle and shoved her fingers in her mouth, sending out a shrill whistle. She watched the man wince, so she did it again – and again. She kept up the signal in the hope her friends would hear it and come running.

'Shut yer row!' the man said as he lunged for her.

Dora moved back out of his way and whistled more urgently. She dared not take her eyes from the man intent on robbing her.

Just then, the whistled reply came and she heard pounding feet. Breathing with relief, Dora saw her friends appear behind the man. Just as quickly, he saw them too as he turned.

'Having trouble, Dora?' Fingers asked as they all pushed past the man in the walkway.

'He wouldn't let me through,' she answered, pointing to the scowling man, 'he wanted my basket.'

'Shame on you, trying to rob a young girl!' Fingers said.

'I weren't! I just wanted to get past her.'

'He's lying!' Dora said hotly.

Fingers, Skinny, Carrot and Lofty stood side by side in front of Dora, Queenie and Owl, showing a united front. 'I think you should try going another way,' Fingers suggested.

'Bloody kids! I'd tan your arses if you were mine!' the man growled as he turned away from them.

'I'd turn you in to the coppers as a thief if I were yours,' Fingers called out.

Once the man was out of sight, Dora put the basket on the ground and began to shake, the shock now taking over.

'It's all right, he's gone. Come on, let's get you into the house,' Fingers said gently.

'I didn't know what to do, so I whistled, hoping you were there and heard it.'

'That was quick thinking,' Lofty put in encouragingly.

Skinny picked up the basket and Queenie grabbed Dora's hand. She felt safe now her friends were here, but she still had to walk home. What if the man was waiting for her?

As if reading her mind, Skinny said, 'You ain't going home on yer own. I'm coming with you.'

Dora smiled with thanks, relief flooding her small body.

'Good idea, Skinny, Dora has had quite a fright, I think,' Fingers added.

Once indoors, Dora emptied the basket while Owl fetched some plates. Queenie made some weak tea and everyone enjoyed their food. Then Dora told them her reason for visiting.

'I love coming to see you all anyway, but I need your advice on something.'

Everyone settled to listen to what Dora had to say.

'I'll start at the beginning,' she began, before going on to tell them about discovering her gran's will and what she'd read. Gasps sounded as the tale unfolded before them; hardly able to believe their ears, the children continued to listen intently. When she'd finished speaking, it was Skinny who said, 'You and your mum will always be welcome here.'

'Thank you. My question is: should I tell Mum about it?'

Glances passed between the children as they considered their answers.

'My personal opinion is yes,' Fingers said at last, and Dora noticed the nods of agreement from the others.

'She'll be cross with me,' Dora said miserably.

'I don't think she will,' Fingers replied, 'not when she knows what's written in the will.'

'I can't believe your gran could be so spiteful,' Queenie put in.

'Some people are just wicked, and your gran is one of them,' Carrot added.

'Can I just ask – what's a will?' Skinny piped up.

The boy's question eased the tension all had been feeling. With a warm smile, Fingers wrapped an arm around the boy's shoulder before he began to make things clearer by giving a detailed description.

## 20

Fingers supplied the explanation in a way Skinny would understand, and the boy nodded as he talked.

'A will is a legal document. In this case it says that when Dora's gran dies, the house and everything in it will go to the church.'

'Shouldn't it go to Mary and Dora?' Skinny asked innocently.

'Usually parents leave their property and belongings to their children, but in this instance Mrs...?' Fingers began.

'Pitt,' Dora supplied.

'Mrs Pitt has chosen not to do that.'

'Why not, though?' Skinny asked, looking confused.

'Forgive me, Dora, if you think I'm speaking out of turn, but I believe it to be one last act of spite against you.'

'I think you're right,' Dora concurred, 'but it's my mum I feel sorry for. After looking after my gran for so long, she's going to be left with nothing and turned out onto the street.'

'Oh, Dora. You and your mum will be welcome here if that day ever arrives. But if you tell Mary now, then at least she will have time to consider your options.'

Dora nodded at the sound advice. 'Thank you, I think that would be best. I'd better go home before it gets dark.'

'Let's all go!' Queenie suggested.

Dora grinned at the idea and Skinny grabbed the empty basket before they trooped out into the fading daylight.

As they walked, Fingers decided to keep them entertained. With a broad smile, he asked, 'Riddle me this. What was given to you, belongs only to you and yet is used more by your friends than yourself?'

Puzzled frowns crossed the other children's faces as they considered the conundrum. Then Dora laughed as she shouted the answer. 'Your name!'

'Aw, yes,' groaned Owl.

'Ask us another,' Skinny said enthusiastically.

'What is it you can keep after giving it to someone else?'

'I don't know,' Skinny said sulkily.

Dora beckoned to him and whispered in his ear, then he yelled, 'Your word!'

Peals of laughter sounded, and Fingers said, 'Correct. Well done, Skinny.'

On they went, with Dora setting the next question. 'What goes round the house, comes in the house, but never touches the house?'

Eventually they gave up trying to guess, and Dora said, 'The sun.' She grinned at the groans amid the laughter, before suddenly realising they were home already. At the gate, she gave her thanks and watched as her friends ambled away. All at once, she felt the loneliness wrap itself around her yet again. Her pals had not even reached the end of the street and she missed them already.

With the basket given back to her by Skinny over her arm, Dora walked up the drive, knowing full well Edith would be watching her. Entering via the back door, Dora replaced the basket in the scullery and called out, 'I'm home.'

'Hello, love, did you have a nice time?' Mary asked as she trundled into the kitchen.

'I did, Mum.'

'Good. Are you hungry?'

'Famished,' Dora replied.

'How about some sausages and onions on fresh bread?'

'Ooh, yes, please!'

Mary set about peeling and chopping onions once the sausages were in the pan on the range, listening as Dora told her about the jokes and riddles the children shared on the way home.

The aroma of cooking must have reached the other room, because it wasn't long before they heard Edith call out, 'Are we having supper?'

Dora rolled her eyes and Mary yelled back, 'Yes.'

'Hurry up then, I'm half starved!'

*That'll be the day!* Dora thought.

'Mum, when Gran's in bed, can I talk to you?'

Mary frowned at the request and her daughter's serious expression, but nodded. 'Of course, sweetie. Have you something on your mind?'

'Yes, but I don't want *her* to hear.' Dora cocked her head towards the kitchen door.

'All right. I'll come to your room when I have your gran settled for the night.'

Whilst they had supper, Dora began to feel nervous about divulging her secret. In her heart, she knew it had to be done. She must let her mum know about the will and the sooner the better.

A few hours later, there was a gentle tap on her door before Mary walked in. Once she was sitting on the bed, she asked kindly, 'Now, what did you want to say to me?'

Dora's eyes slid to the closed door before she began in a whisper.

Mary's mouth dropped open as she listened, then tears welled in her eyes.

'I'm sorry, Mum, I didn't mean to upset you, but Fingers said you should know.'

'You discussed this with...?'

'I had to, Mum! I didn't know what else to do!'

Mary emitted a long, drawn-out sigh before nodding. 'I know, it's just that... oh, Dora! How could your gran do this to us?'

'I told you how awful she is to me and we all think it's her way of ensuring I suffer, even after she's gone.'

'No, surely not.'

'Mum! Stop defending her! Go and see for yourself tomorrow. Find the will and read it and you'll know I'm telling the truth!'

'I believe you about the will, Dora, I just can't understand why.' Mary rubbed her forehead as she spoke.

'The *why* doesn't matter, Mum, it's the *when* that's important. We have to plan for that unless...'

'What?' Mary asked.

'Well, I've been thinking, we could always destroy the will after she's gone.'

'Dora!'

'Nobody would know, and you deserve this house after all your years of taking care of her,' Dora said, her young mind trying desperately to find a solution.

'Except you, me and all your friends would know. Besides, she could have a copy lodged with a solicitor.'

'Oh, I didn't think of that. What are we going to do then, Mum?'

'Right now, I don't know, but let me think about it. Then maybe we can make a plan for our futures.'

Dora threw her arms around Mary's neck and felt the little kisses in her hair. 'I love you, Mum.'

'I love you too, sweetheart.'

After saying goodnight, Mary went wearily to her own bedroom. Once dressed in her nightgown, she stood by the window and gazed out into the night. The moon was a large cream ball amid a carpet of twinkling stars, its silver beams casting shadows onto the garden. Clouds scudded past, covering the white orb for a moment, before it was revealed again in all its glory.

Mary thought again about all that Dora had told her, including the offer from Fingers for them to move to Doe Bank. It was a kind offer and Mary realised it might well come to pass. She wished she'd never come back to this house, but she'd had no other option open to her at the time. She regretted never having learned a trade so she could have earned money enough to send Dora to school. Mary had received an excellent education and wanted the same for her daughter, but as it was not to be, she had taught Dora herself.

After years of being ordered about by Edith, who was cruel and abusive to Dora, all Mary had to look forward to now was being tossed onto the street with nothing but their clothes.

'Damn you, Mother!' she whispered. 'After all I've done for you – you do this to us?'

Sitting in the chair by the window, Mary allowed her tears to fall. Abandoned by her husband, used by her mother who intended to leave her homeless and penniless, Mary cried her woes to the moon, unable to comprehend the wickedness of the people who were meant to love her.

\* \* \*

Whilst Dora and Mary had been in hushed discussions, the Doe Bank children were doing the same over weak tea and Dora's cake.

'I can't believe how cruel Mrs Pitt is,' Lofty said, pushing his brown hair out of his eyes.

'I know. Wicked old bugger,' Carrot said.

'What can we do to help?' asked Owl, her green eyes gleaming in the light of the solitary candle on the table.

'Nothing as yet,' Fingers replied. 'All we can offer is a home for Mary and Dora once the old girl has passed on.'

'Well, they can share with us, can't they, Owl?' Queenie asked and was glad to see her friend nod her agreement.

'Until then, they are living under the threat of eviction, knowing it will come, but never knowing when,' Fingers added.

'Dora's gran needs a good kick up the arse!' Skinny snapped.

'It's such a shame; Dora and Mary are such good people,' Queenie muttered.

'We just have to continue to make them welcome whenever they call round. I don't see what else we can do,' said Fingers sadly.

Their conversation went on quite late and eventually the girls left for their own house and their mattresses. The boys also retired, but all had the unfortunate Dora and Mary on their minds as sleep eluded them. All of them were thinking how it would be with Mary and Dora living with them. It would be like having a sister and a mother, and the thought was comforting as eventually they succumbed to the pull of sleep.

## 21

The following morning, Dora was asked by her mother to go to the market for some fresh fruit and to the baker's for bread.

A little nervous after her encounter with the stranger the previous day, she swallowed her fear and set off. She had not mentioned the incident to her mother, knowing Mary would curtail Dora's outings to Doe Bank.

Entering the marketplace with its streets lined with stalls, Dora walked on, enjoying the sunshine. Buying her fruit, she then moved on to the baker's barrow. All around her came the shouts of the vendors endeavouring to entice customers to buy from them. Freshly cut flowers scented the air before the aroma was replaced by bread and cakes. Having bought a loaf, Dora walked on; it was a good chance to browse. She heard the rattle of tin pots and the clatter of crockery.

A yell from a barrow-boy had her move aside as he trundled past, pushing a wooden wheelbarrow filled with dirt-laden potatoes.

Stopping to stare at the sweet stall, Dora's eyes roved over the different sections of boiled sweets, liquorice and toffee on display.

Her mouth watered and she wondered about buying two ounces of one or another. She resisted, though, knowing the change in her dress pocket belonged to her gran.

'They smell heavenly, don't they?'

Dora turned and her face lit up with a smile.

'Hello, Elijah, how are you?'

'I'm well, Dora, thank you for asking. Are you buying today?' The old man tilted his head towards the confectionery.

Dora shook her head. 'No, just looking.'

'I see. I think I might indulge myself. What would you suggest?'

'Oh, boiled, definitely, they last so much longer and they taste delicious,' Dora gushed.

'Boiled it is, then.'

Dora watched as a quarter of a pound of sweets were weighed and tipped into a paper cone. Elijah paid and, opening the cone, he offered it to Dora, who took a sweet with her thanks. The old man popped one into his mouth, then bent the paper over to seal the cone.

'I'm just doing a little shopping for Mum,' Dora mumbled, the sweet pushed between her teeth and cheek.

Elijah nodded. 'How are things with your gran now?'

'Worse than ever!'

'I'm sorry to hear that.'

'You'll never guess what she's done.' Then, realising what she'd been about to say, Dora clamped her lips together.

'What has she done?'

'Nothing.'

Elijah kept his counsel. Clearly Dora couldn't or wouldn't say – yet, but he felt confident she would tell him if he was patient.

'My sweet tastes of strawberries,' Dora said to change the subject as quickly as possible.

'Mine is apple. Very refreshing,' Elijah returned.

'I must get home now or Mum will worry about me. Thank you for the sweet. It was nice to see you.'

'I've enjoyed your company and I hope to see you again soon.'

As Dora turned away, she didn't see Elijah slip the bag of sweets into her basket. She only discovered them when unpacking the goods onto the kitchen table.

'Dora, have you deviated from the shopping list I gave you?' Mary asked crossly, spying the confectionery.

'No, Mum, I swear!' Dora told her all about her meeting Elijah in the market and how he must have hidden the sweets.

'I'm sorry, I shouldn't have jumped to conclusions,' Mary apologised.

'It's all right, I can see why you would,' Dora replied. 'It was nice of Elijah, though.'

'Yes, it was. Right then, let's get some bread and cheese cut, otherwise your gran will be yelling *my belly thinks my throat's been cut!*'

Dora laughed at her mum's imitation of her grandmother before going to fetch the butter and cheese from the cold slab.

\* \* \*

Whilst Dora and Mary prepared lunch, Elijah wandered home. Washing and then changing out of his beggar's clothes, he dressed in more formal attire, ready to go about his business. Deciding to first have a bite to eat and a cup of tea, his mind remained on Dora and what Edith *had done now*.

'George, you would have loved watching Dora grow,' he whispered into the quiet of the kitchen. His thoughts were drawn back over the years once more. He and George Pitt had been pals from their school days and remained close until Edith came on the scene. Elijah never did discover why she took a dislike to him, all he could reason was she was jealous of the friendship he had with George. Best man at their wedding, Elijah had tried his best to win Edith over, but to no avail. Keeping his distance, Elijah had watched as Mary was born and grew to be a lovely young woman.

It was early one morning when George knocked on his friend's door.

Elijah played the pictures in his mind, he heard again the words spoken, and he smiled at their eventual reunion.

'I've left Edith. I've fallen in love with a lady called Constance.'

Invited in, George explained why he hadn't sought out his friend before.

'Edith told me you had designs on her and you tried to force your intentions on her. She had no option but to ban you from visiting.'

Elijah's heart ached as he recalled how Edith had thought it all right to traduce him.

'George, my friend, surely you knew I would never have done such a thing!'

'In my heart, yes, but Edith's strong character has beaten me down over time. I'm so sorry, Elijah, please forgive me.'

Elijah had of course forgiven him, and they resumed their friendship from that day on. Mary was quite young when George had left home and he and Elijah watched her from afar.

George had tried his best to stay in touch with Mary. He had called round to the house many times to see her, but Edith had ranted and raved, chasing him away. Having to battle his wife each time so he could have contact with his daughter soon took its toll on George's health, and in the end he'd been forced to give up. Despite being unable to visit, George had never stopped loving Mary. Sadly, shortly after Dora's birth, George had passed away.

A huge sigh escaped Elijah's lips on that last thought. 'I miss you, my friend, but I cherish the times we shared. You'll be glad to know I pop in on Constance from time to time and she's well. She misses you too.'

He placed his cup and plate in the sink to wash later. He had never wanted a cook or maid, much preferring to take care of himself. Happy enough in his own company, he had a routine which suited him admirably. Elijah left the house for his office. But Dora was still on his mind. How could he find out what Edith was up to now? He didn't dare visit the house for fear of the old crone recognising him and causing trouble for Mary. Perhaps Dora had confided in the young boy she had introduced him to – Skinny was his name. Did he know about her latest upset? He suspected he would, and hoped that he would meet the boy again so he could question him – discreetly, of course.

Something was tickling the part of his brain which warned him to be careful. He knew how callous Edith could be and his concern was for Mary and Dora. Elijah remembered Dora explaining that her dad had died, but he knew different. He was aware that Jim Parsons was living across town. All these years, Jim had resided alone, and Elijah had often wondered if he was still in love with Mary. So much unhappiness caused by one bitter old woman.

Shaking himself from these thoughts, Elijah hailed a cab – his work was calling.

At the office, Elijah was greeted by a young man. Mason Covington-Smythe was Elijah's sister's boy. Never having married, Annie Covington-Smythe had been left abandoned and pregnant. She had brought up her son with Elijah's help, and they had retained the family name. Both men had mourned the loss of Annie two winters previously when pneumonia took her from the land of the living. Eyes and hair so dark they appeared black, Mason sported a constant smile. He worked alongside Elijah and helped keep the business running smoothly, having a winning way with the office staff as well as the barge and narrowboat owners.

'You look perplexed, Uncle Eli,' Mason said, 'is it anything I can help with?'

'I don't think so, but I welcome the offer.' After a moment, Elijah decided against divulging Dora's business and said instead, 'It can wait, it's not important. Now, how is business?'

Elijah listened to his nephew, but all the time his mind remained on Dora and what she had *almost* told him.

## 22

Over lunch, Dora told her mum about her trip to the market and all the things she'd seen there. Then, after helping to clear the table, she went to the attic to rummage in the boxes once more.

Mary watched Edith's eyes close and when she finally heard snoring, she slipped quietly from the sitting room. Running up the stairs, her long skirts lifted to prevent a trip, Mary rushed into Edith's room. Lifting the mattress, she found what she was searching for. Looking at the document in her hand, Mary swallowed. She had to know. She had believed what Dora had told her, but she had to see for herself.

Opening the folded paper, she scanned the writing. There it was, in black and white. Everything was bequeathed to the church!

Taking a deep breath, Mary replaced the will in its hiding place and went back downstairs to the kitchen. Making tea like an automaton, she considered the implications of what she'd read.

When Edith died, Mary and Dora would be out on the street. Would the church allow them to stay in the house? It was most unlikely, as Mary had no job and no money for rent.

Naturally she had no idea when that time would come, but she must be prepared for it. The question was – how could she prepare? Where would she and Dora go? How would they survive? Would they both end up in the workhouse? She knew the workhouse in Wednesbury had closed thirty-two years ago, but the Union in Wolverhampton was still in use. The thought made her shiver. No, whatever the outcome, Mary would *not* take Dora to that dreadful place.

As she sipped her tea, Mary wondered if they should pack up and leave now. It certainly would serve Edith right for being so cruel. The old woman could be left to fend for herself, and Mary and Dora could move on and try to build a life.

A long sigh escaped Mary's throat as she considered the idea. They could always take Fingers up on his offer for them to move to Doe Bank. She knew Dora would love that, but to live in a derelict house with no means of support? However would they manage? Then again, the long and short of it was – they might have to.

Then the feelings of guilt set in once more. Edith was her mother, after all, and she'd taken Mary and Dora in when they lost their home. It was true Edith treated them both like slaves, but at least they had warm beds and food in their bellies.

Biting back tears of anger and frustration, Mary was no nearer to a solution to her dilemma.

Closing her eyes tight, Mary tried to ignore Edith calling her name, but the old girl was now wide awake and her shouting was persistent. Dragging herself to her feet, Mary shuffled off to answer the call.

'Didn't you hear me? I've been shouting for ten minutes!'

*You're a liar, Mother!* 'What is it now?' Mary asked.

'I could do with a drink.'

Mary nodded and returned to the kitchen sadly. A moment later, Dora appeared.

'There you are, sweetheart, I wondered where you had got to,' Mary said with a warm smile.

'I was upstairs.' Dora didn't want to say that she'd been in the attic; it was her special place and she didn't want her mother to stop her going up there.

The tray set, Mary asked, 'Would you mind taking this through, please? On second thoughts, maybe I should do it.'

'It's all right, Mum, I don't mind.'

Dora lifted the tray quickly, not wanting to go over the same old argument, and carried it into the sitting room, laying it on the table.

'Pass me my knitting,' Edith instructed, and Dora obliged wordlessly. 'What have you been up to?'

'Nothing.'

'Hmm. I haven't forgotten about trying to get you into service somewhere.'

'I won't go!'

'You'll do as you're told, madam!'

Dora turned to walk away when Edith spoke again. 'I expect you'll follow in your mother's footsteps and get pregnant before you're wed, then birth children like popping peas.' Dora stopped mid-stride and clenched her teeth. Would this woman ever stop trying to rile her? 'Of course, it was all your father's fault. The filthy beast couldn't keep his hands to himself.' Dora considered her gran's words an inappropriate conversation to be having with a young girl. 'Tell Mary I want some cake.'

Dora ran from the room, her mind in a whirl. Relaying the message, Dora then gave a dry sob.

'What's she said now?' Mary asked.

Explaining why she was upset, Dora waited and watched the fury cross her mum's face.

'Well, I suppose it's true what she said, lovey. I was pregnant before I was wed, but we were both to blame. We just wanted to be together. To raise a family was the only wish we had, and we were so very happy when you came along.'

'And Joseph?'

'Yes, darling, and Joseph.' Mary's eyes misted over at thought of the boy lost to her.

'Why didn't you have more children?' Dora asked innocently.

'God didn't see fit to bless us further.' The explanation was easier than to go into the whys and wherefores of the truth – that Jim had left her.

'I'm sorry, Mum. I wish Joseph hadn't died, I would have liked having a brother,' Dora said quietly.

'I wish that too, sweetheart, but it was not meant to be.'

Dora wrapped her arms around Mary and gave her a big bear hug. 'I love you, Mum,' she whispered.

'Same here, darling. You are the light of my life.'

Letting go, Dora asked, 'Shall I take that cake to Gran?'

'I'll do it, you enjoy your slice,' Mary said.

In the sitting room, Mary slammed the plate on the table and glared at Edith.

'What?' the old woman asked.

'Do *not* discuss adult things with Dora, she's not old enough to be having conversations of that sort. Besides which, it's my business – not yours!'

'The girl should know. She'd find out sooner or later, anyway.'

'If I want her to know anything, I will tell her!' Mary raged.

'Then tell her the truth about her father!'

'No, I can't. It's too late now and you won't say a word either!' Mary's anger bubbled up but also fear that Edith would divulge her secret. How could she explain to Dora that Jim was still alive? It was true she had no idea where he was, but would Dora accept this?

Edith bit into her cake, an eyebrow raised as she watched the emotions flitting across Mary's face.

With a sigh, Mary stalked back to the kitchen. 'Bloody woman!' she muttered under her breath.

Dora stared at her mum in surprise and, as Mary's eyes met hers, she said, 'Now you know how I feel.'

Mother and daughter burst out laughing and both felt the relief of sharing their pent-up frustration.

\* \* \*

Over at Doe Bank, Skinny had arrived home from the market loaded down with goodies again. The usual cheese, bread and vegetables in his box, Skinny was pleased with his haul. Emptying the contents onto the table, he took the box with him to search for kindling on the heath. *It's a good day to be alive*, he thought, feeling the sun on his face.

Collecting wildflowers as he went, he knew the girls would like them. Returning with a box full of twigs and a posy, he set the flowers in a cup of water with a smile.

A whistle sounded and he dashed outside to see Fingers with a young boy by his side. Their leader had found another orphan to join their coterie.

Skinny noted the stranger was about ten or eleven years old, although small for his age. He was a sullen-looking character with blue eyes and brown hair. The rags he stood up in were shabbier than his own and Skinny immediately thought of some clothes he'd grown out of. They would do nicely for their new housemate.

'Skinny, this is Peter Titmarsh,' Fingers said by way of an introduction.

'Hello,' Skinny responded warmly.

The boy nodded a greeting.

'Come on indoors, you can meet the others when they get back,' Fingers said.

That evening, Peter was introduced to everyone as they sat down to a meal of cabbage and potatoes.

'You don't smile much, do you?' Owl asked.

'What's to smile about? I've been on the streets for twelve months now after my folks chucked me out.'

'Why did they do that?' Queenie asked.

'Because my dad was beating my mum and I kicked him in the...' Peter glanced at the girls, then went on, 'anyway, he couldn't walk for two days and he lost his job on the railway.'

'So your parents sided against you?' Lofty asked.

'Yeah.'

'Blimey!' Carrot put in.

'So Peter is coming to stay with us. I take it there are no objections?' Fingers asked as he glanced at the faces watching him. 'Good, we'll have to get him a mattress but for now he can share mine.'

As the evening wore on, each related their sorry tale of how they had come to be living together, then Skinny told Peter about Mary and Dora Parsons so Peter wouldn't be surprised when they visited. A long discussion then took place about Dora's grandmother and how wicked some people could be.

Peter related how he'd slept in doorways and folk had passed him by like he was invisible. He had begged on street corners for a few coppers so he could eat.

Fingers went on to explain how they endeavoured to earn a living and Skinny's expertise at scavenging food.

'We all have nickersnames so we'll have to find one for you,' Skinny said.

Frowning, Peter thought Skinny might be a bit slow in the head but dismissed it. 'I've got one already. My mum used to call me a whippet 'cos she could never land a slap.'

Everyone grinned and the hours passed as the gang got to know their newest member.

## 23

The next day, Whippet accompanied Fingers to the wharf in search of work and Skinny set off for the market. The weather was still warm, but the early morning mist and chill heralded the onset of autumn. Skinny was enjoying wandering between the stalls despite the change in weather.

'Hello, Elijah,' he called as he spied the beggar walking towards him.

'Well, now, Skinny, isn't it?'

Skinny nodded. 'This is a coinkidenky seeing you.'

Elijah smiled. *It's no coincidence*, he thought, *I've been looking for you*. Instead, he asked, 'No Dora today?'

'No, I think she's at her lessons with Mary 'cos we'm all out at our work.'

'Ah, of course. Is she well?'

'Ar, as far as I know, although she's a bit worried,' Skinny said, as his eyes scanned the ground for any dropped coins.

'Oh, why is that do you think?'

Without realising that he should be keeping Dora's business

private, Skinny divulged what Dora had told them about her grand-mother's will.

Elijah feigned shock; he was not truly surprised at what he heard, knowing Edith of old. She had ever been a termagant and clearly the years had not softened her nature.

The two chatted a while before Skinny said he had to get on. Saying their goodbyes, Elijah watched the boy go about his scavenging, before turning for home.

As he ambled back to his house, Elijah thought about what Skinny had said about Edith. Dora must have found the will to know what it contained, for he was sure Edith would have kept its contents to herself. Did Mary know also? If so, what would mother and daughter do about it? Would they stay tight-lipped and continue on as they were? He assumed they would have to rather than leave, for they had nowhere else to go and Mary, he knew, didn't work. The time to worry would be when Edith died. That would see Mary and Dora out on the streets.

Indoors at last, Elijah made tea and continued to ponder. There was nothing he could do to help – for now, anyway. He didn't want Dora to find out Skinny had unwittingly shared her business and so land the boy in hot water with his friend.

There was also his promise to George to consider, that he wouldn't interfere in Mary and Dora's lives. He had wealth enough to share and could have helped, but that oath stayed his hand. He was torn between wanting to aid George's family, which would mean divulging his true identity, as well as breaking his promise to his old friend, or keeping his word and hoping things would work out for them. At least that way he could step in if things got considerably worse.

The best he could manage was to continue to watch from afar and hope Edith lived for many more years to come. That way, at least Mary and Dora would have a roof over their heads and food in their bellies, and time to come up with a plan.

\* \* \*

Back at the house, Dora was at her lessons with Mary. Given the title of 'My Life in Pompeii', Dora was busy writing a story, imagining herself living in the shadow of Mount Vesuvius, and how she escaped its eruption in 79 AD.

Mary chopped vegetables nearby, casting a proud glance at her daughter every now and then.

'I need the privy!' came the all too familiar screech.

Dora looked up from her paper and Mary shook her head. 'You carry on, I'll see to your gran.'

Mary helped Edith to the lavatory. She returned to the kitchen immediately afterwards, not wishing to be drawn into a contretemps with Edith.

'I've finished,' Dora said, laying down her pencil.

'Good girl. Just complete these arithmetic questions, then you can go and play outside.'

Dora sighed. 'I'm too old to be playing by myself now, Mum,' she said before tackling the paper of numbers in front of her.

Mary was taken aback at the statement, and a little saddened to realise Dora was right. Her daughter was growing into womanhood and Mary wondered how she had missed its onset. At eleven years old, Dora could be starting her monthlies in the next couple of years and so the all-important discussion around the birds and bees would need to take place. Mary took a deep breath – there was no time like the present.

'Sweetheart, I think as you're a young lady now it's time to treat you as such, but first we need to have a little talk.'

Dora pushed away her completed paper and listened carefully as Mary took a deep breath and ploughed on.

Eventually, as Mary finished her speech, Dora said, 'Queenie explained a lot of it already, Mum, but I'm glad you told me as well.'

Delighted that Dora had dealt with it in such a grown-up fashion, Mary then asked, 'How do the girls manage their monthlies?'

'They just tell the boys it's their time, so they'll understand if the girls feel unwell. It works well, Mum, and there's no silly giggling or teasing. It's a part of life they just get on with.'

Mary was amazed at how the children at Doe Bank appeared to have thought of everything.

'I'm so proud of you, Dora,' Mary said with a catch in her voice.

Rising from her seat, Dora went to sit on her mum's knee, her arms around Mary's neck. 'I love you, Mum.'

'I love you more,' Mary said quietly. Despite everything, there were times still when Dora just needed a cuddle.

After a lunch of cheese and fresh bread, pickled onions, ham and tomato chutney, Mary asked, 'How do you fancy a walk?'

'Where to?'

'Doe Bank?'

Dora beamed with pleasure. 'Ooh, yes!'

'I'll go and tell your gran, then.'

Dora followed Mary and listened to the conversation.

'What about me?' Edith growled. 'You can't keep leaving me alone, I might have another fall!'

'You won't if you stay in your chair. We won't be long.' With that, Mary walked away, smiling at Dora standing in the doorway.

They left the house, Edith's yells ringing in their ears.

'Will she be all right, Mum?'

'Yes, she's only trying it on in an effort to make me feel guilty.'

'And do you?'

'No. After what I read in her will – I don't feel in the least guilty.

In fact, I thought to try to find some work so you and I can make a plan to leave.'

Dora was astounded. 'Where would we go, though?'

'If I can earn some money, we might be able to rent a room somewhere. It wouldn't be as comfortable as your gran's house, but at least we'd be free of her and her spiteful ways.'

'I could get a job too,' Dora volunteered.

'I'd prefer it if we could afford to get you into school.'

'I'd like that, but earning a wage would be more important.'

'We'll see. For now, let's enjoy our walk and hope there's someone in at Doe Bank.'

Having grabbed her purse before leaving, Mary suggested they call in at the market and buy some groceries to take to Dora's friends.

Arriving at their destination, Dora whistled loudly and was delighted to see Skinny come running. She and Mary were welcomed warmly and, as the afternoon wore on, the others arrived home. Introduced to the newest member, Whippet, everyone exchanged news of their day's exploits.

Delighted with the food parcel, Queenie made them all a hot drink. She had been worrying that Skinny's scavenging had not been going too well, although she would not risk upsetting the boy by saying so.

After an hour or so of chat and laughter, Mary and Dora left and strolled home. The sun had gone down and the sudden cold wind had them shivering. The leaves on the trees had begun to change from green to gold and it wouldn't be long before they started to fall.

The lamp-lighter would be starting his work earlier now the seasons were changing, and Mary made a mental note to sort out warmer clothing.

'I wonder what Gran will say when we get back,' Dora said.

'Frankly, I don't care,' Mary responded. 'Like it or not, I'll be putting her to bed after she's had a hot drink. Then I think you and I should light the fire, snuggle up and read a book.'

'I'd love that!' Dora said, already increasing her pace, eager to be having a cuddle as Mary read to her.

## 24

It was early the following morning when Mary left for a visit to the Servants' Registry to give her details, pay her fee and enquire after work.

Dora took a tray of tea and biscuits through to Edith.

'Where's your mother?' Edith snapped at the child.

'Out.'

'Out where?'

'Just out.' Dora knew exactly where Mary had gone but had no intention of divulging that information to Edith.

'You think you're so clever, don't you?' Edith said.

Dora could see the old woman was spoiling for a fight, but she was not about to be cowed again. With luck, she and her mum wouldn't be here much longer.

'I'm more intelligent than you, is what I think,' Dora replied.

A shocked look spread across Edith's face, so Dora knew she had hit her mark. 'You cheeky young bugger!' Edith grabbed her walking stick and was out of her chair in a flash.

Dora tried to flee but the stick caught her left forearm with a resounding crack. She screamed as the pain shot up to her shoulder and down to her fingers.

'I'll teach you to back-chat me, my girl!' Edith rasped as she hefted the stick again.

'Don't you dare!' Mary's voice stayed Edith's hand.

Dora was sobbing her heart out, holding her injured arm with her right hand.

'She was...' Edith began.

Mary ignored her mother, going instead to her daughter. Touching Dora's arm and wincing at the howl from Dora, she said, 'Come on, we need to see the doctor.'

Edith sat down again after Mary had led the child out of the room. In a minute, she saw them walking down the drive and grinned. *That will teach you not to mess with me, you foul little brat!*

Mary hammered on the door to the doctor's house a few streets away, and a moment later they were admitted by a maid. Shown into a room Dr Dingley used as a surgery, they waited. The doctor came in, still drying his hands, his shirt sleeves rolled up to the elbows. A handsome man, Dr Dingley was in his forties, his dark hair showing signs of greying. His brown eyes smiled as he asked, 'Now then, what can I do for you?'

'My gran hit me with her walking stick!' Dora blurted out.

'Oh, my! Well, we'd best take a look, don't you think?'

Dora nodded but was reluctant as she was in a great deal of pain.

'I'll have to feel around your arm to see if anything is broken.'

'It really hurts,' Dora said with a sniff.

'I'm sure it does. What's your name, little miss?'

'Dora Parsons.'

'Right, Dora, tell me all about yourself.'

As Dora began to speak, the doctor gently probed her arm. Dora tried to be brave, but the pain caused her to yell out and tears started to fall once more.

'You are very courageous, Dora, but I'm sorry to say it's broken.'

Mary gasped, hardly able to believe what she was hearing. Edith had overstepped the mark this time.

'What we have to do now is set the break and put your arm in plaster. After a few weeks, we can take the plaster off and see how well it's healed.'

Dora glanced up at her mum, fear written all over her face.

'Just think how jealous your friends will be that you have a plaster and they don't,' Mary said, trying to placate her daughter.

Dora tried to smile but couldn't quite manage it.

'Now, I need you to be extra brave for a minute because this is going to hurt,' Dr Dingley said. Without giving Dora time to prepare, he gave her arm a sharp tug.

Dora let out a piercing scream and then began to sob.

'Well done, that's the worst over. Now we'll put the plaster on.'

As he worked, fitting a plaster cast on Dora's arm, he coaxed her into telling him exactly how she had sustained the injury.

'I was arguing with my gran and she walloped me for being cheeky,' Dora said, watching intently what the doctor was doing.

'Oh dear, and were you?' the doctor asked, endeavouring to keep Dora occupied whilst he worked.

'No. I wasn't really being cheeky, I was only answering her questions. Gran lost her temper with me then. My mum told me not to answer Gran back, but I couldn't help it.'

Having finished, the doctor placed her arm in a sling, which he tied neatly around the back of her neck, and Dr Dingley scrubbed his hands clean before accepting payment.

'There you go, choose.' The doctor held out a large jar full of confectionery.

'Thank you,' Dora said as she picked out a boiled sweet.

Mary repeated Dora's words and nodded when the doctor said, 'Make sure this does not happen again.'

'I will, you can bet on it,' Mary replied.

On the way home, Dora noticed the stares from people passing by.

'They probably think you've fallen over,' Mary said as she saw Dora's discomfort.

Shoving the sweet into her cheek, Dora asked, 'How did you get on this morning?'

'They will contact me if any work becomes available,' Mary replied. 'How are you feeling now?'

'It doesn't hurt so much,' Dora replied as she glanced down at her arm.

'Good,' Mary said as she led Dora through the market, where she stopped at the sweet stall. 'Choose what you'd like.'

Dora grinned. 'Chewing nuts, please.' She watched as two ounces of tiny balls of toffee covered in chocolate were tipped into a paper cone, the top folded over to prevent spillage. 'Thanks, Mum,' Dora said as she grasped the precious confection and slipped it inside her sling for safekeeping.

Mother and daughter shared a smile before Mary said, 'Right, let's get home. I have a bloody big bone to pick with your gran!'

Dora laughed aloud at her mother's expletive, and they set off together to the house.

Reaching home, they heard the call, 'Is that you, our Mary?'

Closing her eyes for a second, Mary drew in a long breath through her nose and let it out slowly.

'Time to do battle,' she said as she stalked into the sitting room.

Mary snatched up the walking stick, which was leaning against Edith's chair, and without a word she strode through the house and out into the garden.

Dora followed behind, wondering what her mum was going to

do with the stick. The answer came when she saw Mary pick up the small axe. Laying the cane across the old tree stump and holding one end, she brought the axe down time after time until the walking aid was reduced to kindling. Gathering the pieces, she stamped back to the sitting room and threw them into the grate.

'What the hell!' Edith gasped as she stared at the bits of wood.

Mary didn't see the look of shock on Edith's face, she didn't dare look for fear of what more she might do.

Mary and a grinning Dora returned to the kitchen. Taking two shawls from where they hung on the back door, Mary herded her daughter out of the house.

'Where are we going?' Dora asked.

'Doe Bank,' Mary replied, the pent-up anger dissipating when she saw Dora's beaming smile.

## 25

Walking through the busy streets, Mary glanced up at the darkening sky. The wind had picked up, heralding the oncoming storm. Stopping just long enough to wrap one shawl around Dora and the other about herself, Mary continued on.

Dora trotted along beside her mother, who had not spoken a word since leaving the house.

A lightning strike slashed through the bank of black clouds and a moment later thunder rolled overhead. Large raindrops began to fall and Mary pulled their shawls over their heads before they increased their pace. Like everyone else, they wanted to reach their destination before the heavens opened. However, it was not to be. The thunder crashed again and the rain pelted down, soaking them to the skin.

Dora kept her head down as they rushed on, praying there would be someone at home when they got to Doe Bank. If not, they would have to retrace their steps through the storm. She wondered if they could shelter in the boys' house and sit out the foul weather, but she didn't think her mum would agree. Mary wouldn't want to go into their home unless invited to do so.

Unable to keep her counsel any longer as they hurried through the lashing rain, Dora asked, 'Mum, what if nobody is home?'

The sudden storm had fuelled Mary's anger once more and she snapped her reply. 'We're going to see your friends; you should be a little more grateful!'

'Sorry,' Dora mumbled.

Mary stopped dead in her tracks and turned to Dora. 'Oh, sweetheart, I'm sorry. I didn't mean to be so sharp.'

'It's all right. Let's get out of this rain,' Dora said.

As they strode on, Mary felt wretched. They wouldn't be out in the heavy rain at all had it not been for Edith's quick temper. The fact that she had been unable to keep Dora safe tore at Mary and she felt tears sting her eyes. She had destroyed Edith's walking cane but it should never have come to that. The question hovering in Mary's mind now was – could she prevent Dora suffering any more abuse at her grandmother's hands?

Eventually the houses came into view and the rain began to ease off as the storm moved away.

'You'll have to whistle, Mum,' Dora said as she lifted her arm, nestled in its sling.

Mary did so as they stepped onto the heath and heaved a relieved sigh as Owl and Queenie spilled out of the door.

'Come in quickly! God, you're both drenched!' Queenie said, ushering them inside.

Owl went to fetch a towel and Queenie lit the already-laid fire. Before long, steam began to rise from the wet shawls draped on the chair near the grate.

Mary and Dora sat on the old peg run and warmed themselves while Queenie made tea.

'Whatever have you done?' Owl asked as she pointed to Dora's cast.

Dora enlightened her friends, who were shocked at the ferociousness of her grandmother's attack.

'Does it hurt?' Owl asked with concern.

'Not now, but it did,' Dora replied, not even trying to spare Mary's feelings. She no longer intended to hide behind the worry of upsetting her mum; Dora determined to speak out should there be any further incidents with her gran. She also made up her mind to stay well away from the nasty old crone – and this time she meant it.

One by one, the others returned and the food they had was shared with their visitors. While they ate, Fingers watched Mary closely. Dora's broken arm would be the straw that broke the camel's back, he was sure of it. He had the feeling that things in Edith's house were about to change radically and he wondered how it would affect himself and his friends.

Skinny was fussing over Dora, making sure she was comfortable, and Mary watched over them before saying it was time they left.

'Thank you for your hospitality, especially as we arrived unannounced,' she said as she collected their shawls.

'You are most welcome, as we have said many times before,' Fingers replied.

All their chatter stopped abruptly as Mary dropped onto the chair and, burying her face in her hands, she burst into tears. Years of misery and unhappiness poured out as Mary cried herself into exhaustion.

The children stood around with shocked looks on their faces, unsure what to do. Then Dora broke the spell by rushing to her mother. 'Mum, please don't cry! Everything will be all right!'

Mary sniffed and dashed the tears from her cheeks. 'I'm so sorry,' she managed eventually.

At once, they all rushed to reassure her that it was fine and that she shouldn't worry.

'We really should be going home now. Come on, Dora – thank you again.' With that, Mary hurriedly left, dragging Dora with her. She couldn't believe she had embarrassed herself in such a manner. Walking back to Spring Head, Mary wondered what she should do now.

Edith would struggle to get around without her stick and Mary considered buying another. That, however, would put Dora in danger once more, so she dismissed the idea. Edith would have to manage the best she could. The most pressing problem for Mary to decide was whether to leave or stay.

Again the arguments raged in her mind. If they stayed, then Edith would continue with her belligerence; nothing much would change. Their life would alter radically if they left, for the only place they could go to was Doe Bank, at least until they had saved the money to rent a small room. The thought of living as the children did made Mary shudder, but at least they wouldn't have to suffer Edith's wicked tongue.

Leaving the old woman to care for herself gave Mary a stab of guilt, but a glance at Dora's broken arm made her anger bubble up yet again.

By the time they reached home, Mary was no closer to finding a solution to her dilemma.

'Mary?' came the call as they walked in through the back door. 'Is that you? Where've you been?'

Mary clenched her hands into fists and closed her eyes tight for a second. Turning to Dora, she said quietly, 'You are forbidden to go anywhere near your gran, no matter what.'

Dora nodded.

'You do not answer her call, you do not stay in the same room as her. Do you understand me?'

'Yes, Mum.'

With a solitary nod, Mary began making them all something to eat while Dora set a tea tray.

Watching her mother work, Dora thought about the events of the day. She'd never seen Mary so angry and then so distressed. She thought at one point that they would stay at Doe Bank with the others, but then her mum had jumped up and ushered her back here.

Mary made tea, took the tray to Edith and returned to the kitchen without speaking a word. She did the same with Edith's meal of cheese, cold meat and salad.

Dora had heard her gran trying to engage her mum in conversation, but Mary had ignored her. She wondered if the two would ever speak to each other again.

Just as she began her own meal, Dora looked up at a knock at the front door.

Mary frowned then went to see who was there. When she returned, Mary's face was as white as a ghost.

## 26

Mary sat at the table and laid the letter given to her by the man at the door next to her plate.

'Mum?'

'Eat your dinner, pet, it's nothing for you to worry about,' Mary said, ignoring Edith's yells to know who had come knocking.

'Mary! Will you answer me?' Edith shouted.

Walking as if in a dream, Mary went to the sitting room.

'So who was that?'

Mary shook her head.

'Mary, what's the matter with you?'

'Jim's dead.' Mary's voice was hardly more than a whisper.

'Jim who?'

'My Jim! My husband!' Mary snapped.

'Oh, him. How? When?'

'His kidneys gave up.'

'Oh, well, that's one thing less for you to worry about,' Edith said callously. 'Who told you?'

'His solicitor,' Mary answered, trying her best to control her emotions.

'I need another cup of tea,' Edith said, totally oblivious to Mary's battle to keep her temper in check.

Going back to the kitchen, Mary put the kettle to boil.

'Mum, what's happened?' Dora asked tentatively.

Looking at her daughter, Mary knew the time had come to reveal the truth. Dora needed to hear it all and now that Jim had passed there would never be a better opportunity. 'Let me take some tea to your gran then I'll explain everything, all right?'

Dora nodded and continued to finish her meal as she eyed the envelope on the table. Whatever was going on, that letter was part of it. Dora wondered when her mum would get a break from all the misery and worry dogging her. Mary was so kind and loving, she didn't deserve to be so unhappy all the time. Now the knock on the door had brought more sadness into their lives. When would it all end?

Tea taken to Edith, Mary hoped it would keep her quiet for a while as she sat once more in the kitchen. Taking a deep breath, she began. 'You know you've always thought your dad died when you were little...?'

Dora nodded, a frown creasing her forehead.

'Well, that wasn't true, I'm afraid,' Mary went on, seeing the puzzled look cross her daughter's face. 'He left me when you were small.'

'Why?' Dora asked astonished at the revelation. 'Was it because I survived and my twin didn't?'

'No, sweetheart, it was because of your gran.'

Dora's temper rose like a volcano. 'Gran again!'

'Your dad had had enough of her interfering in our lives, he said.' Mary's emotions were building as she recalled that sad time.

'So where is he now?' Dora asked, daring to feel excited at the possibility of seeing her father at last.

'I'm sorry, darling, but he passed away a few days ago. That was what our caller came to tell me. It seems he'd been very poorly for some time and eventually his kidneys stopped working.'

'Oh,' was all that Dora could manage. She had got her hopes up in an instant and just as quickly they had been dashed. 'Is that what the letter says – is it to tell you he'd died?'

'I don't know, but there's only one way to find out.' Picking up the envelope, Mary tore it open and pulled out the contents. She immediately recognised Jim's handwriting and tears welled in her eyes.

*My darling Mary,*

*If you are reading this, then you will know I have passed on from an illness suffered over many years.*

*I'm sorry for the hurt I put you through so long ago and wanted you to know I have never stopped loving you and our beautiful daughter Dora.*

*If I could turn back time to that fateful day I would, and things would have been very different. I wanted so badly to come back to you – would you have taken me back?*

*In a heartbeat*, Mary thought, as she nodded and blinked away the tears, feeling them roll down her cheeks. She read on.

*All that stopped me was the prospect of having to live beneath your mother's shadow again, which I knew I could never do.*

*I carry my love for you and Dora to my grave where it will rest with me for all eternity.*

*Jim*

Mary laid the letter on the table, then pushed it to Dora to read. Her silent tears slid down her face to drip from her chin into her lap.

Dora picked up the paper and, after reading it, she replaced it on the table, then went to hug her mother as best she could with her good arm. The two cried quietly, holding each other tightly for a long time before the mood was split wide open by Edith's screeching voice.

'Mary! I need the privy!'

'I swear to God, one day...' Mary left the sentence unfinished.

Dora read the letter again and thought to herself, *I wish you had come back, Dad. We could all have gone away. Somewhere far from Gran where we could have been happy.* She wondered if he had thought of it and, if so, why hadn't he done it? Why had he not come back for them? Was it just down to Edith? Or was there more to it than that?

\* \* \*

Later that day, whilst Mary was trying to cope with the devastating news of her husband's death, Fingers and the others were discussing Mary and Dora's visit.

Skinny was pacing the room, threatening all sorts of ill he'd like to do to Edith for hurting Dora as she had.

'Calm down, Skinny, there's nothing we can do,' Fingers said.

'I'm mad as hell, Fingers!' Skinny replied sharply.

'I can see that, but it's Dora who needs our support now.'

'How? What can we do to help?' Lofty asked desperately.

'The best I can suggest is that one of us stays home every day in case Dora needs a bolthole,' Fingers said.

'We could draw up a rota,' Queenie put in.

'That's a good idea,' Fingers praised.

'We can go to the printers tomorrow and see if they have any scraps of paper we can use,' Owl said as she pointed to Queenie then herself.

'Excellent.' Again, Fingers ensured praise was given for the ideas coming forth.

'Well, when I go up the market I'm fetching Dora with me! I ain't havin' her stay in that house with that old woman any longer than is necessary!' Skinny had stopped his pacing as he spoke, then he sat down on the rug.

'Skinny, that's a brilliant idea,' Fingers said, patting his friend on the shoulder.

'My heart went out to Mary when she burst into tears,' Queenie said.

The others nodded in agreement.

'I don't understand why they stay there!' Skinny said.

'Because they have it better than we do,' Carrot put in. Turning his eyes to Fingers, he added, 'Don't get me wrong, I'm grateful to be here, but Mary and Dora have plenty of food, gas light and warm beds.'

Fingers nodded, saying, 'The question is what will happen when the grandmother dies? Where will they go? How will they live?'

'That's three questions,' Carrot said, trying to lighten the mood.

'They would come here to us – wouldn't they?' Owl asked.

'You would hope so,' Fingers answered.

'It might be as well for us to prepare for that day,' Queenie mused.

'In what way?' Whippet asked tentatively. Being the new boy, he had been reluctant to speak for fear of being told to keep out of it.

'Well, if Dora and Mary *do* come here to live with us, they'll need a mattress each,' Queenie said kindly.

'I could move mine into your room and they could share my room,' Owl suggested.

'That would be fine by me,' Queenie replied.

'Thank you, girls, that's most kind of you but for the moment all we can do is watch out for Dora. We have to try our best to keep her safe,' Fingers said.

'I'll collect Dora first thing and show her how to scavenge,' Skinny said, feeling excited at the prospect.

As the chatter continued, Skinny began to imagine what life would be like with Dora and Mary living with them. He already saw Dora as a sister and he wondered if Mary would assume the role of mother to them all. He hoped she would, as the children already loved her as one.

Just then Carrot, still sitting on the floor, lifted a cheek and emitted a resounding fart. The girls leapt on him, slapping him playfully for his disgraceful behaviour. Before long, they moved away as the other boys piled in, and before they knew it, they were play-fighting and rolling around having a fun time.

Queenie and Owl slipped into the kitchen, where they made a hot drink for everyone. Queenie had been a little extravagant whilst shopping earlier in the day and had purchased some cocoa, sugar and milk. With a teaspoon of cocoa powder and sugar, the mugs were filled with boiling water before a generous helping of milk was added. Stirred briskly, the froth swirled and a stream of steam spiralled upwards.

They carried the trays of drinks into the living room, along with a plate of biscuits Owl had baked that morning. All fighting ceased and everyone sat to enjoy the special treat.

Eventually, they drifted off to their respective mattresses and, lying in the darkness, the sound of rain pattering on the roof top lulled them gently to sleep.

## 27

Mary had spoken to Edith only when necessary since the old woman had broken Dora's arm. Harsh words could be ignored but the vicious attack on Dora was unforgivable.

The strained atmosphere was beginning to tell on Edith, who knew she had gone too far that day. Deciding it was time to try to make amends and garner some sympathy, Edith waited for Mary to bring her breakfast.

'That looks nice,' Edith said as the plate of bacon and eggs was laid on her table. 'Before you go, I thought you should see this.' Edith pulled out a little folded card from her cardigan pocket. 'I've paid sixpence a week since I was a girl, so when I die my funeral will be all paid up.'

Mary took the card and glanced at it before handing it back without a word.

'We can't go on like this, Mary! You have to talk to me because I'm going mad!'

'After what you've done, you're lucky I'm still here.'

'I know. I didn't mean to break the child's arm, Mary, I swear!'

Mary bridled. There was no apology and Edith still could not bring herself to call Dora by her name. 'You shouldn't have hit her at all! I'm still of a mind to fetch a constable and report you for assault and battery!' Mary's anger rose again as she spoke.

'I'm your mother!'

'And Dora's my child!'

'We can go over this a thousand times and it won't change anything.'

'It already has. It's altered how I think of you. I've always known you had a sharp tongue but hurting my daughter proves you to be a bully as well.'

'It was an—' Edith began.

'Don't you dare have the audacity to say it was an accident!' Mary thundered.

Edith's handkerchief slid from her sleeve and she dabbed at dry eyes.

Unbeknown to either of them, Dora had crept to stand behind the open door and was listening to every word.

'You wouldn't speak to me like this if your father was here.'

Mary barked a laugh. 'Dad left us because of your nasty ways and foul temper! The poor man led a dog's life with your constant nagging. It's no wonder he fled and I, for one, hope he's happier wherever he is!'

'He's dead and gone! I read his obituary in the paper,' Edith struck back.

The statement hit Mary like a slap. So her dad had passed on as well as her husband. 'Why didn't you tell me this before?'

'What difference would it have made?' Edith answered.

'None, I suppose,' Mary said quietly.

Edith smiled inwardly, feeling a spark of triumph.

That spark was extinguished in an instant when Mary said, 'I've seen your will.'

Dora drew in a breath and her hand covered her mouth.

'You've been poking around in my room!' Edith snapped.

Mary shrugged her shoulders. 'Not exactly. I knew where to look.' There was no use in denying it.

'How? When?'

'It doesn't matter. What's important is what is written in it.'

Edith's eyes narrowed. Was Mary telling the truth? Had she found the will? If so, how would she react now?

'And what's that, then?' Edith asked with a self-satisfied look on her face.

'You're leaving everything to the church.' The colour drained from Edith's face as Mary went on. 'You have not provided for either Dora or me – not a single penny – which means we'll be out on the street after you've gone.'

'It's to teach you to stand on your own two feet and stop sponging off me!'

'You have an answer for everything, don't you?' Mary said.

'You need to learn, Mary...'

'Oh, I've learned all right! It's taken me a lot of years, the loss of a child, husband and father, but I've survived. And I'll be a lot happier once you've departed this world.'

'That's a wicked thing to say!' Edith yelled.

'I learned that from you also: how to be spiteful.' Mary glared at her mother, who appeared to have shrunk into herself. 'You drove my Jim away with your constant derogatory remarks. How he was never good enough for your daughter! Harping on about why he never rose to management. That he should be taking better care of his family. I should have left with him.'

'But you didn't, did you? Instead, you came crawling back to me!'

'Yes, and it was the very worst thing I could have done. I've regretted it every day since.'

'You're still here, though,' Edith said with a tight-lipped smile.

'Dora!' Mary called.

Not wanting her mum to know she had been hiding and heard it all, Dora waited a moment before strolling into the room.

'Did you want me, Mum?'

'Yes, lovey. Your gran and I have been talking...'

*Is that what you call it?* Dora thought.

'...and I've come to a decision at long last.'

Dora looked at her gran's worried face, then back to her mum.

'I want you to go upstairs and pack all of your things. I'll be up in a moment to help you.'

'Am I going somewhere?' Dora asked, feeling fear creep up her spine.

'We both are, sweetheart.'

Dora's fear drained away as she skipped from the room. She had no idea where they were going, but anywhere was better than here.

'You can't leave me alone!'

'Can't I? You just watch me!' With that, Mary went to join Dora upstairs.

Mary folded and packed Dora's clothes into an old suitcase, then she returned to the attic to find another for her own clothes. Neither of them had much, so it didn't take long. Dora shoved her beloved books into a box she found when she retrieved her parents' wedding photograph, which she slipped between the pages of a book.

'Where are we going, Mum?' Dora asked excitedly as Mary carried the cases and box downstairs.

'I don't know yet, love.'

'This is like an adventure!'

Mary smiled. 'It is a bit, but be prepared for hardship, Dora, for we have no money and now – no home.'

'I don't care, because I have you, Mum. We have each other and that's all that matters.' Dora flung her good arm around Mary's waist, and they hugged tightly.

Standing behind the door, Edith scowled. *What a load of rot! I'll give you twenty-four hours before you come back with your tails between your legs!*

## 28

Edith hurried back to the sitting room and grabbed her breakfast plate, which she carried into the kitchen. 'I can't eat this. It's gone cold and greasy.'

'Warm it in the range, then. You'll have to get used to cooking for yourself now,' Mary replied as she dragged the cases across the kitchen.

Edith slammed the plate on the table so hard it broke in half beneath the cold food. Mary raised her eyebrows at the woman's puerile behaviour. Edith scowled and with a grunt she hobbled back to her chair.

Mary followed behind, before saying, 'I've taken five shillings from the household expenses.'

'That's stealing!'

'Let's call it severance pay, shall we? God knows you owe me far more than five bob!'

'You could go to jail if I call the bobbies!' Edith gasped.

'So could you for assault, and you'd be in there a lot longer than me. How do you fancy a few years incarcerated with the lowlifes of the town?'

'You've decided then, you're actually leaving?' Edith changed tack, the thought of jail time making her shudder.

'Yes, and not before time. Goodbye, Mother.' Mary turned and walked out of the room.

Back in the kitchen, Mary opened the back door and was startled to see Skinny standing there, his hand poised ready to knock.

The boy's glance took in the suitcases, before it returned to Mary.

'We're leaving,' Mary explained.

'Where you goin'?' Skinny asked, but the look on Mary's face as she shook her head told him all he needed to know. Instantly taking charge, he said, 'Come on, give them to me.' Grabbing the cases, Skinny stepped away to allow them to exit. Mary picked up the box of books and shoved Dora out in front of her. Closing the door behind them, Mary breathed a sigh of relief. Years of unhappiness lifted from her shoulders with that breath and she was suddenly free at last. She felt light-hearted and young again and, as they walked down the driveway, Mary began to laugh.

Dora and Skinny exchanged a glance before they joined in too. None of them saw the old beggar who stood at the top of the street watching them leave.

Following at a discreet distance, Elijah also breathed a sigh of relief that mother and daughter were at last out of Edith's clutches. The question now was – where were they going to live?

Elijah tailed the trio through the streets until he saw them walk towards two dilapidated houses and his heart sank. They had left a lovely big house with all its comforts to come to this. Whatever had occurred to warrant this must have been very bad. It was then that he saw Dora's arm in a sling and he knew.

After watching them enter, Elijah retraced his steps, heading for the marketplace. He guessed it wouldn't be too long before Skinny went on his regular scavenging hunt. Then he'd be able to quiz the boy and discover exactly what had occurred. As he ambled up the street, he thought how glad he was that he'd chosen to walk by way of the house in Spring Head when he did. A little later and he would have missed Mary and Dora's leaving.

Elijah felt sorry in his heart for Dora and her mum having to live in such squalid conditions, but he'd promised his old friend George only to watch over them. He wished now he had insisted that he should intervene if he felt it necessary.

There was, however, another option open to him. It would mean a visit to someone he hadn't seen for a very long time, and just the thought of it set his heart racing. He wasn't sure what sort of welcome he would receive, but he had to try; he felt he could no longer stand by and watch Mary and Dora suffer.

*Sorry George, my old pal, but it's time to intervene, and under the circumstances I think you would forgive me*, Elijah thought as he hung around in the market on the lookout for Skinny.

* * *

Whilst Elijah was wrestling with his conscience, Mary and Dora were given the usual warm welcome. Skinny set the suitcases on the floor before taking the box from Mary and placing it alongside them. 'I was calling for Dora just as they were leaving,' he said by way of explanation. 'I thought the best thing to do was to bring them here.'

'Quite right, Skinny, well done,' Fingers praised the boy.

Tea was provided by Queenie and everyone settled down to listen to what Mary had to say. Only then would they be about their work for the day.

'I'm so sorry, but we had nowhere else to go,' Mary said, feeling wretched to be foisting herself and Dora onto the happy but poverty-stricken band of children.

'Please don't be, Mary, we had foreseen the possibility and have discussed it at length,' Fingers responded.

'I came to take Dora to the market with me to teach her how to scavenge – just in case like,' Skinny said.

'It was lucky you came when you did,' Dora answered with a smile.

'We'll need to get those mattresses now,' Owl put in.

'I can pay for them,' Mary said, drawing half a crown from her purse.

'Right. Lofty, Carrot, Whippet and I will go and see what we can find,' Fingers said, taking the money from Mary.

'Use the rest for food supplies,' Mary said.

'Thank you. We generally pool our money and Queenie does the shopping for odds and ends that Skinny can't get,' Fingers explained.

'Come on and we'll get you settled in,' Owl said, grabbing one case as Queenie lifted the other. Mary carried the box of books and along with Dora they went next door.

Queenie and Owl shifted the mattress into the other room and Mary glanced around. Whatever had she been thinking, bringing Dora here? She should have held her tongue and they would have still been in Edith's house. Even as she thought it, Mary knew they would have left eventually anyway. They were here now and had to make the best of it. The others lived here quite contentedly, it seemed, so they could too. Part of her wondered how Edith would cope, but one look at Dora's broken arm chased the thought away. She had to concentrate on their new life now, which would leave little time to worry about Edith.

Looking out of the window, all Mary could see was heathland and old coal workings and a disued colliery. This made her think of the winter, not far off, and how they would keep warm. She had to find a job so they could at least have coal during the colder months.

Returning to the downstairs, she explained her plan to Queenie, Owl and Dora.

'There ain't no work to be had, Mary,' Owl said, her green eyes sad.

'I have to try, nevertheless. Maybe it will be easier for me as an adult,' Mary answered.

'I'll scavenge with Skinny, Mum, it will be fun,' Dora added.

Mary forced a smile, but underneath she just wanted to bawl her eyes out. 'For now, what can I do to help?' she asked.

'We need kindling,' Queenie said.

'Right then,' Mary said, looking around. Spotting a box, she grabbed it and hurried out onto the heath where she could shed her tears alone.

'She shot off a bit quick!' Queenie said.

'It's all happened so suddenly...' Dora began.

'Do you think she's regretting it? I mean coming from a big posh house to this?' Owl asked as she spread her arms.

'No, I think she just needs time to adjust. We're both grateful that you've taken us in,' Dora replied.

Queenie smiled. 'I'm away to the shops, we need some tea and bits and pieces.'

'I'd best wait here for Mum to get back, else she'll think I've done a runner again,' Dora said with a tight smile.

'I'll stay with Dora today,' Owl said with a grin. 'We can find something to do, I'm sure.'

Once Queenie had left, Dora and Owl went to unpack the book box. They stood the books on the window ledge, then Owl said, 'You'll have to keep your clothes in the case, otherwise they'll get damp and go mouldy. Watch these as well.' She pointed to the books that stood in an orderly line.

Dora nodded at the sage advice.

'Will you read to us from one of your books this evening?'

'I'd love to. I've been thinking about writing stories of my own. In fact, I've done one or two already.'

'You could read them an' all!' Owl said excitedly.

Dora laughed. 'All right, then you can tell me what you think.'

A while later, the boys arrived back with two mattresses from the pawn shop, plus some blankets. They manhandled them into place and came downstairs as Mary walked in with a box full of sticks.

When the boys had gone for the bedding, Skinny had joined them to walk as far as the market. He had to work extra hard now there were two more to feed.

He was so intent on his work, he didn't notice the old beggar who dogged his steps.

## 29

As his box filled up with his usual haul of vegetables, bread, a couple of rashers of bacon and a few sausages from the butcher, Skinny wound his way back through the tightly packed stalls of the market. He looked up when a man stepped out in front of him.

'Oh, hello Elijah, how you faring?'

'I'm well, Skinny, my boy. You look busy today.'

'Ar, I am. I've two more mouths to feed.'

'Is that so?'

Skinny nodded. 'Mary and Dora have come to live with us, so I'll need to scavenge more now.'

'I see. May I ask how that came to be?'

Once Skinny had told the sorry tale, Elijah looked troubled. 'Is Dora all right? She will heal well?' he asked with concern.

'Oh, ar, the doctor said as she can have the plaster off in a few weeks. She's getting frustermerated with it, though.'

'I'm not surprised. Do send her my regards. Well, I'll not keep you. It was grand to see you.'

'Ar, same here,' Skinny said as he wandered away, his eyes downcast once more in search of anything to add to his box.

Elijah watched him go, hardly able to hold on to the anger building inside him. *Bloody Edith Pitt!*

He stomped away home to wash and change. He needed to sit quietly and digest all he'd been told. He also needed to decide whether he should confront the old virago, or keep his nose out of what she would inevitably say was none of his business. The dolour he was feeling was weighing him down and he ached to be able to approach Mary and tell her the whole truth. He knew he would one day, but that day was not yet nigh, not until he'd visited the one person he was sure would help. The most pressing dilemma was whether to give Edith Pitt the full force of his anger.

With a whisky in one hand and a cigar in the other, Elijah sat by his fireside and pondered the situation.

'That's the mattresses in place, so you boys get off to the wharf and see if you can score some work. I'll follow along shortly,' Fingers said. Once the others had gone, he turned to Owl. 'I don't suppose we could have another cuppa?'

Dora guessed rightly that Fingers wanted a quiet word with her mum, so she mumbled, 'I'll come and help you, Owl.'

Mary looked at the boy, who she'd begun to see as a young man, and wondered if he was about to lay down the ground rules. Was he going to reinforce the fact that he was their leader and Mary should not interfere?

'Mary, we don't have much and I know you must feel that this is a come-down from what you are used to, but please know you are both very welcome.'

*Here it comes*, Mary thought.

'The others look to me as their leader, simply because I was fortunate to have a better education. I like to think of it as a democracy, though – besides, we are all equal in the eyes of God.'

'I don't intend to step on any toes and disrupt the household,' Mary interrupted.

'I didn't think you would. What I'm trying to say is – we could use a woman's touch around here.'

Mary gasped. She had not expected this and was taken by surprise.

'The girls are marvellous at feeding us all and keeping our houses, and us, clean, but there has been something missing – even for them. We all miss having a mother figure; someone who will love us for who we are and who is here to welcome us home when we return from work. I'm pretty sure everyone will agree with me when I say – we'd love for you to take charge.'

Tears sprang to Mary's eyes. 'I was so sure you were about to lay down the law.'

Fingers shook his head and Mary saw then the burden he'd carried for so long. He wanted the weight of caring for the gang lifted from his shoulders. He just wanted to be a child for a little longer before manhood took over.

'I think we should put it to the vote when everyone is home. If all agree, then I'd be happy to take charge.'

In a flash, Fingers rounded the table and threw his arms around her waist.

Mary held him tight and stroked his fair hair.

Behind the door, where Dora felt as though she was spending half of her life these days, she and Owl hugged each other too.

With a quiet, 'Thank you,' Fingers let go and Mary saw tears glisten in his bright blue eyes.

The girls came through with a tray of tea, a delicate cough announcing their arrival. Mary smiled. 'I take it you heard every word?'

Owl and Dora grinned and nodded.

'All right. Tea first then you, young man, should be off to work. The girls and I will sort out an evening meal for when you all get home.'

The tea was poured and the chatter began. As she watched, Mary realised she was about to become mother to eight children. She also knew that the two houses would need a lot of work to make them warm and cosy for the winter. Time was of the essence, as the autumn was already setting in.

'Dora, do you have any paper in your book box?' Mary asked.

'No, Mum, sorry.'

'We could go and beg some from the printers,' Owl suggested.

'That would be grand. Then I can make some notes regarding any repairs that need to be undertaken.'

'Can we go now, Mum?' Dora asked excitedly.

'Yes, but don't speak to—'

'Strangers,' Dora finished with a laugh.

The girls ran from the house and Mary smiled again.

'I'm off too. See you later,' Fingers said.

Left alone, Mary wandered first around the boys' dwelling, then the one she would be sharing. The plaster on the walls was cracked and peeling. There were no curtains or furniture; the floorboards were bare. Little piles of clothes lay on the mattresses and candles stood on cracked saucers. The kitchens had a range in each and a cupboard on the wall for food. The odd pot and pan hung from hooks near the ranges. Outside the girls' house, a tin bath leaned against the wall near the standpipe. Lifting the lever, Mary pushed it back down and was delighted to see clean water spew from the spout.

Back indoors, Mary searched another cupboard and found mismatched crockery and cutlery, next to which was placed an old brownstone sink.

Mary sighed. It was a long way off what she was used to.

*Stop it! You have a whole new life ahead of you so be grateful and don't look back!*

Running upstairs, Mary rummaged in her suitcase for an apron. Then, in the kitchen once more, she rifled through the larder for something with which to make a meal.

Hearing a shrill whistle, Mary went out to see who was back. She waved to Skinny, who was carrying a box, and it looked heavy.

'I got lots of stuff today, Mary,' Skinny said as he placed his burden on the table.

'Well done! Sausages and bacon...'

'There won't be enough for everyone, though,' the boy said, a pained look on his face.

'There will be, just you wait and see. Apples, how about I turn those into a pie for afters?'

Skinny grinned like a Cheshire cat. 'That would be bostin'!'

'All right then, I'll get to work.'

'I will an' all, see you later,' Skinny called as he left.

Lighting the range with the kindling she'd collected, Mary added a few nuggets of coal from the bucket standing alongside it. Then she drew water, found a scrubbing brush and set to work on the table, with a vengeance. Whilst that was drying off, she peeled and cored the apples and left the thin slices in water. She could have done with a drop of lemon juice to prevent them discolouring. She knew they would be expensive, but she might be able to afford just one. Cutting the sausages into tiny portions, she wrapped each in small pieces of bacon and laid them on a baking tray. Pigs in blankets would ensure everyone had a taste. With some potatoes and greens, they would provide a good meal.

Without realising it, Mary began to hum a little tune as she worked, making pastry and filling it with the apple slices. A small sprinkle of sugar and a pastry lid, and it was ready for the oven.

Another whistle sounded and Mary's head popped out of the door to see Dora and Owl running towards her, their arms full of paper offcuts.

'Marvellous, well done, girls!' Mary praised them as she relieved the girls of the paper. 'Can you go next door and bring the boys' table in here next to ours, please?'

Without a word, the girls obeyed. They giggled loudly as they struggled to manhandle the table out of one door and in through another, Dora's cast making her job all the more difficult.

'Do you want the chair as well?' Dora asked.

'No, sweetheart, we can manage without I think, but we'll push the tables against the wall, which will leave room for us to sit on the floor.'

Searching a drawer, Mary found a stub of pencil and made a list of items needed such as gravy browning, salt and pepper, and vinegar. A lemon, too, went on the list, Mary hoping the market would have such an exotic item, as well as herbs and spices.

'Would you mind going to the market and shops for me?' Handing over the list and the other half crown, she watched the girls dash off, chatting as they went. With pie and pigs in the oven, Mary found plates, cups and cutlery which she set on the nearest table.

Before long, the usual whistle heralded the arrival of Queenie with her box of goodies. Flour, sugar, milk and tea. 'Something smells good,' the young girl said, feeling grateful not to be having to cook that day. 'Oh, we have the boys' table here as well.'

'Yes, it will be needed if we are all to eat together,' Mary replied, 'and it will leave room for some furniture when we can afford it.'

'That's good thinking,' Queenie replied. 'Is there anything I can do to help?'

'No, love, you just have a rest. It's a fair trek to the market and back.'

Queenie sat on the back doorstep, enjoying the last of the sun's rays, whilst Mary busied herself in the kitchen.

Owl and Dora returned and Queenie responded to their signal, then the boys came back in pairs, all eager to be home and hoping to fill their bellies.

The tantalising aromas drifted on the air, making their mouths water, and the chatter was loud and excited as they exchanged news of their day.

'Grab a plate each and cutlery, then single file,' Mary said as she stood by the steaming pans on metal trivets on the other table. Dishing out the food, Mary smiled as each child found a space to sit and enjoy their meal. They left the one chair for Mary, and she felt honoured.

'Ooh, this is smashing!' Carrot said as he tucked in.

'Better than the muck you serve up, Queenie,' Lofty said with a cheeky grin.

'Keep it up, Lofty, and you'll be woken up with a cup of cold water on your ugly face,' Queenie retorted in the same playful manner.

Then silence fell as each of the children enjoyed their food, then their apple pie. Loud burps signalled satisfaction as they lolled around on the floor before Fingers spoke.

'Mary and I had a chat earlier and we came to the conclusion that a vote was needed.'

Worried glances were exchanged. Had Fingers asked Mary and Dora to leave? Was he putting his foot down as leader? If so, he would have a rebellion on his hands. The thought came to each individual independently and frowns formed on each of their foreheads as they wondered what was to come.

## 30

'I asked Mary if she would do us the honour of becoming our new leader,' Fingers said. 'And Mary suggested the idea be put to the vote.'

Everyone was surprised but before he could say another word, all hands went up and the yeses sounded loud and clear – including Dora's. Mary couldn't help but smile as Fingers said, 'The ayes have it!' The applause and whistles were deafening and then Mary called for silence.

'Thank you. May I say that Fingers has done a sterling job in keeping you rowdy lot under control.' She smiled as the children laughed. 'Now, I have been thinking about these houses and before the winter sets in there are repairs that need to be done. The windows have to be sealed properly to shut out the draughts, the chimneys need sweeping and a lot more kindling collected and stored. We must have more blankets and some curtains to help keep the heat in and ward off the damp.'

'We never have enough money for extras like that,' Lofty said.

'I know and that's why I wondered if we could start a little business.'

'Doing what?' Carrot asked.

'Anything. Lots of things. I know, for instance, that Owl and Queenie are excellent bakers,' Mary answered. The girls smiled at the compliment as the boys noisily agreed with the sentiment. 'How would it be if the girls did some baking and sold it on?'

'I could help,' Dora put in.

'We could do that,' Queenie said, 'but we'd need money for the ingredients in the first place.'

'Hmm, we would have to think on that. Now we turn to the boys.'

'I'm really great at scavenging!' Skinny said excitedly.

'You are, Skinny, you've kept everyone well fed,' Mary agreed.

The boy beamed and nudged Fingers, who grinned.

'What I need to know is – what else can you all do?'

'I'm good with wood,' Whippet piped up. Mary nodded for him to continue. 'I can make crackets – they're like small stools, and chairs, cupboards. I can carve love spoons.'

'What's a love spoon?' asked Skinny.

'Wooden spoons carved into a design and given to a sweetheart. They are very popular in Wales,' Mary explained. 'Excellent, Whippet. Anyone else have a hidden talent?'

Glances were exchanged and heads were scratched.

'Dora, I wondered if you would keep an account book so we have an idea of any monies coming in and going out,' Mary asked.

'Yes, Mum.'

'And when you're not doing that, I'd like you to write down your stories.'

'Why?' Dora asked with a frown.

'Because we could try to get them printed in book form, it may be they will sell well, you never know.'

'Lofty and I have been working the wharves, lifting and carrying,' Fingers said. 'It earns us a few coppers.'

'Which will be very useful,' Mary said encouragingly.

'That just leaves me,' Carrot put in, 'I've been working with Fingers and Lofty, but how about I tackle the house repairs so we don't have to pay anyone to do them.'

'Wonderful. I can also try to find some paid work,' Mary added.

'Begging your pardon, Mary, but shouldn't you be staying home to take care of us lot?' Fingers asked, seemingly very relieved at not having to do it himself.

'Maybe, but I need to earn my keep.'

'You will be, by looking after us,' Queenie said.

'It'll be nice if you're here when we get home,' Skinny said. 'It's rotten coming back to an empty house.'

'Very well. I'll stay here for now and make sure there's food ready for you on your return,' Mary conceded. 'Now, while I wash the dishes, maybe Dora will tell you a story.' Gathering up the plates and cutlery, Mary took them to the kitchen. She listened as Dora began.

'Long, long ago there lived a...' Dora pointed to Queenie who said, 'Princess!' The boys groaned.

Dora went on. 'Now, this princess was very bored with court life, so she decided to sneak out and...' She then pointed to Fingers.

'Become a pirate!' he said to whoops of delight.

The exciting story finally came to an end, with everyone having added their ideas and spun their tales. The applause was loud as Mary lit the candles against the oncoming darkness.

This would be their first night at Doe Bank. The first of many, she mused, and Mary wondered how she would cope with poverty after being used to the relative luxury of her mother's house.

*I'll make the best of it. These children are relying on me, and I cannot let them down.*

Mary stood by the open back door and called everyone to come and see. They all trooped outside to watch the bats swooping around in the hope of catching a meal on the wing.

After a hot drink, the children went to their mattresses while Mary doused the candles and secured the houses.

Dora had lit the candle stub in their room and was struggling to undress. Mary helped her daughter into her nightclothes before getting changed herself. Settling down, Mary blew out the candle flame, leaving an odour from the burnt wick lingering in the trailing smoke. The darkness closed in, and it seemed even the moon had deserted her. Suddenly the reality of their situation hit her like a punch. This was not a game, it was not a trip out which would end the following day – it was for good.

Feeling suddenly wretched as the excitement of the day wore off and honest truth hit, Mary began to sob quietly, trying not to wake Dora.

Dora, however, was not asleep and, hearing her mother crying, she crawled over and squeezed onto Mary's mattress. 'Don't cry, Mum, please. If you hate it here, we can go back to Gran's house,' she whispered.

Mary sniffed, wrapping an arm around Dora. 'Your gran would never have us back now. Besides, you're safer here. I had to get you away from her, Dora. Look what she did to your arm! The next time it could have been your head! We're better off here, lovey, I just need to get used to it.'

'I love you, Mum.'

'I love you too, with all my heart,' Mary whispered back.

Snug in her mother's arms, Dora fell asleep, safe and warm.

It was a long time before Mary did the same.

## 31

Whilst Mary was trying to come to terms with her new situation, Edith Pitt had waited and waited, convinced her daughter would return with her tail between her legs. When the day became night, Edith started to wonder. Would Mary come home? If not, how would she, Edith, cope? Making meals and hot drinks and going to the privy she could manage, but how would she get on doing the shopping and the other heavy tasks?

It had been a long time, years in fact, since Edith had been into town. Could she walk that far without the aid of her stick? Seeing the remnants of her cane still lying in the fire grate, Edith scowled. It was all that child's fault. *Bloody Dora Parsons!* she thought acidly.

Staring out of the window, Edith began to feel sorry for herself. She was all alone now with no one to converse with. The house felt empty and hollow, its creaks and groans were all the company she had.

Edith awoke, having spent the night on her own for the first time in years, and she had not slept well. Now, in the daylight, she was tired and grumpy.

Edith had no idea where Mary had gone, so trying to look for her was out of the question. Besides, her legs wouldn't be strong enough to allow her to trudge all over the town. She had to accept that Mary was gone and was unlikely to come back. So the options left open to her were to sit and cry about it or get on with living her life as best she could.

With a perfunctory nod, Edith rose, made her way downstairs and into the kitchen to make a hot drink. These were the first steps in a new life of residing alone and she felt proud of herself. She didn't need Mary after all, and now she could prove it.

Edith felt heartened at the thought, but somewhere in the recesses of her mind was a worry. Her concern was about being overwhelmed by loneliness and, if that happened, would she be able to overcome it?

Not for the first time, Edith wondered where Mary could be. Where had she slept that first night? Had she taken a train to another town with the money she had stolen? Or was she still living in Wednesbury?

Making tea like an automaton, Edith returned to her chair in the living room. This would be her life from now on, catering for herself. She would have to do the washing too and knew she would struggle with that task. There was no way she could empty the wash tubs on her own.

With a huge sigh, Edith considered the possibility of hiring a maid. It would cost her, but at least she would have everything done for her. A visit to the Servants' Registry would be needed, which would mean paying the fee as well as for a cab to get there and back. Although a good idea, this independent living was proving expensive before she'd even stepped out of the door!

Sipping her tea, she stared out of the window. Autumn had arrived and the leaves on the trees had already begun to change colour. Gone was the rich green of summer, to be replaced by golds and browns. Soon they would fall and carpet the ground like a mosaic, which meant winter would not be far behind. Edith realised she would have to carry in buckets of coal and light the fires herself as well as clean out the grates and dispose of the ashes.

The more she thought on it, the more she had to accept just how much Mary had been doing for her.

*Edith, you are going to need some help – and soon!*

* * *

Over at Church Hill House, Elijah was also drinking tea and still pondering Mary and Dora's situation.

Unable to sleep, he had risen early and washed and dressed in a fine dark suit, white shirt and fancy cravat. He was about to go visiting and he wanted to look his best.

Placing his cup in the sink, he picked up his top hat and silver-topped cane. Patting his pocket assured him his wallet was safe. Leaving the house, he locked the door behind him and slipped the key into his inside jacket pocket.

Out on the street, he donned his topper and whistled loudly for a cab. After a moment or two, he heard the clip-clop of a horse's hooves and carriage wheels rattling on the cobblestones.

'Whoa, Bess,' the cabbie called as he pulled gently on the reins, drawing the cab to a halt. Tipping his cap, he asked, 'You be wanting a cab, guvnor?'

'Yes, thank you.' Giving the address, Elijah climbed aboard and settled himself.

'Walk on, Bess, my beauty.'

With a lurch, the cab began to roll forward and Elijah considered one last time if he was doing the right thing.

Through the town towards the area known as Mesty Croft, the cab traversed the busy streets and trundled over the bridge which crossed the South Staffordshire line of the London and North

Western Railway. Turning into Piercy Street, Elijah kept his gaze through the window. Dirty houses on both sides leaned against each other with a ginnel between every half dozen, thus giving access to the rear of the properties.

As they travelled, Elijah thought about the woman he was about to visit. He had not seen Charity Lacey for many years, and he hoped she would remember him. He had been great friends with Charity's husband before he had been taken from this world by pneumonia one particularly cruel winter. It was unseemly then for Elijah to continue to call on Charity once she was a widow and so their meetings had ground to a halt – much to his regret.

Elijah swallowed noisily as he wondered if Charity would make him welcome or whether she might tell him to sling his hook.

The cab wound its way up the long driveway and came to a halt outside an impressive building which abutted the allotment gardens. Hady Moor House. He hadn't been here in an age, but the place had withstood the passing of time well.

The cabbie jumped down and opened the door for Elijah to alight.

'Thank you. I'd be obliged if you would wait,' Elijah said as he donned his hat.

'Will do, guv,' the cabbie replied. Climbing back to the driving seat, he filled a small clay pipe. Striking a lucifer, he held it to the tobacco and puffed contentedly, before shaking the match to extinguish the flame, and flicking it to land between two large trees.

Elijah stepped smartly to the front door and yanked on the bell pull. A moment later, the door opened, and he was faced with a pretty young maid.

Stating the purpose of his visit, Elijah waited on the doorstep while the maid consulted her mistress.

'Madam says you're to come in, sir,' the maid said on her return. Closing the door behind him, she led him to the parlour.

*It's like stepping back in time!* he thought as he followed the young woman.

Opening the double doors after a polite knock, the maid stepped aside to allow Elijah entry.

'Elijah Covington-Smythe, as I live and breathe!'

'Hello, Charity,' Elijah replied with a huge grin.

## 32

Elijah took a seat on the sofa Charity indicated, laying his hat and cane beside him.

'I never thought to see you again,' Charity said, her wide smile reaching her blue eyes.

'Nor I you.' He had noted her fine speaking voice, which was just as he remembered. Her coiffed hair was pinned elegantly in the latest fashion and, despite her age, there were few wrinkles in evidence.

The maid brought in a tray of tea and a plate of tiny biscuits before returning to her station in the kitchen.

Charity did the honours by pouring steaming tea into beautiful china cups and, using silver tongs, placed two little pastries on the saucer. Adding a spoonful of sugar and a drop of milk, she passed it to Elijah.

'You remembered, even after all these years!' Elijah shook his head in disbelief.

'One rarely changes one's habits where tea is concerned, don't you agree?' Charity spoke whilst pouring herself a drink.

'You look well, Charity, and it does my heart good to see it.'

'Likewise, Elijah. At least you dressed well for your call and left your beggar's rags at home.'

'How on earth...?' Elijah was aghast that she knew about his other secret life.

'Come now, Elijah, you know me. I like to keep tabs on my friends. I'm aware, for instance, that your business is flourishing.'

Elijah nodded. *Do you know or can you guess why I'm here today, though?* Sipping his tea, he glanced around. 'Nothing seems to have changed.'

'I see no reason to alter the things I like and am comfortable with,' Charity answered.

'Indeed,' Elijah replied, feeling a little nervous beneath the woman's stare.

'Elijah, you didn't come here to remind yourself of my furnishings, so why don't you come straight to the point?'

Placing his cup and saucer on the table, Elijah cleared his throat. 'I need to speak with you about Edith.'

* * *

Having shared breakfast and seen the boys off to find whatever work they could, Mary asked the girls to stay with Dora whilst she popped into the town.

Going straight to the Servants' Registry, she had to inform them she had changed her address, and would now not be needing their assistance. Mary had thought about it long and hard and decided she would not leave Dora alone at Doe Bank while she worked, even if she was lucky enough to be offered a job.

Mary felt she would be better off staying at home and teaching the girls, and the boys if they wished, how to read and write. She would cook and clean and gather firewood, as well as climb the slag heaps looking for coal nuggets for the fires. She would beg the things they needed to repair the houses before the weather turned really cold.

After her visit to the Registry, Mary considered calling in on Edith to see how she had managed on her first night alone. But the idea was quickly dismissed as she recalled the will and Dora's arm. Let the old woman stew in her own juices.

Mary pulled her shawl closer about her shoulders, worrying again at how time was marching on and how winter would soon be upon them. She had to make sure they would all have enough to eat during the long cold months. It was now that she should be pickling vegetables and bottling fruits; with a sigh, she wondered how. They were all living hand to mouth, so there was nothing left over to store.

Tracing her way back to Doe Bank, Mary's spirits dipped again. Chastising herself, she thought about the children. They had been living this way for years and yet they always had a smile and a kind word. *Stop feeling sorry for yourself, Mary Parsons, you have a family to take care of now!*

Having reprimanded herself, Mary strode down the street. She watched a carter pass by and as the cart rolled over a large stone in the road, a crate fell off. The miracle was it didn't burst open and with all the noise of people yelling and whistling, children crying and dogs barking, the carter was oblivious to his loss.

Mary looked around then dashed to the crate and dragged it to the side of the road. Should she take it? It would be stealing. If she didn't, though, someone else would, to be sure. She had no idea what was inside, but it was heavy. Mary tried to lift it, but she couldn't. There was nothing else for it, she would have to drag the wooden crate all the way back to Doe Bank.

'Need some help with that, missus?'

Mary looked around and saw two young boys watching her. 'I'm afraid I can't pay you anything,' she said.

'Fair enough.' The boys turned and walked away, leaving Mary to struggle by herself. Shaking her head, she placed her foot against the side of the crate and pushed. It moved but not far before it wedged against a cobblestone. *Well, that didn't work, so what now?*

Despite the chilly wind, Mary shucked her shawl and, lifting the crate one end at a time, she slipped the garment beneath. Ignoring the stares of folks passing by, she tied a knot firmly, leaving one end long enough for a handle. Giving it a tug, she was delighted when it shifted easily. The shawl would be ruined by the time she got home so she would have to sew or knit another, supposing she could acquire some wool or material, so she hoped her find was worth the sacrifice.

As she hauled the heavy weight home, her mind kept repeating, *This is stealing*. However, Mary reconciled herself that their need was greater than wherever the item had been destined for. All the way back, she prayed the wooden box didn't contain nuts and bolts. *Please let it be food!*

Nearing her destination, Mary sighed with relief but then she still had to get her prize the short way over the heath. Whistling the signal, she waited and when she saw the girls, she crooked an arm, calling them to her. She watched as they ran, laughing, and she saw how happy Dora was. No matter the hardship they faced, Mary was glad of her daughter's cheer.

'What have you got, Mum?'

'I've no idea, but it fell off a cart, so...'

'Mum! You stole it?' Dora asked incredulously.

'Erm – yes, I'm afraid I did,' Mary said sheepishly.

The girls burst out laughing before Owl, Queenie and Mary took a corner and lifted the load. Dora's cast prevented her from clutching the crate itself but she grabbed the shawl and did her best to help. They staggered to the house, where Mary unwrapped the shawl and held it up in despair. It could be mended but it was in a sorry state. 'We need something to open this box with,' she said.

'I know!' Owl said and dashed outside, coming back with a piece of flat iron bar.

'That should do it. Good thinking, Owl,' Mary praised the girl. Using the bar as a jemmy, she managed to lever up the lid. 'Oh,' was all Mary said as she peered into the box.

## 33

Taken aback momentarily, Charity Lacey said, 'What has my sister done now?'

'Firstly, allow me to apologise for bringing my concerns to your doorstep,' Elijah responded.

'This tells me that whatever the problem is, it must be grave indeed.'

'Let me start at the beginning.' Elijah began his tale with his promise to George, Edith's estranged husband, to watch over Mary and Dora.

Charity was aghast. She knew Edith had a daughter named Mary but was unaware Mary also had a daughter. 'Edith and I have not spoken since the day I married,' she said a little sadly.

Elijah nodded and continued. 'George left her eventually.'

'I'm not surprised.'

'Mary's husband did the same, I'm afraid.'

'Why?' Charity asked with a frown.

'Edith's interference, I shouldn't wonder, although I can't vouch for that. Mary and Dora were turned out of their house, which meant they were forced to return to live with Edith.'

'Poor Mary.'

Elijah went on to explain about Edith's treatment of her grand-daughter, Dora running away then having her arm broken, and he finished the story with the contents of the will and Mary taking Dora to live with the urchins at Doe Bank.

'Good God above!' Charity exclaimed. 'I knew Edith could be nasty, but this is pure evil!'

'I'm concerned for Mary and Dora's welfare. They're living on scraps scavenged from the market and with winter just around the corner, goodness knows how they will manage,' Elijah added.

'Are they aware of your identity and your promise to George?'

'No. They only know of me as the beggar from when I returned Dora home after she had absconded. I did consider bringing them home with me, but that would have meant leaving the other children to fend for themselves.'

'I see.' Charity stood and stepped to the fireplace, where she pulled the bell rope to summon the maid. Running her hands down her green bombazine dress, she then returned to her seat, the only sound in the room being the rustle of her skirts and the ticking clock.

A knock preceded the maid's entrance.

'Could we have some more tea, please, Ginny? Oh, and please take a tray out to that patient cabbie.'

'Of course, madam,' the maid replied with a quick bob of the knee. Collecting the tray, she disappeared, closing the door with a quiet click.

Charity had guessed Elijah would have asked the cabbie to wait rather than have to search for another when he left.

'I'm shocked, Elijah, I can't deny. However, I'm at a loss as to what we can do about any of this.' Charity's face was full of concern.

'There's nothing to be done about Edith's will; the property and contents will go to the church. Only after she has passed could we make an offer to buy the house back. I'm sure the church would prefer the money in their bank as opposed to a building they would have to rent out and the possible problems relating to that.'

'I agree.' Charity held up a finger as a tap came to the door and the maid entered with a tray of freshly brewed tea.

'Thank you, Ginny.'

Another bob and the maid was gone.

Stirring the pot, Charity listened as Elijah took up again. 'Edith could live for many more years but I couldn't say the same for Mary and Dora, not whilst they're living in a derelict house out on the heath.'

'After tea, you can take me and show me precisely where they are,' Charity said with conviction. 'Then it might be time for me to call on my sister.'

\* \* \*

'They will come in useful, Mum, I'm sure.' Dora tried her best to lift Mary's mood.

'We can't eat these, Dora,' Mary said as she kicked out at the crate.

'No, but we could sell them,' Queenie put in.

'How? Who to?' Mary asked, looking utterly deflated.

Queenie shrugged, then answered, 'The boys will know. If anyone can find a buyer, it will be Carrot.'

Mary felt a little better then as hope rose in her. One of the lads surely would be able to shift her stolen goods. The thought of being a thief made her shiver, and Dora ran to their room to fetch Mary another shawl.

'Thanks, sweetheart.' Mary smiled as she wrapped the garment around her shoulders. 'I can't believe I've become a common thief.'

'It's not your fault, Mum, it's all because of Gran!' Dora growled.

'I don't think the police would see it that way, and now I'm living in fear of a bobby coming calling to arrest me!' Mary wailed.

'I doubt they would be bothered even if they were informed,' Owl said resignedly.

'Strictly speaking, you didn't steal this crate.' Queenie nudged the box with her toe as she spoke. Seeing Mary's frown, she went on. 'If it fell off the cart as you say, and the carter didn't retrieve it, then actually you found it.'

Knowing what Queenie said was true, it didn't stop Mary feeling like a thief. 'Well, let's push it outside and round the back, out of the way of prying eyes,' she said, getting to her feet wearily.

Her booty hidden from sight, the tired band set out to find some kindling for the fire.

\* \* \*

Over at Hady Moor House, Charity asked the maid to keep the fire burning until she returned. Pinning her hat in place with a pearl-headed hatpin, Charity was helped into a long woollen coat by the maid. Then she and Elijah went out to the cab Elijah had waiting.

The cabbie opened the door and helped Charity inside. 'Thank you kindly for the refreshments,' he said.

'You're welcome.' Charity smiled.

'Doe Bank, please,' Elijah said as he climbed aboard.

'Sir?' The cabbie wasn't sure he'd heard correctly. 'Doe Bank, sir?'

'If you please,' Elijah replied, pulling the door shut.

'Righto, guv.' The cabbie wondered what the toff and this lady wanted in one of the poorest areas of Wednesbury. Clicking his teeth, he urged the horse on. 'Come on, you lazy beast,' he called good-naturedly.

'I can't say I'm looking forward to this,' Charity mumbled.

'You need to prepare yourself, my dear, it might come as a shock.' Elijah patted Charity's gloved hand.

'The visit to my sister I'm looking forward to even less.'

'I can only imagine,' Elijah whispered, feeling glad it was not he who was in that situation.

'So Mary has no work?' Charity asked as the cab rumbled along.

'No. As far as I can make out, she has been carer to both Dora and Edith.'

'Hmm. Clearly she has not been in a position to amass any savings, then.'

'I wouldn't have thought so, hence their residing at Doe Bank,' Elijah answered. 'I'm guessing their penurious state forced them there.'

Charity nodded, setting her hat wobbling. With a long, drawn-out sigh, she gazed out of the window.

Elijah kept his counsel, allowing his friend time to digest all that had been said and hopefully ponder on a solution. He hoped at least that between them, Mary and Dora's luck could at last change.

## 34

The cab drew to a halt on the side of the road, giving its occupants a clear view of the two dilapidated buildings.

'Please don't tell me this is where my niece is living!' Charity gasped.

Elijah nodded.

Charity's hand covered her mouth. 'All because of my sister!'

'If you do decide to visit Edith, then no mention of the will can be made, Charity.'

'Why not? Look at that place and the way Mary and Dora are – surviving!'

'If Edith knows you are aware of what is written on that document, she will ask how you came to be in possession of that information. Consider, if Mary didn't tell you herself, then Edith will guess others are also in the know.' Elijah spoke quietly and patiently.

'Yes, I see what you mean.' Charity glanced again at the houses, and just then Mary and the girls appeared carrying a box of sticks.

'Is that her?' Charity asked.

'Yes. I would bet she's taken on the role of mother to the other children residing there.'

'To be expected, I suppose. I've seen all I need to. Take me home, Elijah, you and I have a lot to discuss.'

Elijah banged his cane on the roof of the cab and yelled to the driver to return them to Mesty Croft.

* * *

Whilst gathering firewood, Mary had been pondering their ideas for starting up cottage industries. It would have been lovely if they had had the money to start them off, but unfortunately every coin earned went towards filling the larder, leaving nothing to serve as capital. For all her grand ideas, none would come to fruition without money. As it was, the best they could hope for was surviving the winter with whatever could be scavenged.

The girls were laughing and joking around her, but Mary could not find it within herself to join in. They were a happy but impecunious family and Mary could see no way to rectify the situation. Short of going back to Edith, Mary was all out of ideas. But she would not return Dora to the danger she had so recently saved her from. Besides, she couldn't abandon these children, who looked to her to take care of them.

As they neared the house, Mary saw a black-painted cab draw away. She frowned, wondering who might be inside and what they were doing down this way. Maybe they were lost, the cabbie having taken a wrong turn somewhere.

Bundling the girls indoors out of the chill wind, Mary forgot all about the cab as she searched for something with which to make a meal. Potatoes peeled and in a pan, Mary added the last of the carrots, then pulled off and discarded the rotten leaves of a cabbage. Vegetables were all very well, but these children needed meat.

It was then that the boys began to arrive home, handing over their meagre earnings to Mary.

'Well done, everyone,' she said as she placed the coins in the table drawer.

Skinny was the last to come back, his box filled with all sorts of fruit and vegetables.

'I got some faggots from Mr Hollingsworth an' all,' he said proudly.

'Excellent,' Mary praised.

'I'll enjoy them,' Carrot put in.

'Fatty,' Lofty said.

'I can diet but you'll always be ugly,' Carrot returned, and everyone guffawed at the boys' playful banter.

Mary took the food to the kitchen. Four faggots between nine of them – it would be a very small helping each, but if she did without then the food would go further.

It wasn't long before the children were tucking into a hot meal while Mary washed the pans and cleaned the kitchen.

'Where's yours, Mum?' Dora's voice behind her made Mary jump.

'I've had mine, sweetheart,' Mary lied.

Dora looked sceptical but didn't pursue the matter.

After they had eaten, the children asked Dora to tell them a story, so she settled herself on the peg rug and began.

'Long ago, in a place called Egypt, there lived a mighty queen. Her name was Cleopatra.'

The others listened in rapt fascination as history was brought to life by Dora's descriptions.

Mary's pride made her catch her breath as she watched her daughter allocate each of her friends a character. Queenie became Cleopatra and Fingers was Julius Caesar. Skinny puffed out his chest as the famous general Mark Antony. Owl was the queen's most trusted hand maiden and Lofty, Carrot and Whippet were centurions in the Roman army.

Rapturous applause greeted her as Dora finished the story, and eventually Mary said it was time to retire for the night.

At Hady Moor House, Elijah, having dismissed the cabbie, who was delighted with his huge tip, was discussing with Charity how they could help Mary and her new family.

'Well, we can have some food delivered anonymously if nothing else,' Charity said.

'That would help, I'm sure, but would Mary see it as charity? If you'll pardon the pun.'

Charity laughed. 'I don't know what else to suggest, Elijah. Those houses need renovating properly and they will need coal for a fire, food in the larder and warm clothes very soon!' Charity was becoming agitated as she thought about the poor children, as well as Mary, suffering through the freezing winter. Then she asked, 'Who do those houses belong to?'

'No one, as far as I can make out. Clearly, if they did, they would have been kept in good repair,' Elijah answered, wondering at Charity's line of thinking.

'Could we get some builders in to do them up a bit? They could say they had been sent by the council but they would report back to you or me,' Charity enthused.

'It's an idea. Then we'd have a better knowledge of how they are living and what more we would need to do to make life more comfortable for them all.' Elijah felt himself caught up in Charity's excitement.

'Elijah, I'm so grateful to you for bringing this to my attention. I am really going to enjoy having such a worthwhile project to concentrate on, and the cherry on the cake – helping my niece!'

The maid came through to light the lamps and the aroma of cooking wafted on the air. The fire roared up the chimney and the curtains were drawn against the oncoming night.

Over a meal, the two then laid out a plan of action, and as the evening wore on they slipped into relaxed companionship.

## 35

The following morning, an excited Charity hailed a cab and went shopping. Stopping at the butcher's and the grocer's, she set up accounts with both in the name of Mary Parsons. Each week, a large order was to be delivered to the two houses set on the heath at Doe Bank. She instructed the butcher to send good red meat, fowl, sausages, bacon, faggots, liver and kidneys. From the grocer, she requested staple foods such as bread and butter, flour, tea, sugar and milk as well as coffee, fruit, seasonal vegetables, cakes, biscuits, cheese, potatoes and condiments. He was to vary his food hamper each week so there was always something different to choose from. Both vendors were sworn to secrecy and told to present their bills to the bank, who would pay them immediately.

Going on to said bank, Charity explained to the manager what she was about and asked he be instrumental in keeping her secret safe. The manager was delighted to aid his very important customer, knowing if he refused, Charity would more than likely shift her fortune to another bank.

Then it was on to her dressmaker. Although Charity had her

dresses made to measure, the shop carried ranges of clothes for both genders, all ages and sizes.

A brief explanation to be kept in the utmost confidence saw the owner excitedly becoming another member of the plot to help Mary and the children.

As she was shown one outfit after another, Charity realised she had no idea of how many children lived at Doe Bank. She couldn't just buy for Mary and Dora, she would have to purchase for them all.

'I'm afraid I have no idea of sizes,' Charity said, annoyed that she hadn't considered this before. Then a bolt from the blue came with a solution. 'Give me a couple of days and your word to say nothing and I'll make it worth your while.'

'Of course, Mrs Lacey,' the owner fawned.

Charity's cab then took her to Elijah's house on Church Hill. She hoped he would still be there, if not then it would be onward to his office.

It was the cabbie who banged on Elijah's front door on Charity's behalf, having been told it was not certain the gentleman would be at home. He was, and a moment later Charity was being helped from the cab and led inside to the parlour.

'What a lovely surprise, I didn't expect to see you here today,' Elijah said. 'Will you take coffee?'

'Yes, thank you.'

'I'll just go and put the kettle to boil.'

'Elijah, you really should get yourself a maid,' Charity admonished.

'I'm too set in my ways now, my dear.' With that, he disappeared. A little while later, he returned with a tray of hot coffee and biscuits. 'Now, to what do I owe this great pleasure?'

Charity explained she needed to discover the number of children and their sizes to purchase them some clothes. 'Therefore, I

wondered if you had a discreet man who could act as a census officer. He could visit in the evening when everyone was at home and
so provide the information we need.'

'What a splendid idea! I have just the person. Leave it with me
and with luck you will have what you need by tomorrow.'

Clinking cups in a congratulatory manner, Charity then went
on to tell Elijah about her adventures so far that morning.

'I've been busy too. I have a family of builders – *from the council*
– visiting Doe Bank tomorrow.' He gave a conspiratorial wink and
Charity smiled.

'Good, have them send the bill to me,' she said.

'Should we not share the expense of all this, Charity?' Elijah
asked.

'I didn't want to presume...'

'Nonsense, my dear lady. I will pay my end and you pay yours. A
good compromise, don't you think?'

'I do indeed. Thank you, Elijah. I'd love to see the look on
Edith's face if she discovered what we were up to.'

'God forbid she should find out; she'd chew my arse ragged!'
Elijah said with a shudder.

Charity burst out laughing. Then, over more coffee, they
hammered out the details of their plan.

Whilst the boys were out scavenging or looking for work, Carrot
had run across town to a builders' merchant. He had a box of
screws and washers to sell. The girls were out collecting firewood
and Mary was cutting down one of her older dresses. She had
noticed Queenie's dress was no longer at the prescribed calf length
appropriate for a girl of her age. Now the hem sat at just above her
knee. She would do the same for Owl once Queenie's new garment

was finished. That done, she could then concentrate on acquiring some wool to knit jumpers for the lads.

It was as she cut and sewed that her mind strayed to Edith and the pangs of guilt bit sharply again. How was the old woman coping? Was she suffering in any way now that Mary was no longer there to take care of her? Had she ventured out to the market for food? If so, how had she managed to carry her shopping?

Mary shook her head, trying to dispel the questions but to no avail; they continued to pester her as she worked. Pricking her finger with the needle, she cursed under her breath. Even just thinking about Edith brought pain.

Laying the needlework aside, Mary went to the kitchen to check the larder. Aside from a little flour, salt and pepper and half a loaf, the cupboard was bare. Her stomach growled from not having been fed the previous day. Should she cut herself a slice of bread? No, it would be needed if Skinny couldn't beg more. Pouring herself a cup of warm water from the kettle, she decided that would have to do for the present. She would eat something later with the others, providing there was enough to go round. Mary was sensible enough to know she had to keep up her strength in order to care for the children.

With a sigh, she went back to her sewing and soon she heard the call sign. She smiled; the girls were back.

Placing the sticks and twigs in the hearth, the girls presented Mary with a bunch of wildflowers. Standing them in a cup of water, Mary gazed at nature's beauty.

'They're lovely, thank you,' she said.

'What are you doing, Mum?' Dora asked as she eyed the dressmaking.

Mary explained her plans for each of them and enthusiastic chatter ensued.

The boys returned in the early evening, and thankfully Skinny was loaded down with a big box full of things, enough for a hearty meal for everyone – including Mary.

Eventually Carrot arrived out of breath and excited. 'I've sold your box of screws and washers, Mary,' he said, handing over ten shillings.

Mary's mouth fell open, then she laughed loudly. 'Oh, Carrot, well done!'

'The bloke is on his way to collect them; he'll be here in a minute with his cart.'

Mary prayed it wasn't the man who had lost them in the first place, but on second thoughts he would be unlikely to buy them back.

When the man arrived, he peered inside the open box. With a nod, he watched as the boys heaved it onto the cart, having hammered the lid on first. A happy builder pulled away and the boys returned indoors to the aroma of cooking food. Liver and onions, potatoes and cauliflower would be shared equally amongst them all.

Their meal finished, Mary was washing the dishes when there was a knock on the door. Drying her hands, she went to answer and was faced with a man in a dark suit. His brown hair was parted down the centre and was greased to his head.

'Good evening, madam. I am from the census board and I need the information pertaining to all those living in these two houses.'

'Please come in.' Mary led him through to where the children were sat on the floor.

Opening his case, the man took out a note pad and pencil as Mary explained who their visitor was.

One by one, the man gathered information on them all. Names, ages, where they were born, height, weight and colouring.

'Do you need those last things for a census?' Mary asked, suddenly feeling uneasy.

'New rulings, madam. Well, that's all, I think, so I'll bid you a goodnight and be on my way.'

Mary saw the man out. 'That was strange,' she said quietly.

'I thought so, too,' Fingers agreed.

'Isn't the census to find out how many people live in a certain area?' Lofty asked.

'What do you know about it?' Carrot teased.

'More than you, clearly,' Lofty responded.

'Oooooh!' the girls chorused.

Picking up her sewing once more, Mary smiled at the antics of her brood, their visitor forgotten for now.

Back in town, whilst the information they needed was being gathered, Elijah had taken Charity to dine in a rather expensive hotel. They took the time to reminisce, Charity talking of her deceased husband, while Elijah explained he had never married but had spent the years building up a thriving business.

Afterwards, they took a cab ride around Brunswick Park and stopped to listen to a band practising on the bandstand.

Then it was back to Hady Moor House. Both were content to be in each other's company after all this time.

## 36

Early the following morning, Elijah's builder arrived at Doe Bank as everyone was having breakfast.

Mary studied the man as he introduced himself as being from the council.

Fingers frowned. 'We've lived here for ages and this is the first time anyone has taken an interest in these properties. Might you tell me what's going on?'

'No use asking me, lad, I just do as I'm told and I've been instructed to survey these houses before work can begin on fixing 'em,' the man said. Short and squat with very little hair, the man called Sam pulled out a homemade notepad and plucked the stub of pencil from behind his ear. 'Now, if it's all right with you, I'll get on. I have to make a thorough inspection of windows, doors, walls, chimneys as well as the lavvie.'

Mary and Fingers exchanged a look of puzzlement as the man disappeared next door to the boys' house.

'This is very odd, Mary, don't you think?' Fingers asked quietly.

'Yes, I'm not sure I understand why all of a sudden people are coming and going. First the census and now this? I find it strange, to say the least.'

'I'm going to hang around here until he's gone, then I'll go out to find work,' Fingers confided.

'No, you get off, all will be well here,' Mary said.

'I ain't going to the market 'til later either,' Skinny put in. 'We don't know who he is, never mind that he says he's from the council.'

'Thank you, boys, I must admit I'll feel a little safer with you here, and we have the money from selling the crate,' Mary admitted.

'That settles it then, we'll all stay,' Lofty added.

'You're just a lazy bugger; anything not to go to work,' Carrot teased.

'Ain't that the truth,' Lofty said, stretching out on the floor where he'd sat to break his fast.

Mary couldn't help but smile, and Dora laughed loudly at her friends' banter.

Sam, the builder, had been about to step into the kitchen but halted as he heard the jovial goings on. Even though he didn't know if all these children belonged to the woman or not, it was clear they were a family. He guessed from the different hair colour that they were not blood relatives, but most likely drawn together from sheer desperation to survive. From what he could surmise, the menfolk lived in one house and the women in the other.

Clearing his throat loudly, he walked into the living room and on up the stairs. He shook his head sadly. There was nothing in the rooms other than old mattresses on the wooden floors and small piles of spare clothes. He made a note. Moving to the window, he checked and nodded at the rotten frame. Taking a quick glance up the chimney, he wrote *chimney sweep needed*. Downstairs again, he walked the perimeter before climbing his ladder to check the roof tiles. Sam's notebook filled up quickly and, as he bade the family farewell, he thought Mr Elijah Covington-Smythe would be having a hefty bill to pay for those houses to be made properly habitable before winter.

Once the builder had left, everyone went about their business, leaving Mary at home alone. The girls went hunting for firewood as usual, while the boys went looking for a day's work and Skinny shot off to the market.

Sewing the last bits of Queenie's dress, Mary considered the activity over the last couple of days and how strange it was. Had the council decided to repair the dwellings at last in order to rent them out? If so, that would mean she and the children would have to move on and find other accommodation. Was it because she and Dora were here? Had the council somehow got wind of them moving in? Had Edith informed on them? No, Edith had no idea where they had gone. Worry creased her brow as she completed the garment for Queenie. Folding it neatly, she put away her needle and thread and went to the standpipe out the back to pump water to wash the breakfast dishes.

'Hello!' a voice called out and Mary walked towards it, wiping her hands on her apron as she went. Now what?

'Mrs Parsons?' a man asked.

'Yes,' Mary answered, perplexed that this stranger knew her name.

'Oh, good. I have the right place, then.' The man began unloading the crates of food from his cart. 'Where do you want this lot putting?'

'I haven't ordered... stop, please!' Mary brushed her hair from her eyes. 'You must be mistaken. I can't pay for...'

'No mistake, lady, and it's all been paid for already,' the carter answered as he trudged indoors and placed the crate in the kitchen.

Mary followed behind, asking, 'By whom?'

'Ain't got a clue, missus. I was told to deliver a big order every week.'

'What? No, you must take it back! I'm sure it must be for someone else!'

'No, it's for Mrs Parsons over at Doe Bank. Look, here's the order.' The man slipped a paper from his pocket along with a pencil. 'I just need you to sign for delivery.'

Mary read the document and frowned when she realised it was indeed correct. 'I don't understand.'

'It's simple, really, you just put your mark right there,' the man said kindly. He was of the opinion that this lady couldn't read or write.

'Not that. I can't understand who has sent and paid for all this for us,' Mary said.

'Look, lady, I ain't able to answer your questions 'cos I only deliver, see, so sign it and let me get on.'

Mary signed and the carter shoved the paper and pencil back in his pocket before unloading the other boxes. With a tip of his flat cap, he climbed onto his cart and waved before telling the horse to walk on.

Mary was in the kitchen, staring at the delivery, when the girls returned.

'Mum, what's going on?' Dora asked as she and her friends gaped at all the food.

'I don't know,' Mary said quietly.

A moment later, they heard a whistle and Skinny came in with a small carton of odds and ends.

'Bloody hell!' he gasped as he saw what the women were staring at.

'My thoughts exactly, Skinny,' Mary whispered.

## 37

'Shall we unpack it?' Owl asked, aghast at the amount of food before her.

Shaking her head, Mary said, 'I can't help thinking the carter was mistaken. It *must* be for someone else.'

'Did he say who it was intended for?' Queenie asked.

'He said my name – asked for me specifically.'

'Then it can't be in error,' Dora said.

'But who sent it?' The same question came to her lips yet again as Mary looked at the faces surrounding her.

'Whoever it was, it's most kind of them, Mum,' Dora put in.

'Let's leave it for a while in case the carter returns,' Mary said. The sight of all the food made her stomach rumble, reminding her that she'd missed breakfast so that the children should have enough.

'There's some tea and milk in there; it wouldn't be missed,' Queenie ventured.

'Besides, the milk will go off if it's not used,' Dora added, 'and look, Mum, there's some bourbon biscuits – your favourite.'

Mary screwed up her mouth as she considered the idea. 'All right, but only those items.'

The girls' grins were wide as they rifled the box and set the kettle to boil. Before long, they were all enjoying a good strong brew and a crunchy biscuit.

\* \* \*

Whilst Mary was trying to work out who their benefactor could be, Elijah was in a meeting with the builder.

'You wouldn't believe it, guv,' Sam said. 'Mattresses on the floors, one blanket apiece. The window frames are all rotten and there's tiles missing on the one roof. There ain't no food to speak of and they ain't got any coal, just a few sticks for the fire and the range.'

'Well, hopefully they should have a food delivery today,' Elijah said. 'Are you able to take on the work, Sam? Those houses need repairing as soon as possible.'

'Yes, guv, I'll start tomorra,' Sam replied.

'Excellent, and remember – it's the council who have ordered this to be done.'

'Can I just ask – what do I say if Mrs Parsons wants to know if they'm being done up for sale?'

Elijah stroked his whiskers. 'That's something I hadn't thought of.'

'I tell you what, I'll tell her the neighbours further up have complained about the state of them, that they'm an eyesore so the council have had to do summat.'

'Marvellous, Sam! Thank you. Present your bill and I'll ensure you are paid immediately,' Elijah said.

'Very good, guv.' Knuckling his forehead, Sam left Elijah, beaming from ear to ear. A moment later, he was back. 'Sorry, guv, but what about coal?'

'I'll get the coal cellars filled straight away, Sam, thank you for the reminder.' Elijah pulled half a crown from his pocket and passed it over.

'Ta, guv.' Sam went away a happy man and Elijah hailed a cab.

'The coal yard, if you'd be so kind.'

Inside an hour, Elijah was on his way to work, having paid for the two coal cellars to be filled that afternoon. The coal jagger had been sworn to secrecy about who had ordered the delivery, a half crown in his pocket sealing his lips tightly.

Charity was also busy at work. She had received the note from Elijah containing the information on all the children living at Doe Bank. The note had been delivered by an urchin runner who was given a threepenny bit as his reward, and now Charity had taken a cab to the town, where she ordered new clothes for all of the children. They also were to be delivered under the strictest secrecy, the possibility of further sales keeping the modiste's mouth firmly closed.

On her return home, Charity sat with tea and thought about how she and Elijah were doing their best to help Mary and Dora as well as the other children. Edith would be livid if she knew, but that didn't worry Charity one iota. If that miserable old bat she called a sister wouldn't help, then she would, and to hell with Edith.

Charity hadn't forgotten that she had decided to visit Edith, and she wondered what kind of reception she would receive when she got there. It didn't really matter one way or the other, she was going and that was all there was to it.

A warm feeling crept over her as Charity imagined the little family enjoying a hot meal and trying on new clothes. They would all be so excited and very puzzled. As far as Charity knew, Mary had no idea she had an aunt and although eventually all her questions would be answered, for now *Mum* was the word.

Charity smiled – she felt like Mrs Christmas and she liked it.

\* \* \*

The boys came back to their home in Doe Bank and were regaled with the tales of the different delivery people coming and going all day. The jagger had filled the coal cellars, new clothes and boxes of food had arrived and no one knew why or from whom they had been sent.

The carter had not returned for the food, so everyone unpacked the boxes. Meat, cheese, eggs, bread, butter, tea, sugar, milk, flour – the list seemed endless.

It wasn't long before Mary had the range stoked and a meal on the go. The aroma of cooking meat had everyone's mouths watering as they tried on their new outfits.

There was great excitement as they showed off their clothes, then in front of a roaring fire they enjoyed the best meals they'd ever had. Queenie had discovered boxes of candles and, as evening wore on, Mary lit a few. The whole room was bathed in flickering light and set the scene perfectly for one of Dora's stories.

'Before Dora begins, I'd like permission to use the money from the selling of the screws and washers to buy some wool. It's my intention to knit you each a winter jumper.'

'Ooh, lovely,' Skinny said.

With all in agreement, Mary nodded her thanks.

'Which story are we having tonight?' Fingers asked.

Dora pondered a moment, then said, 'How about when the Vikings invaded our shores?' The applause told her it was a good choice.

As Mary listened, she silently thanked whoever it was who had taken pity on them and had prevented them from starving.

Seeing the yawns as Dora finished her tale, Mary ushered everyone to their beds. For once, the dishes could wait until tomorrow, she thought, as she climbed weary but happy onto her mattress.

## 38

As the days passed, over in Spring Head, Edith grumbled each time she had had to cook for herself; this was when she missed Mary the most. It was also time she had to face the trip into town to do some shopping.

'I wouldn't have to do this if you hadn't overreacted, our Mary,' she mumbled into the quiet of the kitchen as she donned her hat and coat. Taking the housekeeping money from the kitchen drawer, she shoved it into her bag. 'At least you didn't steal all of it!'

Locking the door behind her, Edith set off with a basket grabbed from the scullery. It was a long walk to the market, and she wondered about hailing a cab, but she shook her head dismissively, too mean to pay the fare. She realised then that she would have to visit the bank and explain that her housekeeper had left and so would not be collecting the usual monies to pay for expenses. This was something else Edith would have to do for herself each week.

No longer having to keep up the pretence of having to hobble, Edith strode out with a scowl on her face. As she walked, she muttered under her breath, drawing glances from passers-by. 'You shouldn't have been so hot-headed. Now look, I'm having to do everything. I ain't long for this world!'

In the distance, the church bell struck ten times and as Edith passed the public house she heard the carousing inside. 'Drinking at this time of a morning! Bloody disgrace!' With a loud sniff, she moved on to the bank situated at the top of Lower High Street. Once her business there was completed, Edith strode through the market. Hearing the vendors calling out their prices, her scowl deepened. 'Daylight robbery!' Nevertheless, she bought what she needed, arguing with each seller about how they were robbing the public blind.

'Take it or leave it, missus, nobody else is complaining,' a man on the vegetable stall said.

'It's thieving! You're stealing from the poor is what you're doing!' Edith snapped.

'Look lady, do you want the veg or not? I ain't got all day to bandy words with you!'

Edith nodded and handed over some money begrudgingly. She stood a moment, counting her change carefully, not seeing the vendor roll his eyes before serving another customer.

Pushing her way through the crowds, Edith halted at the bread stall, where the whole process was repeated. Unhappy at being in the press of unwashed bodies, she couldn't wait to be home, but she *had* to get her groceries. She was causing havoc everywhere as she challenged retailers about their prices. Other shoppers were complaining and the shouting began.

'Come on, get a bloody move on! Some of us have families to see to!' a woman yelled.

'Wait your turn!' Edith railed.

Another woman shoved Edith in the back as she tried to get to the front of the queue.

Edith turned on her and hissed like a snarling cat. 'You do that again and I'll land you one!'

'Hurry up and mek your decision, then!' the woman retaliated.

'I can take as long as I want, so you shut your trap!' Edith spat nastily.

A crowd had begun to gather, seeing a bit of sport to be had, but Edith ignored them.

Turning to the vendor, the woman said loudly, 'You'm losing custom 'ere cos of this old bugger!'

The saleswoman, drawn unwittingly into the debacle, had to agree. 'She's right, so if you ain't buying then make way for them as is.'

Out came the obligatory handkerchief from her coat pocket and Edith dabbed her eyes. 'It's not right speaking to an old lady like that, especially one with a heart condition,' she said on a sob. Instantly the crowd was on her side with calls of 'you should be ashamed' and 'give the old girl a minute'. Edith smiled inwardly, as she took her time choosing a loaf and a lemon drizzle cake.

As she began to move away, spontaneous applause rang out from the crowd surrounding her and Edith waved as though she was the queen.

So busy was she enjoying the adoration, Edith didn't see Skinny and Dora watching from a little way off.

'I wonder who that was causing all the trouble,' Skinny said as they wandered away.

'My gran,' Dora answered.

'Blimey! No wonder you came to us,' Skinny replied.

'Let's go home,' Dora said and turned for Doe Bank.

At the fruit stall, Edith stood perusing what was on offer. The crowd had followed along, jostling to be at the forefront of another potential confrontation. The seller, having witnessed the furore at the previous stall, waited patiently.

Edith cast her eye over the fruit laid out before her and wrinkled her nose. 'You ain't got much of a choice, have you?'

'Seasonal, missus, all the soft fruits have finished,' the saleswoman answered, her arms crossed beneath her breasts.

Edith began to pick up and replace apples and someone took offence, as she had hoped they would.

'Don't go handling them if you ain't buying!' a young woman said sharply.

'I need to check they aren't rotten,' Edith returned.

'Well, I ain't paying good money for apples she's been pawing. You don't know where she's had her hands!'

Edith spun round, making the woman step back into the crowd. 'My hands are clean, young lady! I may be old, but I make sure to wash regularly, which, judging by your appearance, you don't!'

The crowd clapped and whistled at the rejoinder.

'Some of us can't afford good clothes like you,' the woman yelled.

'It costs very little to wash what you *do* have!'

Again, the applause rippled around the marketplace.

Whilst the argument raged, the vendor took the opportunity to serve others who were waiting.

Edith turned away from the blushing woman and bought the apples she had inspected. All along the market, the crowd followed, hoping their enjoyment would be extended to other stalls. By midday, Edith had completed her shopping trip and she hobbled out of the market to find a cab, her gait having reverted to a shuffle after the first contretemps. It all added to the persona of being a sick old lady who was managing the best she could. The sound of cheering filled her ears as she made her way slowly towards a waiting cab. The sound grew louder as the cabbie jumped down, took her basket and helped her inside before returning the heavy carrier. Tipping his hat to the crowd, the cabbie climbed aboard and clucked to the horse.

Edith grinned widely. She had dreaded going out but, much to her surprise, she had thoroughly enjoyed herself. She had realised Mary was not the only one she could argue with, there were lots of others she could upset. She determined to venture out again in another few days to see who else she could rile. If she was lucky, this could become a most pleasurable pastime.

## 39

Dora and Skinny returned to Doe Bank and told Mary what they had witnessed in the market. Despite the food parcels delivered from an unknown benefactor, Skinny had taken Dora to show her how to scavenge. This was something they would have to do again once the free food had all gone, he'd explained.

'So your gran has found someone else to bully,' Mary said as she wiped her hands on her apron. The conversation was interrupted by the sound of banging, and rushing outside, Mary saw a man on the roof.

'Excuse me, what are you doing?' she called out.

'Fixing the tiles, missus,' the builder said, and Mary realised it was the same man who had completed the survey a few days previously.

'I didn't request this; I can't afford it.'

'Courtesy of the council. We'll be doing the windows and doors next,' Sam yelled back.

'Oh. Well, thank you very much.' Mary frowned as she went back indoors. 'It's all very odd,' she said to Dora.

'What is, Mum?' Dora asked as she tried to push a finger beneath the plaster on her arm to scratch an itch.

'Why are the council suddenly interested in renovating these properties when they've been derelict for years?'

Dora shook her head as she glanced around for something more suited to getting at the infernal itch.

'Do you think the council will devict us?' Skinny asked worriedly.

'I can't see how they could evict us, Skinny,' Mary answered. 'I'm not sure these are even council tenancies.'

'Why not?'

'If they were, wouldn't the repairs have been undertaken a long time ago? Surely they would have had families renting them by now.'

'Does that mean they were privately owned at one time?' Dora asked as she carefully manoeuvred a taper into a gap between plaster and arm.

'I suspect so,' Mary answered as she continued to roll out pastry for a pie.

'So why are the council doing the repairs?' Skinny asked.

'That's what I can't work out,' Mary answered.

With a sigh of relief as the itch subsided, Dora said, 'Maybe we shouldn't question it. The work is being done and we don't have to pay. That's what's important, isn't it?'

'I suppose so.' Mary filled the pie with meat, vegetables and gravy before putting a pastry lid on and shoving it into the range. However, the questions would give her no peace. Maybe when she got a minute to herself, she'd ask at the council to see if they could shed any light on it. Scraping potatoes, Mary listened as Dora and Skinny, Owl and Queenie chatted amongst themselves. Then she called out, 'We could do with some kindling.'

'All right, Mum,' Dora called back and she and the others ran outside and over the heath, laughing loudly.

Mary smiled. Dora was so much happier here; she had never once complained of the cold or lack of the luxury of an indoor privy. It warmed her heart to hear Dora laughing all the time. Gone were the long faces and moping about looking for something to do. These were things of the past. Mary was glad they had been able to move in with the others and she was slowly coming to terms with living a life of poverty.

The roof repairs took very little time and already the occupants of the houses noticed the difference. There were no more howling draughts and they no longer worried about the roof leaking when it rained. Not before time, either, as the weather began to turn colder. Mary knitted sweaters as fast as her hands could move so all the boys were warmer when they went out to find work. The temperature dipped sharply at night and early mornings saw a fine layer of frost which coated everything in sight. Winter was coming and Mary's fear about how they would manage increased.

Her worry was raised further when one day, around mid-morning, the boys arrived home in a panic. 'Scarlet fever has broken out in the town,' Fingers explained.

'Then you all did the right thing in coming back,' Mary said. 'We're pretty much isolated here so we should be all right, but you'll all have to stay put until we hear it's been eradicated.'

'Don't it just affect little'uns?' Skinny asked.

'Usually, but we'll take no chances. If any of you have a sore throat you must tell me. If you feel sick or have a headache, let me know.'

'I've always got a headache,' Carrot put in. 'It's called Lofty!'

Giggles sounded as Lofty landed a punch on Carrot's arm.

'I'm serious, boys, there will be no more work until it's gone. Oh, and everyone check your chest and stomach regularly for a rash.'

'How will we go about earning a few pennies?' Whippet asked.

'We can't, so we'll have to do what we can with what we have. I'll go to the town when we need anything,' Mary answered.

'But what if you catch it, Mum?' Dora asked, clearly concerned.

'I won't, but I'll try to make sure none of you do, either. So, use your own towel, don't use each other's. The same goes for plates, cups, utensils. Wash your hands thoroughly and often. I know it will be awkward, but don't get too close to each other.'

'Why not?' It was Owl who asked.

'Scarlet fever is passed by droplets when you cough, sneeze or exhale so just be aware. I'm not trying to frighten you, I'm simply telling you how to stay safe. I'm not expecting anyone to contract this disease, because it usually affects younger children as far as anyone knows. Having said that, it pays to be vigilant. Any questions?'

'Yes, what do we do with our time now we can't go to work?' Skinny asked.

'Lessons?' Mary queried.

Groans at the idea made her smile. 'The old crates stacked out the back could be made into chairs, so that's you lads sorted out. Girls, you can knit or cook – Dora, you can write your stories down to entertain us all at night.'

'Mary's right, we have to make the best of it,' Fingers added, 'and now is a good time to start.' He led the boys outside, and it wasn't long before hammering and banging could be heard.

Mary set the girls to pickling vegetables to be stored ready for use in the worst of the winter months. As she worked, providing an evening meal, she heard Whippet giving instructions on constructing stools. The laughter sounded loud when someone hit a thumb with a hammer and cursed.

Mary's mind returned to the scarlet fever outbreak and

although she felt her little household would be fairly safe, she couldn't help but wonder how many youngsters would succumb. There was no doubt there would be mourning in many houses before the disease had finished its lethal trek through the town.

They had plenty of food in the pantries, thanks to their anonymous benefactor, the deliveries coming each week as regular as clockwork. The cellars were full of coal which, with luck, would last them a long time. The children had some good clothes now and she would continue to knit sweaters, hats, gloves and scarves to help beat off the cold. Any scraps of wool left over could be pegged into a rug and any old clothes which no longer fit would be turned into quilts for the mattresses. At least this would keep them all busy whilst they were isolated.

Once the meal was prepared, Mary set the girls to unpicking one of her old dresses and cutting it into squares. These would be stitched together to make the first quilt. Mary checked the money in the table drawer and, seeing there was sufficient, she grabbed her basket.

'I'm going to the market for some more wool for cardigans for you girls. I'll also see what old clothes I can get for quilting. You must all stay home whilst I'm out – is that clear?'

The girls nodded and Mary went outside to tell the boys the same.

'I can come and carry your basket,' Skinny offered helpfully.

'Thank you, but no, Skinny. I need you to remain here where I know you are safe. You can, however, keep an eye on that lot.' Mary tilted her head and winked at Fingers, who smiled in return.

'Will do, Mary,' Skinny said self-importantly.

With money in her pocket, shawl around her shoulders and basket over her arm, Mary set off for the market. Overhead, dark clouds gathered and the sharp wind bit through to her bones.

Increasing her step, she endeavoured to outpace the oncoming storm, but she knew it was not going to happen when she felt a few drops of rain suddenly begin to fall. Looking up at the louring sky, Mary resigned herself to the fact that by the time she got home she could well be soaked to the skin.

## 40

Whilst Mary was organising the work details at Doe Bank, Elijah had called in on Charity. They had discussed, over hot chocolate, what had already been achieved to help Mary and her adopted brood; now they considered whether there was anything more they could do.

'I have food being delivered each week,' Charity assured her visitor. 'Other than that, I don't see what else can be done to help.'

'That's wonderful, Charity, but it won't come cheap.'

'I'm not concerned with the expense; this is my niece we're talking about. If my sister won't look out for her, then I will.'

Elijah nodded as he stroked his silver beard. 'As will I.'

'I'm so glad you came to me regarding Mary's plight, Elijah. I'm also grateful for your keeping watch for so many years.'

'I promised George...' he began.

Charity waved a hand. 'I know you did, but how many men would have adhered to that oath? The question I keep asking myself, however, is why has Edith chosen the church as the bene-ficiary?'

'Perhaps she sees it as her ticket into heaven when she dies,' Elijah said.

Charity shook her head. 'I can't see the old battle-axe being admitted when she arrives at those pearly gates.'

Elijah couldn't help but smile at the image Charity's words conjured up – Edith arguing with St Peter!

'There could well be a queue there, I'm sorry to say, with scarlet fever raging through the town,' he said.

'I fear you're right. The undertaker could find himself busy with the construction of little white coffins,' Charity added sadly.

'Oh, I pray not. I think Mary and those kiddies will be safe enough, however.'

'Indeed. Now, is there anything more we can do to help?' Charity asked.

'I suspect not, but I'll keep an ear to the ground.'

Charity gave a single nod. 'Stay in touch with me and if there's anything...'

'I'll be sure to let you know,' Elijah assured her before taking his leave.

Charity sat for a long time, thinking about Edith. How could two sisters be so different? Where Charity was light-hearted and jovial, Edith was miserable and rude. Charity's husband had passed over, whereas Edith's had left her. Elijah had thought that Mary's husband could no longer put up with Edith's interference and had also left, and poor Mary had taken Dora and returned to Edith where she was treated like a slave. It was the child, however, who bore the brunt of Edith's spite, and that was what rattled Charity the most. Dora was the innocent in all of this and yet she had suffered the most.

* * *

Whilst Charity was brooding, Mary had bought some wool and was sorting through the second-hand garments on one of the stalls in the market. Quite suddenly, a quiet descended and Mary looked up to see a man carrying a small white casket, his distraught wife following behind, being held up by two other women.

Men wearing caps removed them and held them to their chests in respect as the funeral cortege passed by. All activity in the market stopped as hundreds of pairs of eyes watched the sad procession. The first of many more to come, Mary thought sadly, and she guessed everyone would be fearing the same.

Traffic halted in the street as the man trudged on wearily. Bystanders held their breath as he stumbled and they only exhaled when he moved on. A carter offered his service and helped the man and his wife onto the back of his cart, the little coffin held tightly across their laps. The other mourners walked behind as the cart moved on.

Slowly the market came back to life as the cart disappeared, but the mood was subdued. Vendors called out but not as loudly as before. Women muttered prayers for the bereaved as well as for their own families.

'Watcha lookin' for, missus?' the stallholder asked Mary quietly.

'Anything to make into bed quilts for my children,' she answered. It was the first time she had referred to the Doe Bank kids as her own and it gave her a warm feeling. The vendor nodded and sorted out a couple of long woollen coats.

'How much?' Mary asked, aware she had little money left.

Seeing the bedraggled state of Mary and how thin she was, the woman said, 'Nuthin. You have 'em with my blessing.'

'Thank you,' Mary mumbled her gratitude as she hung the coats over her arm before moving on. When she was given three cotton dresses by another stallholder, Mary realised how much the funeral cortege had touched everyone's hearts. With the money she'd saved, Mary went to the confectionery stall and bought half a pound of boiled sweets. She knew it was frivolous, but she felt the children would deserve a treat after all their hard work.

The clouds had come to nothing, but the breeze was still cold. Gathering strength, its eldritch sound echoed loud in the ginnels between the houses as Mary walked home. It picked up detritus from the street and flung it high in the air before allowing it to fall again. On the cobbles, the whistling wind swirled dust into eddies before racing away.

Mary hurried after it, wanting nothing more than to be home by a warm fire with the children around her. Life could be taken in the blink of an eye and it was up to her to ensure the children were kept safe. It was a big responsibility but one she would not shirk. Taking care of these outcasts and orphans had become her mission in life, and it was one she would tackle with relish.

The signal given, Mary smiled as her family came out to meet her. Skinny took the basket and Owl and Queenie carried the clothes.

Indoors at last, Mary breathed a sigh of relief as she warmed her hands by the fire. She related what she'd seen in the market, and everyone listened with sadness, while Dora managed to make tea with her good arm which Mary accepted gratefully.

'We have a surprise for you,' Fingers said with a smile as Skinny clapped his hands like a toddler.

Whippet, Carrot and Lofty came through, each carrying a stool made from the old crates. Placing them down, they sat on them, legs and arms crossed, wide grins on their faces.

'Oh, boys, well done!'

'These are for the girls,' Whippet said, 'and once we get more wood, we can all have one.'

'That's very thoughtful of you, and it makes me very proud. Now

I have a surprise for you.' Going to the basket, Mary pulled out the bag of sweets.

Skinny clapped harder than ever when he saw the treat. Quiet descended as each child sucked contentedly on their boiled sweet.

'One each every day,' Mary said as she placed the bag on the table. She grinned as the sound of sweets rattling against teeth was all that could be heard, interspersed with the odd slurp.

After their evening meal of belly pork, potatoes and vegetables, Mary suggested Owl and Queenie try on the woollen coats. They fitted well and Mary said they should keep them; the cotton dresses would do for quilting.

By the light of candles and the fire, Dora read them the tale of Jack the Ripper from a newspaper that they had found in the food box. It was only last year that his victims had been found in the Whitechapel and Spitalfields areas of London.

*Another reason to stay close to home*, Mary thought as they all headed for their mattresses. It would be another chilly night, so Mary banked the fire up in case it was too cold to sleep upstairs. She did the same in the boys' house, reminding them all to check their bodies for a rash. Then she went to help Dora undress and slip into her nightdress, before doing the same herself.

It was about an hour later when, wrapped in their blankets, Owl and Queenie met Dora and Mary by the living room fire. It was freezing up in the bedrooms and Mary guessed the boys would likely be sleeping by their fire too.

## 41

The following morning, Charity thanked the driver who helped her from his cab. 'Please wait. I have a feeling this won't take long,' she said. The cabbie knuckled his forehead and climbed back into the driving seat.

Charity knocked on the front door of the house in Spring Head and waited.

The door opened and a booming voice declared, 'Well, I never thought to see the day.'

'Hello, Edith.'

'What do you want?'

'That's a nice welcome for your sister, I must say. Are you going to invite me in?'

Edith turned and walked back to the living room, leaving Charity to close the door after stepping inside. Following Edith, Charity took a seat and watched Edith do the same.

The women eyed each other with suspicion as Charity removed her gloves and laid them on her bag in her lap. Both noted how age had caught up with them, their lined faces testament to the years gone by.

'Well?' Edith finally broke the strained silence.

'I thought to visit as neither of us is getting any younger,' Charity replied. 'I wanted to see how you are.'

'You've seen now, so you can leave,' Edith growled.

'Still the same, nasty as ever. I had hoped you might have mellowed, but clearly I was mistaken.'

Edith didn't answer.

'Are you not pleased to see me?' Charity asked.

'Not especially,' Edith said ungraciously.

Another silence followed Edith's remark and Charity wondered why she had bothered to come at all.

'You continue to live alone?'

'Do you see anyone else here?'

Charity sighed. This was going to be harder than she had thought.

'How have you been?'

'I'm still breathing, am I not?'

Charity tried again to elicit a decent conversation. 'You are managing well enough?'

'Yes.'

*Blood and stone springs to mind!* Charity thought, as she glanced around the room. The furniture was old but serviceable. The rugs had seen better days, but they were clean. The whole room had a dingy feeling to it.

'Tea would be nice,' Charity tried yet again.

'The kitchen is through there. If you want tea, make it yourself.'

'Why are you being so horrid?' Charity snapped.

'I don't want you here! I don't know why you've come, but it was not by invite from me!'

Charity swallowed her anger. Falling out further with her sister would not furnish her with the information she sought.

'I came to assure myself you were still in the land of the living.'

'I am, so now you're assured, you can bugger off back to your fancy house and leave me in peace!' Edith spat back.

'How is your daughter?' Charity asked pointedly.

Edith shrugged her shoulders.

Frowning, Charity went on. 'Do you not see her?'

'No, not any more.'

'Why is that?' Charity probed.

'None of your business.'

'I see.'

'What?' Edith asked, suddenly suspicious of the woman she hadn't laid eyes on in years.

'I take it that you've alienated your daughter as well, then,' Charity answered.

'Mary upped and walked out, left me to cope on my own, and after all I did for her and that brat of hers!'

So this was the way to extract what she needed to know – by riling Edith.

'I thought she had married.'

'She did, but he left her. Then she came crawling back to me.'

'Ah, that's a shame. Is there no chance of a reconciliation between them?'

'Not now – he's dead.'

'How very sad. So where is Mary now?' Charity pushed, hoping to learn more.

'I don't know and I don't care!' Edith blasted. 'I'll see her in hell before she'll get anything more from me!'

'That could prove awkward in the event of your death.'

'How so?' Edith asked, her eyes narrowing to slits.

'This place,' Charity said as she waved a hand around the room.

'That's all taken care of.'

'Really?' Charity asked nonchalantly.

'Yes. I'm leaving it all to the church.'

'The church! What about Mary?' Charity asked, feigning surprise.

'What about her? She'll have to fend for herself, like I had to.'

'Edith, she could be in the workhouse! Have you no compassion?'

'Evidently not,' Edith said with a sickly grin. 'Look, Charity, whatever it is you want, you can't have it, so I'd be obliged if you'd just bugger off!'

Charity curled her lip. Drawing on her gloves, she stood to leave. She'd heard enough. Edith had told her what she wanted to know; she had confirmed that the church would inherit everything.

Without rising to see her sister out, Edith called over her shoulder, 'And don't bother to come back!'

Charity was helped into the carriage once more by the cabbie and, as she was jogged along, her mind whirled. Rather than mellowing with age, Edith had become harder. The lines on her face had formed from constant scowling and she was more argumentative. Her selfishness had surpassed itself with her bequeathing her property to the church. It was certain now that Edith Pitt would die a lonely woman, and Charity thought she deserved every bit of it.

*I'll worry about you no more, you spiteful old crone. My concern will be for Mary and Dora in the future.* Charity glanced out of the cab window as she determined to discuss with Elijah how best to further aid Mary and her coterie.

Once home, Charity sent a note, inviting Elijah to dine with her that evening. The urchin runner had been told to try the house first, and if he received no answer to then go on to Elijah's office. The bedraggled boy sped off, saying he knew where the properties were and after some time he returned with the message: *I'll be glad to.*

\* \* \*

Over their meal that evening, Charity said, 'I had to go, Elijah, I needed to hear it for myself.'

Elijah nodded. 'I guessed you would, and I'm betting you didn't receive a warm welcome.'

'Indeed not. It is as we feared, Mary stands to inherit nothing.'

'The question now is – where do we go from here?' Elijah asked, feeling perplexed.

'I don't see what more we can do, for now, at least. We just have to ensure they don't starve and have enough fuel to last them through the winter.'

'I wonder whether we should make ourselves known to Mary,' Elijah said after a short pause.

'Maybe in the future it will come to that, but I wonder if she might see our help as charity and refuse it. Then we'd be back to square one.'

Elijah sipped his wine before he said, 'Possibly. So we continue as we have been doing, and aid where we can from afar.'

'Do you think it unlikely you will see Dora or her friends because of the scarlet fever outbreak?'

'I do. I think Mary will keep the children at home for the foreseeable future,' Elijah returned.

'That means there will be no money earned.'

A frown formed on Elijah's face as he contemplated the ramifications of Charity's statement. 'They'll have food and coal, what more could they need?'

'Boots, winter coats, woollens, and ladies need certain other things too,' Charity said, raising an eyebrow.

Elijah muttered something unintelligible and flushed to the roots of his silver hair.

'I'll open an account at the bank in Mary's name and send her the bank book, so at least she'll have access to some funds,' Charity said, ignoring Elijah's discomfort.

'May I contribute?' he asked.

'No need, but thank you for the offer. I was left well provided for, as you know. Besides, I've made a decision. Everything I have will go to Mary when I've gone, so she might as well enjoy some of it now.'

'That's very charitable of you,' Elijah said.

'Not really – she's family.' Charity grinned at his pun. Then she rang the hand bell for the maid to clear their plates.

They spent the evening reminiscing about times gone by, and Elijah felt he could happily stay here forever.

## 42

The next day, Charity visited the bank and set up an account in the name of Mrs Mary Parsons, 2 Doe Bank Cottages, Wednesbury. In it, she deposited the amount of fifty pounds and was given the bank book by the manager, who was given a brief explanation as to what Charity was doing and why. Once home, her maid, Ginny, whistled for a runner.

The stick-thin boy stood in the kitchen and waited. His clothes were rags and his boots were held together with string. Dirt was ingrained on his hands and face, and he constantly sniffed.

'I'd be obliged if you would deliver this to Mrs Parsons at Doe Bank,' Charity said, holding out a sealed envelope.

'Will do, missus,' the boy said as he took the envelope.

'Ensure it is Mrs Parsons before you hand it over, mind.'

'I will.'

With a firm nod, Charity gave him a shilling and smiled as the urchin tested it between his teeth. Happy the coin didn't bend, so proving its validity, he tipped his ragged cap before he turned to set off.

'What are you called, lad?'

The boy eyed the woman suspiciously. Why did she want to know his name?

'It's all right, I can't just call you boy or lad, can I?'

Understanding now, he replied, 'Billy Fitzwarren, but everybody calls me Fitz.'

'Well, Fitz, are you hungry?' Charity asked, knowing full well he must be starving.

The ragamuffin nodded.

'We'll sort that out in a minute, but firstly, where do you live?'

The thought of having something to eat helped Fitz to relax a little and he said, 'I live with a few others in an old empty house on Alma Street, until the council move us on, that is.'

Charity heard the grumble of his empty stomach, and she rang for the maid.

'Take Fitz to the kitchen and give him something warm to eat, please, my dear,' Charity addressed the maid, who was looking down her nose at the scruffy boy. Then to Fitz, she added, 'Please don't forget your errand.'

'Ta, missus, I won't,' Fitz responded eagerly as his belly growled again.

Charity requested tea and went to sit by her fire in the parlour. With luck, Mary would spend her money wisely. Charity hoped that, by the end of the week, all at Doe Bank would be sleeping in proper beds, at least. Of course, there was no way she would know for certain, but she remained hopeful.

Then her mind returned to Fitz and his runner friends. Was there anything she could do for them? This was something she would have to ponder at length.

A little while later, a note arrived from Elijah, inviting her to dinner and a trip to the theatre. Charity sent her reply: *I'd love to.*

\* \* \*

Over at Doe Bank, Mary had received the envelope from the runner. Sitting at the table, she opened it and gasped.

Dora, Queenie and Owl exchanged a glance as they watched Mary's hand cover her mouth.

'Mum?'

Mary looked up from the bank book, then she passed it to Dora.

'Blimey! Mum, who's doing all this?'

'I don't know, sweetheart,' Mary answered quietly.

Queenie and Owl peeped over Dora's shoulder, then looked at each other in shock.

'I'll have to take this back to the bank and tell them it's a mistake,' Mary said as she retook the little book.

'It's in your name, Mum, so it can't be an error,' Dora said.

Mary shook her head as her eyes rested on the amount once more. Fifty pounds! She could barely believe her eyes. 'Maybe I can find out who was kind enough to set up this account, at least.'

Grabbing her shawl and bag, Mary set off for the town, leaving strict instructions for everyone to stay home. No sooner had she gone than Dora, Queenie and Owl rushed next door to tell the boys of Mary's good fortune.

'That's an enormous amount of money,' Fingers said.

'Who gave it to her?' Skinny asked, having no idea exactly how much fifty pounds was.

'We don't know. That's why Mum's gone to the bank, to see if she can find out,' Dora answered. 'In the meantime, I suggest we light the fires and make it cosy for her return.'

* * *

Mary hurried through the streets, the cold wind whipping her long skirt against her legs. Having tied her shawl around her chest, she shoved her hands in its folds to keep them warm, her bag over her arm.

Arriving at the bank, she strode purposefully towards a teller who was working quietly behind the counter. Mary pushed over her bank book and the teller looked up.

'How can I help you, madam?' he asked politely as he peered through his round spectacles, which made his eyes look enormous.

'Are you able to tell me who set up this account, please?' Mary asked as she passed over the little book.

The teller frowned. 'May I ask your name?'

'Mary Parsons.'

The bespectacled man opened the book and squinted at the name written there. 'Are you trying to be funny?' he growled.

'Excuse me?'

'This is your book, with your name on it, therefore I'm surmising you opened the account!' the teller snapped, all signs of politeness gone.

'That's just it – I didn't! It was delivered to me this morning.'

'Really? Let me see if the manager can shed any light on it for you.' The teller's words dripped with sarcasm. Walking towards an office, the teller started to feel contrite about having spoken so rudely to the customer. He knew he would be in hot water if the manager found out how badly he had behaved. Tapping the door, he walked in and a moment later he was back. 'I'm afraid the manager has no knowledge of this either,' he said, then in a whisper added, 'although I doubt that – he knows everything that goes on in this place.'

'Would it be possible to speak with him?' Mary asked.

The teller shook his head. 'He'll tell you nothing more than you already know.'

'But that's the thing, I don't know anything about it!' Mary said as she held up the bank book which had been returned to her.

'Look, madam, take my advice and enjoy your money. Someone felt you should have it, so go out there and spend it.'

He was right, of course, Mary thought, as she considered his words. There was so much they needed and now they had the money to buy those things.

With a nod, Mary made up her mind. 'In that case, I'd like to withdraw fifty pounds, please,' she said, pushing the book over the counter once more.

The teller grinned and, marking her book, he then counted out the money, both of which he passed over. He watched as Mary shoved them to the bottom of her bag. 'Enjoy your shopping,' he said out of the side of his mouth.

'I will,' Mary said with a smile.

By the time Mary arrived home, she had nine beds on order, along with good mattresses and pillows, as well as plenty of blankets, sheets, pillowcases and bedspreads. Five were to be delivered that afternoon and the rest the following day, having to be brought in from the manufacturer's other premises.

When she returned to Doe Bank, everyone rushed out to meet her and Mary explained about her trip to the bank. 'I want all the mattresses taken out of your house, boys, and taken onto the heath and burned.'

'We'll have nothing to sleep on,' Skinny protested.

'Oh, you will, Skinny, beds and linen will be delivered today. Ours, girls, will be coming tomorrow.'

Applause and cheers sounded before the boys set to manhandling their old mattresses down the stairs and out to a safe place where Fingers set light to them.

Smoke plumed up high into the sky as the boys kept a careful watch on the fire, ensuring a spark didn't stray and ignite the heath.

Indoors, Mary began to prepare food for their lunch. She decided hot stew would go down a treat on such a cold day.

It was shortly after they'd eaten, that carts arrived one after another carrying the cast iron bedframes, mattresses and linen. The children watched with glee as these were hauled into place. It was a tight fit for the room containing the three bedsteads, but eventually they were crammed in.

Mary and Queenie made up the beds while Owl and Dora made tea and provided cake.

As darkness approached, they sat around the fire awaiting their evening meal, the boys eager for bedtime to roll around so they could enjoy a good night's sleep in a proper bed at last.

## 43

Whilst Mary was serving stew to her brood, Elijah and Charity were having dinner together in a fine hotel.

They sat in the dining room surrounded by other guests, all dressed in their finery. Ladies in their colourful dresses and dripping in jewels, their male companions in smart dark suits.

Crystal chandeliers twinkled in the light from the gas lamps and candles in glass holders lit the tables. Wine and water glasses, Sheffield steel cutlery and small flower displays also adorned the tables.

'Mary's account is all set up with a fifty-pound balance, the bank book was delivered to her this morning,' Charity said before sipping her wine, savouring the excellent vintage.

'My sources inform me that she's ordered beds for them all, the last of which are to be delivered tomorrow,' Elijah commented.

Charity sighed contentedly.

'You're enjoying this, aren't you?' Elijah asked.

'What?'

'This cloak and dagger stuff,' he said, waving his knife around.

'To be truthful, I am. It's given me a new lease of life, Elijah. I suspected I would end my days quietly at home, having done nothing of import, and having no one to leave my money to.'

'And now?' he asked with a smile.

'I have something worthwhile to concentrate on. Helping Mary and Dora is giving me an inordinate amount of pleasure.'

'Does it bother you that she doesn't know where that help is coming from?'

'No. I rather like the intrigue. Besides, she will know me one day, I'm sure.'

Elijah studied the woman sitting across from him. Her blue eyes twinkled in the light from the candle on their table. Her shining grey hair was expertly piled up in an elegant fashion, and the laughter lines at the outer edges of her eyes were visible, giving her a constant smile.

As they ate, he recalled how, very many years before, he had first met Charity Lacey. Daniel Lacey had approached Elijah to conduct some business of carrying cargo from his tube works around the country. Elijah's narrowboat and barge company was the ideal mode of transport, the boats sailing the criss-cross network of canals to the major towns and cities. The arrangement had continued even after Daniel's death, but Elijah now dealt with the foreman of the tube works.

His first meeting with Charity had been at a debutante ball given by a wealthy couple who were bringing their daughter out into society.

Elijah had been enchanted by Charity at the outset and all three had become firm friends. He thought how, back then, he had been a little in love with her, but because she was married he had kept his emotions in check.

Now, as he gazed at her across the table, all those old feelings flooded back and he realised with a jolt that perhaps this lady was the reason he had never married. He had never met anyone quite like Charity, and no other woman could match up to her.

'What do you think?' Charity's question snapped him back to the present.

'I'm sorry, my dear, I was miles away for a moment there,' he answered, embarrassed at allowing his attention to roam.

Charity smiled. 'Should I introduce myself to Mary while I still have the chance?'

'I don't understand,' he said with a frown.

'Before I die, Elijah! Should Mary know me now rather than learn about me after I've gone?'

'That's your decision to make, of course, but you'll live many more years yet.'

'I'm older than Edith, you know,' she said, laying her cutlery neatly on her empty plate.

*If I didn't know, I would never have guessed*, Elijah thought but said instead, 'Let's have no more talk of death, but if you want to meet with Mary then I think you should do so.'

'Would you come with me?' Charity dipped her chin and looked at him, moving only her eyes.

Elijah's heart melted at the coquettish gesture, and he knew right then he'd do anything for the woman who'd stolen his heart so long ago. 'If you wish it, then of course I will.'

Charity beamed with pleasure and watched as Elijah replenished her glass. 'Why did you never wed, Elijah?'

The question came out of the blue and took him by surprise. Was this the time to confess all? Or should he keep his counsel and brush it off with a joke?

Sipping his wine, Elijah took his time before answering. If he told her the truth, that he had loved only her all these long years, would it ruin the good relationship they had? Might it be that she could secretly harbour feelings for him? He shook his head in disbelief at that last thought. Then, taking his courage in both hands, he said quietly, 'Because you hold the key to my heart and have done since the day I first met you.'

He watched for her response and was taken aback that she wasn't surprised.

'I think I've always known,' she said on a sigh.

'You never said anything,' Elijah mumbled.

'Neither did you,' she responded with a warm smile.

'I couldn't. You were married to Daniel, who was my good friend, and when he passed – well, it wasn't appropriate for me to continue to call. After that, I assumed you didn't wish to rekindle our friendship.'

'Elijah Covington-Smythe, there's nothing I would have liked more!' Charity said in a loud whisper.

Elijah grasped her hand across the table and asked, 'Charity, would you walk out with me?'

With a nod, she answered, 'I'd love to.'

Neither had seen the waitress approach and they were unaware of her presence until they heard her catch her breath.

Looking up, they saw her brush away a tear, then grin down at them.

\* \* \*

Whilst Elijah and Charity were enjoying a scrumptious dinner in the hotel dining room, over at Spring Head, Edith was grumbling under her breath as she cooked her evening meal. Her back ached from standing peeling potatoes at the sink, knowing it would be worse still the next day when she had to clean out the ashes from the range.

'I wouldn't have to be doing this if you hadn't gone off in a huff, our Mary!'

Sitting on a kitchen chair to ease the pain, the only sound to be heard was the bubbling of the water in the pan. Edith sighed loudly, propping her elbows on the table and resting her chin in her hands. In the time Mary had been away, Edith had seen no one other than when she had gone to the market, and the unwelcome visit from her sister. Realising she had no friends, as though the thought had only just occurred to her, she wondered why. Her mind travelled back across the years, and she acknowledged she had never had friendships that had lasted.

The hiss of the pot boiling over had her on her feet. Draining the potatoes and too lazy to make gravy, Edith added a knob of butter instead. Looking at her meal, a pork chop and green beans alongside the buttered potatoes, she sighed again before beginning to eat.

Once she had finished her meal, Edith made tea and took it with some biscuits to her chair in the living room. The empty plate remained on the table to be washed whenever she felt inclined.

Staring at the wall, Edith couldn't deny she missed Mary. The girl was useful to have around the place and was an excellent cook. She never would have left had it not been for that brat, Dora. Edith scowled at the thought of the child she hated so much.

*It's her fault I'm on my own now! I hope the bloody kid rots in hell!*

Sipping her hot tea, Edith's upper denture slid out and landed with a plop in the cup. Closing her eyes for a second, she groaned before fishing out her false teeth, burning her fingers in the process.

'Bloody hell! This day is going from bad to worse!' she mumbled after shoving her teeth back in place. The trouble was, she knew tomorrow would be no better, nor the next day, nor the one after that. 'Best get used to it, because Mary isn't likely to be coming home any time soon.'

Edith slipped into a morose mood, feeling the world was against her, and the only reason for that as far as she could see was because of Dora Parsons.

'That child should have died at birth!' she grumbled nastily. 'Then there would just be me and Mary and all would be well.'

Before long, Edith fell asleep, not aware that her teeth had escaped her mouth once more and now lay in her lap.

## 44

Over the next weeks, 154 cases of scarlet fever were reported as the disease waged war on the town. Eventually, it disappeared, leaving the populace to lick its wounds. Some said it was the sudden cold temperatures that had killed off the infections, others disagreed, saying it always struck in winter and spring. Whatever the reason, the fever moved on from Wednesbury, much to everyone's relief.

Then, of course, it was the weather that folk grumbled about. The temperature plummeted at night, coating the streets and buildings with a layer of frost which twinkled in the lamplight. Smoke swirled from almost every chimney, floating lazily for a while before being carried away on an icy wind.

Thick woollen shawls were brought out, as were jackets and, for those who could afford them, coats. Scarves and gloves, caps and hats, and socks and boots replaced summer footwear. Everyone was in a hurry to conduct their business so they could return to a warm fireside. In the inky blackness of night, the sky would light up fiery red as furnace doors were thrown open.

At Doe Bank, Mary was thankful that the children had escaped contracting scarlet fever. Now they resumed their search for work each day, wrapped in warm outdoor clothing.

On one of her shopping trips, Mary had called in at the council offices to enquire about the work that had been undertaken. She remained baffled when the officer said that as the properties were once privately owned, it was not down to them to repair or maintain them.

Each member of the household now slept in a proper bed. Mary had tried to ration the coal but, as the weather moved further into winter, she gave up the idea, saying it was imperative to keep both themselves and the houses warm and dry. Besides, if they ran low, she now had the money to order more.

Their food parcels still came every week as the delivery man had told Mary that first day, and she was still no wiser as to who was paying for it all. Either no one knew or they had been sworn to secrecy, although 'why' was the question which plagued Mary the most. Who was it that was being so kind to them? Why had they not come forward to introduce themselves? Was it someone Mary knew? Or was it a stranger who had seen or heard of their plight? The questions rattling around in Mary's mind were a constant source of frustration, and try as she might, she could not rid herself of them.

It was one very cold morning that the mystery was finally solved. The boys had gone to the wharf to find work, and the girls were at home with Mary, who was teaching them spelling. Hearing a knock on the front door, Mary went to answer it, the girls trailing behind her. As the door opened, it was Dora who spoke first.

'Elijah!' she gasped, taking in his changed appearance in one glance. From his shiny boots, black trousers and knee-length woollen coat, scarf, gloves and walking cane to his top hat, Elijah was the epitome of an immaculately dressed, well-to-do gentleman.

'Hello, Dora, Mary,' he replied with a beaming smile.

Dora's gaze moved to the woman standing next to Elijah. Also well-dressed in an olive green full-length coat, the dark green piping matched perfectly with her leather gloves, bag and boots. A large hat held a few silk roses and was perched on a perfect coiffure of grey hair.

'Please pardon the intrusion...' Elijah began.

'I'm sorry, please come in out of the cold,' Mary cut across, suddenly finding her tongue again. The change in Elijah had had Mary glued to the spot for a moment before he had broken the spell.

Closing the door, Mary ushered the girls to sit quietly on the peg rug whilst Elijah's companion was offered the chair. Queenie dashed next door, coming back with the boys' only original chair, which she offered to Elijah.

'Queenie, kettle on, please, Owl – biscuits. Dora, go and help, thank you, girls.'

Charity and Elijah watched the activity in silence as Mary issued her orders then built up the fire.

'This is a surprise,' Mary said at last as she waved a hand towards Elijah's attire.

'Mary, this is Mrs Charity Lacey from Hady Moor House in Mesty Croft,' he said.

'I'm very pleased to meet you, Mrs Lacey,' Mary said gracefully, while all the time more questions raged in her mind. Was Elijah actually a businessman who played at being a beggar when the mood took him? It certainly looked that way. But why would anyone do that? Who was Charity Lacey and why had Elijah brought her here? What did they want with Mary?

A tray of tea and biscuits was brought through and placed on the table. The hot drink was accepted gratefully and, as they drank, Charity cast a glance around her.

'Forgive my asking, Elijah, but...' Mary began.

Raising a hand to forestall her, Elijah said, 'I realise there's a lot of explaining to do before everything becomes clear, but firstly Mrs Lacey has something she wishes to say to you.'

Mary inclined her head and her eyes moved to Charity. The girls sat quietly on the floor by the fire, listening to every word.

'Mary, I've known about you from the day you were born. What I didn't know was that you had a daughter, not until very recently, anyway.'

Mary looked at Dora with a smile, then back to Charity.

'It was Elijah who brought your predicament to my attention, for which I will always be grateful,' Charity went on.

'I'm sorry, but how do you know about me when I have never met you before today?' Mary asked impatiently.

'Because Edith Pitt is my sister. I'm your aunt, Mary.'

* * *

Whilst Mary was only now learning she had an aunt, Edith was cooking herself a late breakfast. She had spent an hour trying to light the fire in the parlour, the damp kindling fighting her all the way. Eventually, the fire took hold and began to blaze. The range she kept burning night and day, so it was ready for her pan of bacon and eggs and kept the kitchen warm. Cutting bread that was a little stale, she knew she would have to venture to the market again very soon. The prospect of going out in the cold made her shiver, but the thought of a contretemps with someone or other made her smile.

Still in her cotton nightdress, dressing gown and slippers, Edith decided to dress in front of the fire once she had broken her fast.

Slapping her food on a plate, she sat at the table and poured a cup of tea. Having enjoyed her meal, she added her cup and plate to the ever-growing pile of dirty dishes in the sink. With a sigh, she dismissed the idea of washing up in favour of sitting by the fire, which she justified to herself as aiding digestion.

Gazing out of the window at the murky yellowing sky, Edith predicted snow would fall before the day's end. Would she have time to shop before the first fall of flakes?

With a groan, she eased herself out of her chair and began to dress, glad that her day clothes had been warming. Banking the fire up, Edith threw on her hat and coat, and with purse and basket she set off.

Blowing out her cheeks at the nip of cold to her nose, she trudged on, only the chance of causing a ruckus keeping her going. She was up for an argument with somebody, and she didn't care who it was.

The opportunity presented itself at the bread stall, where she pushed herself to the front of the gathered women waiting to be served.

'Hey, there's a queue here!' a woman protested.

Edith ignored her and snapped her fingers at the vendor, who glared at being summoned in such a way. 'Give me that cottage loaf and a fruit cake,' Edith called.

Muttering broke out behind her, and Edith turned to stare down the culprits. At once the grumbles ceased and Edith turned back to the vendor. 'Oi, did you hear me? Come on, I don't have all day and I mustn't get too cold, having a bad heart an' all.'

The saleswoman sighed and with an apologetic look at her other customers, she served Edith. 'Anything else?'

'Yes, I'll have...' Edith deliberately took her time in deciding and was pleased to hear the groans start up again but more quietly this time, '...that batch of scones.'

'What, all six?' she was asked.

Edith nodded.

'Greedy cow!' someone muttered, and it was enough to set Edith off.

'Who said that?' The silence was heavy, so she asked again. 'Not brave enough to come forward and say it to my face, eh? Coward!' Turning again, Edith collected her goods and paid her money. She stood to count her change, much to everyone's annoyance. Moving off, Edith permitted herself a tiny triumphal smile.

Stepping smartly between the stalls, she stopped at one selling wet fish. 'Here, weigh me that haddock,' she yelled.

'Wait your turn!' a large woman said as she shoved Edith back a step.

Edith exaggerated the movement, adding a little tilt as if she might fall. Another younger woman caught her and asked if she was all right.

'Ooh, I think so, but I thought I was over for a minute there.'

The younger woman turned on the larger lady with, 'You should be ashamed of yourself, pushing an old lady like that!'

'Bugger off and mind your own business before I give you a cockaiver!'

The threat of being struck didn't deter the young woman as she yelled, 'Come on, then, and I'll have you arrested! I ain't frightened of you!'

As the two women squared up to each other, Edith nodded to the saleswoman and pointed to the haddock. Paying her money, the wrapped fish in her basket, Edith slipped quietly away as the two women continued to shout at each other.

*I can't believe all these years I didn't know shopping could be so enjoyable*, she thought as she wound her way out of the market and set off for home.

## 45

'My aunt?' Mary was shocked to her core.

Elijah gave up his seat so she could sit down. How was it she had never known her mother had a sister? Why had Edith not told her? Then, after a moment, everything began to make sense. 'So are you responsible for the repairs to the houses?' Mary asked.

'No, my dear, that was Elijah. We have a lot to tell you, Mary, so all I ask is that you be patient while we explain,' Charity said.

For the following hours, Charity and Elijah were able to answer most of the questions that had dogged Mary. She was told about Elijah's business and his disguise as a beggar as well as his promise to George, Mary's father.

As the discussion went on, the boys arrived back, cold and hungry. Sitting on the rug, they listened too while Queenie and Owl cut them sandwiches and made more tea.

Mary was astounded when she heard how Edith and Charity had not spoken a word to each other since Charity's wedding, until the other day. She was not surprised, however, at the cold reception given to her aunt by her mother. Charity related how Elijah had sought her help, having heard Mary and Dora had left Spring

Head. How she had relished aiding them all with the food boxes, clothes and Mary's bank account.

When Charity and Elijah had finally come to the end of their story, Mary blew out her cheeks with a long, drawn-out sigh. 'I can hardly believe it,' she said at last. 'Why didn't Mother tell me about you?'

'I expect it was jealousy. She was always envious of me, I'm afraid, although I never gave her cause to be. I married into money – Edith didn't but George was a nice man, nevertheless. We quarrelled all the time as girls, and I realised on my visit that Edith is more argumentative and ruder than ever before.'

'How did you know Dora and I had left Spring Head?'

'Erm, that'd be 'cos of me, Mary,' Skinny piped up. 'I motioned it to Elijah one day in the market.'

'Did you also mention the reasons?' Mary asked, but not unkindly.

'Ar, was I not opposed to?' Skinny asked, feeling he might have let Mary down.

'It's not important, Skinny.' Mary assured him she wasn't angry with him.

Fingers patted his friend's arm as further reassurance that all was well.

Mary took the bank book from the table drawer and handed it to Charity. 'It's minus the amount spent on the beds and linen,' she said, 'but I will pay that back somehow.'

Charity's eyes brimmed with tears at the gesture and, pushing the little book back into Mary's hands, she said, 'Please take it. Allow me this, Mary, let me help you and your family. Give me the opportunity to enjoy getting to know you all.' The threatened tears tumbled over her dark eyelashes and ran down Charity's cheeks.

'Oh, please don't cry!' Mary said as she wrapped her arms around Charity.

Charity hugged her niece and in those few moments a new bond was forged. As they released each other, Elijah came to offer his handkerchief to Charity and slipped his arm around her shoulder. It was Dora who went to hug her mum.

'Thank you, Aunt Charity, for all your help,' Mary said.

Charity beamed. 'I like the sound of that – Aunt Charity. Now, I suggest you all join me for dinner this evening. Elijah will collect you around seven, is that all right with you, darling?' she asked the man now holding her hand.

'Of course, my love,' he responded.

Mary and Dora exchanged a surreptitious glance at the endearments before seeing their visitors out. Everyone waved as the cab pulled away, taking Charity and Elijah home.

Back indoors, the chatter was loud and excited, full of the amazing revelations and how lucky Mary was to have a rich aunt.

Clapping her hands for their attention, Mary said, 'I want all boots polished and your good clothes brushed down. I also want best behaviour this evening.' She looked at Carrot and Lofty, who grinned back at her. 'All right, off you go.'

Whilst the children were busy, Mary had a few minutes to herself to digest all that she'd been told. She wondered what her life would have been like if she'd known about Charity whilst growing up, and suspected Edith would have stood in the way of her ever having a relationship with her aunt, even if they'd known about each other.

Meanwhile, in their cab, Charity was thinking much the same thing and voiced her thoughts to Elijah.

'Maybe it wasn't meant to be back then that you and Mary should meet.' Seeing Charity's frown, he went on. 'I doubt very much that Edith would have allowed Mary to visit you, which might well have been worse. Imagine having an aunt who you were forbidden to have any contact with.'

'I see your point,' Charity agreed.

'It's my belief you were meant to meet now because *now* is when Mary needs you. I noticed how much weight she'd lost since the last time I saw her. It's my guess she had been feeding those children and going without herself, so your food hampers came at just the right time.'

Charity shook her head slightly. 'I still can't believe how cruel Edith has been to her own flesh and blood.'

'I wouldn't worry too much about Edith, she's like a cat – always landing on her feet. No, sweetheart, it's Mary and Dora we need to be concerned about.'

'As well as the other children. Did you see how well-behaved they were? And that house – despite the lack of furniture, it was as clean as a new pin. I'm so looking forward to them coming to dinner!'

Elijah smiled. 'So am I.'

* * *

That evening, everyone lined up in front of Mary for inspection. She nodded her approval as the knock came at the door. Elijah had hired two cabs to take them all to Hady Moor House.

Mary had banked up the fires with slack, water-soaked coal chippings, which would smoulder slowly until they returned. One good stab with the poker would then see it burst into life.

Trudging across the small expanse of heath to the cabs, they were careful where they placed their feet so as not to trip or turn an ankle. In the darkness, the candle jars attached to the front and back of the waiting cabs beckoned.

The streets were not as busy as earlier in the day, but carters still trundled past in the opposite direction. Men strode out in their working clothes, either coming from work or searching out a tavern for a well-earned pint of porter.

Eventually they came to Charity's house in Mesty Croft, and everyone gasped. It seemed every room in the place was lit up in welcome. The warm glow spilled through the windows, bathing the driveway with enough light so they could alight the cabs safely.

Fingers helped Mary step down from their cab, and Skinny aided Dora. The other boys jumped down easily, leaving Elijah to extend a hand to Queenie and Owl.

Charity was standing in the open doorway and ushered them all inside to the parlour with its roaring fire. The maid served an aperitif, sherry for the adults and orange juice for the children. Mouths watered as the aroma of roasting meat floated on the air.

'Welcome,' Charity said, raising her glass in a salute.

'Thank you, Aunt Charity,' Mary replied, pleased to see the honorific accorded the older woman light up her face.

'I hope you all like roast beef, for that's what Cook has prepared.'

A chorus of yeses came from all the young mouths as they stared around the room. Plenty of overstuffed chairs and sofas afforded everyone a seat. Small tables dotted between allowed for glasses to rest and the mantlepiece held an impressive array of ornaments. Paintings adorned the walls and heavy brocade curtains were pulled across by the maid to help keep the heat in.

'Children, you may go and explore the house, but please don't enter the servants' quarters at the top. The cook and maid won't thank you for nosing in their rooms,' Charity said with a grin.

'Quite right, too,' Fingers answered. Then, with great excitement, they shot off, leaving the adults to chat quietly.

A short while later, the dinner gong sounded and everyone gathered in the dining room where places were set for each of them. Cut glass and bone china sat on the huge table and down the centre nestled small flower decorations. The gas lamps filled the room with bright light, which made the crystal chandelier twinkle.

Charity had hired the maid's sister to help out for the evening and, before long, shallow dishes of onion soup were brought in on a large trolley.

'Ooh, my favourite,' Owl said as she tucked in.

'You should wait 'til everybody has one. Ain't that right, Fingers?' Skinny still looked to the other boy as his leader at times, a habit hard to break after so long.

'Yes, Skinny, in polite company one would normally wait until everyone is served before eating.'

'Sorry, but I'm starved!' Owl retorted.

'Please don't stand on ceremony – get stuck in,' Charity said with a little laugh. So they did. Napkins tucked in collars, they slurped the hot soup with relish.

Elijah served wine whilst the empty dishes were cleared away. Even the children were given a glass, heavily watered down.

Next came plates loaded with beef and Yorkshire pudding, roast potatoes, and a variety of vegetables all smothered in gravy.

Having eaten so little for so long, Mary felt overfaced by the huge plate of food. Seeing Charity watching her, she gave a tight smile and picked up her cutlery.

The children were eating as though the food might disappear before they'd had their fill, and conversation was limited.

Charity watched the people around her table and suddenly realised how much she'd missed giving dinner parties. She determined to rectify that by arranging more and often.

The empty plates were removed. Mary groaned inwardly as a couple of cheese boards and bowls of fruit were brought out, but the children were delighted, pointing out to the maid which varieties they would like to taste. Mary wondered where they put it all as she sipped her wine.

Then it was time for a few games, so everyone trooped into the parlour. A circle was formed, with Elijah in the centre. He closed his eyes and a slipper was passed from person to person behind their backs. When Elijah opened his eyes, the slipper stopped and Elijah then had to guess who was holding it. His first guess was incorrect and so the game continued. The next time around he was right, and Mary took centre stage. Laughter and excitement filled the room as the slipper was rushed from person to person.

Next came Blind Man's Bluff. Fingers had a silk scarf tied around his eyes and everyone scattered around the room. He then had to carefully move to catch a 'prisoner'. He caught Owl almost immediately as a chair got in the way of her retreat. With the blind-fold on, Owl proceeded to search for another 'prisoner'.

All too quickly, it was time to go home.

'I will accompany you to ensure you get home safely,' Elijah said to Mary.

'There's no need, really.'

'It's no bother, my dear.' To Charity, he added, 'I will see you tomorrow.'

'I look forward to it,' she said with a smile.

Profuse thanks were given for such a marvellous meal and a lovely evening spent in delightful company.

But their mood soon darkened as they travelled through the town when their cabbies had to give way to the horse-drawn fire wagon, its bell clanging loudly in the still of the night.

## 46

Skinny jumped down from the stationary cab and shouted up to the cabbie. 'Where are they going, can you see?'

'Looks like they're headed for Spring Head,' the cabbie called back.

Mary heard the exchange and whispered, 'Oh, my God!' Then, louder, she yelled, 'Skinny, tell the cabbie to follow the fire cart!'

Skinny obeyed and climbed aboard as the cab began to move once more.

Silently, Mary prayed that the occupants of the house on fire had escaped and added another prayer that it was not her mother's residence.

As the cab stopped again, everyone piled out and Mary's heart sank. She took to her heels towards the blaze, oblivious of the shouts to stay away. A man caught her around the waist to prevent her going any further. 'Whoa there, missy, that's far enough!'

'No, please, you have to let me go! That's my mother's house!'

'There's nothing you can do. Let the firemen do their work and don't put yourself in danger,' the man said.

'Mother! Mum!' Mary yelled as she struggled to free herself from the man's grasp.

Suddenly, Elijah was at her side. 'Thank you, young man, I'll take her now,' he said as he wrapped a sobbing Mary in his arms.

The children watched from a safe distance as men took it in turns to work the plunger to force the water from the massive barrel on the cart. The men soldiered on, pumping water onto the now raging inferno. Smoke plumed white against the inky black sky, and yellow-tipped flames fought their way through broken windows in an endeavour to devour the building.

People poured from nearby dwellings and stood wrapped in blankets, watching the devastating scene.

Mary's howls of despair carried over the roar of the burning house and the people discussing how it might have happened.

The water slowed to a trickle from the hose – the barrel was empty. The fireman shook his head as he began to move back towards the wagon.

'Hey! You get back here and put that fire out!'

Mary couldn't believe her ears. Struggling away from Elijah's hold on her, Mary rushed towards a solitary figure. Edith stood on the driveway in her nightgown, shawl and indoor shoes.

'The barrel's empty, missus, I'm sorry,' the fireman said as he walked away.

'Mum!' Mary called as she closed on the irate woman. 'Are you all right?'

'Of course I am, but I can't say the same for that!' Edith flung out her arm towards the house.

Mary dragged her further down the drive as loud crashes sounded; the floorboards had given way and the bedroom was now in the kitchen.

'Come on, let's get away from here,' Mary said, leading Edith to the cab. She felt the old woman shiver, so she removed her coat, which she draped around Edith. Shock was beginning to set in, and Edith babbled nonsense as she was pushed into the cab alongside Mary and the others.

'I'll get off home, Mary,' Elijah said, trying not to be seen by Edith. 'I'm sorry about...' He tilted his head towards the blaze and they both winced as the roof collapsed, sending showers of sparks everywhere.

'Thank you, I'll take Mother home with us and see if I can find out what happened.'

Saying his goodnights to the children, Elijah walked away, the rumbling of the carriage wheels loud in his ears.

Back at Doe Bank, Skinny poked the sleeping fire in the grate. A burst of sparks, and the flames reached up the chimney. Queenie and Owl hung the kettle on the fire crane to boil, as it was quicker than re-lighting the range, and prepared teacups.

Dora fetched a blanket from Mary's bed as per her mum's instruction, then as Edith was cocooned inside, Dora hung up Mary's coat.

Mary rubbed Edith's cold hands, all the while whispering, 'It's all right, you're safe now. We'll have some tea and then you can rest.'

The boys stood around, not knowing what to do or say. Skinny glared at Edith, thinking this was the person who had bullied and abused Dora, who had run Mary ragged over the years, and now she was here under their roof. His mind was full of questions – would the old crone stay? Had Mary forgiven her mother? Would Dora be safe? It was most likely she would stay, as all she had left was what she stood up in. She had nowhere else to go, and he felt sure Mary would not see her in the workhouse or out on the street. One thing was certain – life here would change drastically now and Skinny was not at all happy about it.

Edith was given tea then Mary settled her into her own bed.

Downstairs once more, the discussion was started immediately by Dora. 'I don't want to sleep in that room with her!'

'Dora, sweetheart...' Mary began.

'No, Mum! I won't do it! It's been so lovely living here and now Gran is here it will spoil everything!'

Queenie laced an arm around Dora's shoulder. 'You can share with me,' she said quietly.

'I'm sorry, everybody, but you see my predicament,' Mary said as she glanced from face to face.

No one spoke, but it was as clear as crystal that Edith was not welcome.

The following morning, Elijah took a cab to Mesty Croft. He needed to inform Charity that her sister was now homeless due to the fire. Whatever had caused the blaze was still unknown, but he had no doubt the reason would come to light in the fullness of time.

He met with Charity in the parlour and, over coffee, he related the dreadful scene they had witnessed the previous night.

'Is Edith all right?' Charity asked.

'Well enough to chastise the firemen when they had to walk away once the water barrel was empty. There was nothing more they could do. A blind man could have seen there was no saving the house.'

'So where is she now?'

'Up at Doe Bank with Mary and the children.'

Charity nodded and ran her tongue around her teeth as she considered what to do. Edith, Mary and Dora were once again all under the same roof, along with Queenie and Owl. That would not make for good relations and would, if Charity was not mistaken, lead to all-out war eventually.

'Something needs to be done about that situation and quickly,' she said. 'We have to find Edith somewhere else to live.'

'Well, don't look my way. We'd most likely end up trying to kill each other!' Elijah was quick to say.

'I agree. She can't come here, either, for much the same reason,' Charity went on.

Elijah looked at the woman he had loved for so long and marvelled that age had not diminished her beauty. He had been considering asking for her hand in marriage, but it would have to wait; now was not the time, and Dora's safety came first. Between them, they had to find a way to separate the young girl and her grandmother.

'I need to buy another house, something small – in fact, just big enough for one person,' Charity said at last.

'It will be hard going getting Edith out of Doe Bank once she realises Mary and the children will take care of her.'

'Yes, I think you're right. I'll send a note to Mary asking her to call on me at her earliest convenience to discuss the matter. In the meantime, I need to visit the estate agent.'

'Would you like me to accompany you?' Elijah asked.

'That would be grand. That way, the property seller won't try to take advantage of this dear old lady,' Charity said, tongue in cheek.

Elijah burst out laughing. 'I pity anyone who would attempt any such thing with you.'

Charity grinned, then said, 'Let's away, then. The sooner we find Edith another dwelling, the better it will be for all.'

\* \* \*

In the meantime, Edith had woken in an unfamiliar bed, and she was suddenly overwhelmed by the memory and horrors of the fire. Looking around the dingy room, she thought, *I've seen worse. At least*

*Mary will take care of me again now I have nowhere else to go. It won't take me long to stamp my authority here and have everyone at my beck and call.*

Settling back onto the comfortable pillow, Edith smiled as she waited for Mary to bring her some breakfast.

## 47

Mary had slept in Dora's bed while Dora shared with Queenie, and in the morning she began sorting out some underwear and a skirt and blouse for Edith, which she hoped would fit.

The boys came round when the aroma of cooking bacon carried to them on the breeze. 'Mary, we had a chat last night and decided we needed to talk to you about Edith being here,' Fingers said, clearly feeling uncomfortable.

'I understand, but can it wait? After breakfast, I need to take Dora to the doctor to get her arm checked. Hopefully she might have the plaster removed today.'

Fingers looked to each boy in turn, and they all nodded, understanding the pressure Mary was under. With all the children enjoying their food, Mary took a plate of bacon and eggs and a cup of tea upstairs for Edith.

'Oh, Mary, I've had such a time of it. I was terrified I would burn to death in that house,' Edith wailed as she sat up and accepted the tray gratefully.

'Well, you didn't, but I have to ask – how on earth did the fire start?' Mary asked, laying out clothes for her mother to try on.

'I don't know. I think it must have been a hot coal which rolled onto the carpet. It's lucky I fell asleep in the chair, because if I'd been in my bed – well, I wouldn't be here now.'

'Eat your breakfast, get dressed and come down when you're ready,' Mary said, keen to get on with the day and not let her mother dominate her time.

As she washed the dishes, Mary wondered about her mother's explanation of how the fire had started. Could Edith have committed arson in her own home? Good grief, no! Who would do such a thing? However it had started made no difference to the outcome, anyway – they were together again, only this time Edith was in their home. Now there was the problem of impending rebellion from the children, and Mary guessed that no end of discussion would change their minds. They would vote in favour of ousting Edith after what she'd done to Dora. And she was sure their argument would be that where she would go and how she would live would not be their concern. And there was a part of Mary that agreed with them.

Dora had given up the use of the sling and Mary had washed it, ready to return to the doctor. Now, both with thick woollen shawls about their shoulders, they prepared to set off. 'While we're gone, ignore my mother. Don't answer her calls and do not get drawn into a contretemps with her.' Seeing the nods, Mary and Dora left them to it, Mary hoping they'd follow her advice and that her mother would be too frail to cause trouble.

As they walked to the doctor's house, Dora didn't speak.

'Are you worried about the plaster coming off?' Mary asked.

'No.'

'Then what's wrong? You're very quiet this morning.'

'Mum, if you decide Gran can stay, then I think we may all be asked to leave Doe Bank.'

'I was thinking much the same thing,' Mary confessed.

'What shall we do?' Dora asked, concern written all over her face.

'First things first. Let's see the doctor, then we can decide about your gran.'

Dora nodded, placated for the moment.

Inside the surgery, the doctor asked Dora to wriggle her fingers, then requested she pick up the paperweight from his desk. Satisfied the actions caused her no pain, he said her plaster could come off, provided she was careful not to overstrain the arm.

The colour drained from Dora's face as she saw the large pair of snips.

'Don't fret, my dear, this won't hurt, it's to cut through the plaster. Then you can have a good scratch!'

Dora grinned and held her arm still while the doctor snipped away the plaster cast. Then he felt all along her arm and nodded. 'It's healed well,' he announced as he washed and dried her arm. 'Now, you go steady with it for a while, young lady.'

'I will, thank you,' Dora said, already giving her skin a gentle scratch.

Mary paid the doctor and they left for home.

'My arm feels as light as a feather,' Dora commented happily as they wound their way through the busy streets.

Mary merely nodded, her mind back on Edith and the problems she could cause now she was reliant upon Mary once more.

Dora was happy to be able to give the call signal whistle again as they neared home and was delighted that all the children came to greet them.

Edith was downstairs, dressed in the clothes Mary had loaned her, and sitting on the one chair as opposed to a stool. She noted the lack of plaster on Dora's arm, but made no mention of it.

'Mary, a note came for you while you were out,' Fingers said, handing over the sealed envelope.

Opening it up, Mary read the contents. 'I have to go out,' she said, her eyes pleading that no one ask where she would be going.

'Again! You've only just got in!' Edith rasped.

'When I return, I'll take you to the bank. You need to make a withdrawal and buy yourself some clothes,' Mary answered.

'I don't have my bank book, it burned along with everything else!' Edith said with a sniff.

'Do you really think the manager won't know who you are?' Mary asked pointedly.

*Once seen, never forgotten!* Dora thought as she caught Queenie's eye. She tilted her head and the two girls disappeared upstairs.

'What's going on?' Queenie whispered.

'Help me move my books into your room, please,' Dora replied.

'Why?'

'Just in case. I don't want Gran destroying them.'

Queenie nodded and did as her friend asked.

Dora breathed a sigh of relief once the task was completed, and pulling out her parents' wedding photograph, she showed it to Queenie. 'I'm glad I took it now, otherwise it would have been lost in the fire.'

Pushing the books under the bed frame, Queenie said, 'They'll be safe there. Come on, else we'll be missed.'

The two returned to the living room, where the argument between Mary and Edith was still going on.

'I can't walk all the way to the bank!' Edith raged.

'You managed well enough when you went shopping in the market,' Mary shot back.

'How...?'

'Dora and Skinny saw you,' Mary cut in.

Edith aimed a look at Dora which could have fried bacon.

'I refuse to continue this discussion, Mother. Be ready for when

I get back.' Turning to the others, she said, 'I won't be long, I'm going back to where we were last night.'

Skinny was about to speak but Fingers nudged him in the ribs and shook his head and the boy understood the unspoken instruction to button his lip.

'Where were you last night?' Edith questioned.

'That's none of your business. Don't try to wheedle it out of the children either because they won't tell you,' Mary answered firmly. Grabbing her shawl, she left to visit Charity Lacey, the note shoved into her skirt pocket.

## 48

'Well, don't just stand there gawping. One of you make me a cup of tea!' Edith demanded, as soon as Mary had gone.

'Please!' Dora remonstrated.

'Just do it!' Edith snarled.

'It costs nothing to say please,' Dora said, feeling confident in the company of the others.

Edith was on her feet in an instant, her arm outstretched ready to clout Dora.

In that same instant, the boys stepped swiftly forward and in front of Dora, showing a united front. 'We'll have no violence here, if you don't mind, Mrs Pitt,' Fingers said quietly.

Edith's arm lowered to her side and she glowered at the boy who'd spoken. 'Give me time and I'll see you all out on the streets,' she whispered into his face.

'I doubt that. You see, these houses belong to us and you are just a visitor. Therefore, if anyone will be leaving, it will be you.' Fingers remained calm, not at all intimidated by the woman who was visibly seething.

'Ah, but that's where you're wrong. Our Mary won't see me homeless, I'm her mother, after all.'

'Gran, stop it!' Dora called from behind her protective barrier of friends.

'You shut your whining!' Edith shouted as she jabbed a finger in Dora's direction.

'You leave her alone, you old bat!' Skinny yelled back, unwilling to have Edith bully Dora for one more minute.

'You can close that stupid mouth of yours as well!' Edith rounded on him.

'This could get out of hand very quickly if we don't do something,' Lofty whispered to Carrot who nodded his agreement.

'Fingers, maybe we should all get off to work,' Carrot said.

'I ain't going and leaving the girls here with this... varmint!' Skinny said, his rage building inside him.

'We'll all wait here for Mary,' Fingers said, 'because I have a feeling she might have something to tell us. Now, ladies, if we might have some tea, please.' Fingers glared at Edith who sat once more, her eyes drawn into slits. He knew by her look she was trying to figure out what news Mary would bring back with her. He also knew that the not knowing would drive her mad.

The tea was made and drunk in silence before the children went off together to find some kindling, leaving Edith alone to brood on her circumstances. They didn't go far and kept the houses in view all of the time so they could watch for Mary's return and hear her whistle.

In the meantime, Edith was fuming at the way those urchins had stood as one against her. It was going to be a lot harder than she had thought to make her mark here. There was only one way to deal with this and that was to divide and conquer. She had to find ways of setting the urchins against each other and then she could take them down one by one.

* * *

Whilst Edith plotted and planned, Mary had arrived at Hady Moor House. Given entry by the maid, Mary joined Charity and Elijah in the parlour. Coffee was quickly delivered, and they settled to discussions about the fire at Spring Head, Edith and the problems it would cause having her live at Doe Bank.

'How did the fire start?' Elijah asked.

'Burning coal on the carpet, Mother said,' Mary answered.

'I understand that you had to take Edith home with you, Mary, but you must realise she cannot stay there.' Charity watched Mary closely as she spoke.

'I do, but I can't see a way out of it. She has nothing left except a little money in the bank.'

'There is a lot more than you think,' Charity said. 'Let me start at the beginning and then you can decide what to do with the information.'

Mary frowned, wondering what she might learn.

'Elijah and I went out to find a house for Edith, but we made a detour first and so that is where we shall begin. Did you know your father, George, had a string of shops?'

'No! I thought, like my husband, he worked on the railway.'

'Oh, he did, but his stores were run by a board of executives. George had little to do with the running of the business, but he benefitted financially, as has Edith since his passing,' Elijah explained.

'You mean Mother has kept this secret for all these years?' Mary asked incredulously.

'Apparently so,' Charity answered. 'Elijah suggested we visit the company offices to inform them of Edith losing her house to the fire. It was then, as Edith's sister, I was able to learn of the fortune she has amassed.'

Mary stared, unable to take in what was being said to her.

'Mary, there is more than enough to buy Edith another house,' Elijah put in.

'Well, the church won't be getting the other one now,' Mary mumbled.

Elijah and Charity exchanged a glance and, at a nod from Elijah, Charity went on. 'She could never have done that anyway. That house was bequeathed to you by your father, which means Edith's will would have been fraudulent.'

'Oh, this just gets better and better!' Mary said with a shake of her head.

'Actually, it does, because all the money she has accumulated doesn't rightly belong to her.'

'What?'

'Everything paid out from that company is yours. Your father ensured that it would all come to you eventually.'

'Then why has it been going into mother's account?'

'It hasn't. The account is made out in the name of Mary Parsons.'

'Oh, my God! So she's been stealing my money?'

'It would appear so, my dear,' Charity said sadly.

Mary blew out her cheeks in disbelief.

'That's why we thought you should know,' Elijah said.

'Edith has nothing more than the clothes on her back,' Charity said.

'Even those are mine,' Mary muttered.

'Now you know the all of it, it's up to you what you do with this information,' Charity said, relieved everything was at last out in the open.

'Thank you both for all you have done to help me. I can never repay your kindness,' Mary said as tears welled in her eyes.

'You can do that by getting Edith away from Dora and her friends,' Charity said with a note of finality.

'I will, don't worry, and I think I know just how to do it!'

## 49

Elijah hailed a cab, saying he would drop Mary off on his way home, and as they travelled he kept his counsel; it was clear Mary was trying to digest all that she had learned.

'Thank you, Elijah,' Mary said as he helped her from the cab at Doe Bank. Suddenly she threw her arms around him and the impulsive gesture took him by surprise. He hugged her back, enjoying the feeling of what it must be like to be a father.

He climbed aboard once more, the cab rolled away and in the privacy, Elijah shed a tear of his own. *I don't know what Mary will do about all of this, George, but I think you would have been so very proud of her.*

Reaching home, Elijah was delighted to see he had a visitor waiting. Paying the cabbie, Elijah walked up to the handsome young man standing on his doorstep.

'Mason, my boy, how wonderful to see you!' The two hugged, then Elijah unlocked the door and they went indoors. Despite working together, it was unusual for Elijah's nephew to visit him at home. 'Sit and I'll make some tea,' Elijah said as he busied with cups and cut some cake. 'I didn't expect to see you today, lad.'

'I was worried, Uncle, you haven't been into the office for a while,' Mason returned.

'Ah, yes. I'm sorry about that but I've been rather busy.'

Mason regarded his uncle, then, with a laugh and a clap of his hands, he said, 'You've found a lady to court!'

Elijah blustered, 'Well, yes, I have…'

'Bravo, Uncle!'

'There's more to it than that, though. Look, let's have tea then I'll explain everything.'

Sitting in the comfortable parlour, Elijah began his tale. From his friend George and the promise to watch over Mary and Dora, he told of Edith and how she had abused her granddaughter and her bequeathing her house to the church – the house which had since burnt down, but as it turned out, belonged to Mary, as did the money in the bank.

'Good grief! No wonder you've had no time to work!' Mason said good-naturedly. 'But how about this lady you've been courting?'

'Her name is Charity Lacey,' Elijah said.

'Of Lacey's Tube Works?'

Elijah nodded.

Mason's eyebrows raised and he nodded approvingly.

'She's Edith's sister.'

'Ah!' was all that Mason could find to say, and the two men shared rueful smiles.

\* \* \*

Whilst Elijah was regaling his nephew with the tale of Mary and Dora Parsons, Mary had marched into the house. Moments later, the children came running indoors, their arms full of kindling.

'It's about time! These buggers left me on my own and I'm dying for a drink!' Edith was at Mary the moment she stepped inside.

Mary fetched another shawl and threw it at Edith, causing the children to exchange glances. 'Come on, we need to get to the bank before it closes.'

'We can go another day...' Edith began.

'We will go now!' So sharp was her tone that Edith thought twice about arguing.

'Please, girls, would you mind sorting out a meal?' Mary asked.

'Yes, of course,' Queenie replied.

Mary gave a curt nod and walked out of the house, Edith trotting along behind.

'Mary, we should get a cab,' Edith said as she emphasised her panting.

'I can't afford it!' Mary snapped.

'Slow down, I can't keep up with you!' Mary complied with the request but said nothing. 'What's the hurry?'

'You need clothes and the shops will be closed if we don't get a move on. Besides, I have the children to see to.'

'They can look after themselves.'

Mary bridled but she would not get drawn into a quarrel as they walked through the streets. As time had passed since leaving Charity's house, the anger in Mary had slowly been building. She was holding on to it by the skin of her teeth and the last thing she needed was for it to burst its banks now.

Eventually, they came to the bank, and walked towards the teller.

'May I help you?'

'Yes, please. I'm afraid my mother's house has burned down so she will need a new bank book.'

'I'm sorry to hear that. Can I take her name?'

'Edith Pitt,' Mary said as she pushed her mother forward.

'I'll just consult with the manager,' the teller said before disappearing into his superior's office. A moment later, he was back. 'If you ladies will follow me, please.' The teller led them behind the counter and into the office where the manager sat. Invited to take a seat, the women nodded their thanks.

'Mr Hodges has informed me of your plight, Mrs Pitt, and I'm sorry to hear of your misfortune. My difficulty here is that we do not hold an account in the name of Edith Pitt.'

Mary glanced at her mother, who had the good grace to bow her head, realising she had been caught out in her fraudulent dealings with both Mary and the bank.

'I'm guessing the account is in the name of Mary Parsons – my name.'

Opening a drawer in a cabinet by his desk, the man drew out a folder. 'Yes, this is the account in that name.'

'May I ask how a person' – a glance at Edith then back to the manager – 'can withdraw money from someone else's account?'

'I don't understand,' the man frowned.

'That account in my name has been plundered by my mother! In fact, I was unaware of the existence of the account until this morning.' Mary's anger was threatening to erupt.

'My goodness! I don't... I can't...' The manager was shuffling papers in his embarrassment.

'The money from my father's business has been paid into this account for over twenty years and this knowledge was kept from me! All of that time, Edith Pitt has been drawing from it.'

'I don't see that this is the fault of my bank.'

'Never once has she been challenged or asked to prove her identity!' Mary exploded. 'She has been stealing my money! Now, if it is not the fault of your bank, then pray tell me whose fault it is!'

Edith quailed under Mary's tirade. How had she found out?

Who had told her? Someone else must have known for Mary to be aware of it now.

'Please calm yourself, Mrs Parsons, I'm sure we can sort this out.'

'Mary, you're overreacting again as usual,' Edith said, having decided that attack was the best form of defence.

Mary's head shot round, and she glowered with fire in her eyes. 'Mother, I suggest you keep quiet, you're in enough trouble as it is.'

'Don't be so melodramatic! That money has fed us all and kept us warm!'

'You stole it! You're a thief, Mother! Don't you understand what that means?' Mary's mind brought forth the box of screws and washers she had dragged home, but she pushed the thought away. This was an entirely different situation.

'Ladies, please! Can we not clear this up calmly?' The manager was almost beside himself and was worried that violence could break out at any moment.

'Yes, we can,' Mary said, bringing her attention back to him, 'and the way to do it is to send for the police straight away!'

## 50

'Your mum really was angry,' Skinny said.

'I know; it's rare for her to be like that. Something is going on and I'm dying to know what it is,' Dora replied.

'I think we'll know soon enough,' Fingers added.

'Should we be trying to find some work?' Lofty asked.

'Not yet. When Mary returns will be time enough. Besides, I think we should take a vote.' Fingers had again assumed the role of leader in Mary's absence.

'On what?' Whippet asked.

'On whether Mrs Pitt is allowed to stay here with us,' Fingers said.

'I vote no!' Dora was quick to answer.

'No,' Skinny said as he sidled up to Dora.

'No,' Queenie added.

'No,' Owl said.

Carrot, Lofty and Whippet agreed, and Fingers cast his vote to the nays. 'Now we just have to tell Mary.'

A collective sigh filled the room as all eyes turned to Fingers.

'I'll tell her,' Dora said to everyone's surprise. 'None of you should have to carry that responsibility, and anyway it might be better coming from me. After all, Gran and I have a history.'

'That's very cageous of you Dora,' Skinny said with a smile.

'Courage has little to do with it, Skinny, it's about doing what's right. You were all so kind to take Mum and me in when we were desperate, and it would be wrong of us to abuse that kindness by having Gran disrupt all of our lives now.' Dora glanced at each one in turn and saw the love burning bright. She felt tears prick the back of her eyes as she went on. 'We are a family, and no one will ever come between us and spoil that. Promise me, here and now, that we will always come to the aid of each other if needed.'

Oaths were sworn as they stood in a circle, their arms around each other, holding on for all they were worth.

\* \* \*

Over at Mesty Croft, Elijah had taken Mason to meet Charity. They were invited in and agreed to stay for lunch, which Charity had announced was roast pork with all the trimmings.

Although Charity knew of Mason, this was the first time they had actually met. They hit it off immediately.

Over the years, she had made it her business to watch from afar Elijah's progression through life. Elijah and her husband had worked together many times, Elijah's barges having transported Lacey steel tubes all over the country. Even after her husband's death, these transactions had continued under the watchful eye of her works manager.

Charity had also known right from their first meeting how Elijah had felt about her, but as a married lady she could not encourage him. Then, when she had lost her husband, as Elijah had said, it would have been unseemly for a relationship to blossom between them. Now, after many years of widowhood,

Charity was in love once more, and was delighted that Elijah felt the same. Her one wish was that Elijah might find the courage to propose to her.

Mason sipped his wine, then out of the blue he said, 'Uncle Eli, I think you should take this lovely lady for a wife.'

Charity grinned as Elijah spluttered and began to cough. Dabbing his mouth with his napkin, Elijah said in response, 'I think that's not your business, young man.'

Charity wondered then if marriage was not on Elijah's mind, after all.

'Why wait? You've loved Miss Charity for so long and... you're not getting any younger.' Mason's eyes crinkled in a loving smile.

'You cheeky bug... devil!' Elijah corrected himself.

'I always knew there was someone special but out of reach, and now I know who and why.' Mason had no intention of letting the subject rest.

'Mason! For goodness' sake! Charity, I'm sorry for...' Elijah began.

'It's all right, Elijah, Mason is having a little fun with you, aren't you, dear?' Charity sent a withering look Mason's way for embarrassing his uncle.

'Yes, Miss Charity. I'm sorry, Uncle Eli, please forgive me, it was quite thoughtless of me.'

'I should think so too!' Elijah blustered before finishing his wine in one gulp. 'Now, if you don't mind, Charity, I think we should be getting back to work.'

Elijah and Mason gave their thanks and left rather quickly. Charity was left wondering if Elijah would ask for her hand now or whether Mason had ruined it for them.

\* \* \*

Over at the bank, the manager was trying to console a weeping Edith and persuade Mary that it was not necessary to involve the constabulary.

'If someone stole money from your bank, would you not call a policeman?' Mary asked heatedly.

'Well, yes, of course, but—'

'Precisely! In effect, Edith Pitt has been taking money from your bank that does not belong to her. In my mind, that constitutes theft!'

'Very well,' the manager said reluctantly and rang the little hand bell on his desk. When the door opened and a head appeared, he said, 'Please send someone to fetch a constable.' With a nod, the head disappeared and the door closed.

'Mary! You can't turn me over to a bobby!' Edith wailed.

'I can and I will.'

'You're my daughter! You should look after me in my old age!'

'I've done that for years and look where it's got me.' Mary could not bring herself to look at Edith as she spoke.

The manager drew out his pocket watch, flipped open the lid and checked the time before snapping it shut and replacing it in his waistcoat. *How long does it take to fetch a copper? I hope he's here soon!*

'I'm not waiting here to be arrested!' Edith said, getting to her feet.

In a flash, Mary had pushed her mother back onto the chair, a hand on Edith's shoulder holding her in place. 'You stay right where you are or so help me...!'

The manager leaned as far back as he could in his chair, afraid he might be assaulted. He gave a sigh of relief when there was a knock at the door and a policeman strode in. The manager sat quietly as Mary explained again about Edith and the account.

Edith tried to interrupt on occasion, but each time she was silenced by the constable. Eventually he said, 'I'm afraid you'll have to come along with me, madam.' Helping Edith to her feet, he removed the handcuffs from his belt and snapped them around her wrists.

'All right, Mary, that's enough! You've had your little joke, so can we go home now?' Edith was almost pleading now.

'It's no joke, Mother. You chased my father and my husband away, you bullied my daughter to the point of breaking her arm, and now I discover you've stolen my money. So no, Mother, we can't go home. The only place you're going is to jail.'

Mary closed her eyes as the constable dragged a yelling Edith away.

'Mary! Mary, you'll pay for this!' Edith's voice grew fainter as she was hauled away to the police station.

\* \* \*

It was later that afternoon that Elijah gave Charity a surprise when he turned up at her house once more.

'I came to apologise again for Mason's behaviour at lunch,' he said.

'Please don't fret, it was only his little joke,' Charity answered.

'It was in bad taste.'

Charity inclined her head, not wishing to add to his discomfort. 'Was there something more?'

'Actually, yes.' Elijah gave a little cough as he grabbed his courage with both hands.

Charity waited with hope in her heart.

Elijah rose and walked to where she sat. Taking her hand, he drew in a breath. 'Charity, would you do me the great honour of becoming my wife?'

With a smile that lit up her face, Charity nodded. 'I will, Elijah, and just to say – I thought you'd never ask!'

Elijah breathed a sigh of relief before his sonorous laughter echoed through the house.

After a chaste kiss, Elijah said, 'I'm taking Mason over to Doe Bank to meet Mary and the children.'

'Good idea. Will I see you tomorrow, my love?'

'You will, darling.'

With another kiss, Elijah left his betrothed, eager to share their good news.

## 51

The children looked at each other in puzzlement when Mary arrived home alone. She was pale and shaking and Queenie immediately set the kettle on the fire crane. Hot sweet tea was clearly the order of the day.

'Mum, where's Gran?' Dora asked gently as Mary was led to the chair.

'I've done a terrible thing,' Mary muttered, before a paroxysm of tears overtook her.

Everyone was thinking the same thing. Had Mary hurt her mother or worse – committed murder? Perhaps Edith had riled her daughter one time too many? Surely it wouldn't be long before the rozzers discovered the body and came looking for Mary. Dora and her friends would have to get Mary away from Doe Bank as soon as possible.

At last, Mary's tears eased, and Dora tried again. 'Mum, what have you done?'

'I've had your gran arrested.'

The children all breathed a sigh of relief.

'Why?' Dora's voice was calm and low so Mary would not burst into tears again.

None of them uttered a word whilst Mary regaled them with the debacle at the bank.

It was as she finished that there was a knock on the door. All their eyes widened in fear of it being the bobbies come to arrest Mary – what lies had Edith told?

'Hello, anyone home?'

Elijah's voice carried on the air and the children sighed with relief as one. Skinny went to answer and returned with Elijah and another man.

Spotting Mary's red and puffy eyes, instantly Elijah understood there had been an upset and at the same time he noted that Edith was nowhere to be seen. He wondered if the two were linked. 'Please forgive us arriving unannounced,' he said, 'but I've brought my nephew Mason to meet you all.'

'You are very welcome any time,' Mary said, doing her best to pull herself together.

The girls busied themselves making yet more tea after the introductions were made.

'I've some good news to share also. Charity and I are to be married!' Elijah said excitedly.

Mason's mouth dropped open in surprise. His uncle had said nothing of this to him on the journey over. He shook his head with a smile when Elijah gave him a wink.

There were shouts of joy and they all congratulated Elijah heartily before Elijah asked warily, 'What's happened, Mary?'

Taken aback for a moment, Mary then steeled herself and explained yet again about Edith's arrest. She didn't notice Mason staring at her, but the children did.

When she had finished, Elijah said, 'We all know it's no more than she deserved, Mary, and you mustn't blame yourself.'

'I feel so guilty, though, Elijah,' she answered quietly.

'Put it this way: did Edith care about driving off your father and your husband? Did she feel guilty at abusing Dora so badly? Was she at all concerned about stealing your money and trying to leave the house to the church?' Mary shook her head in response. 'Well, then. Edith will be tried at the Assizes at the Victoria Law Courts in Birmingham, where she will be sentenced.'

Mary gasped at the prospect of her mother spending the rest of her life in jail.

'I think you are going to have to come to terms with it, Mary, and move on with your life. You have these children to think of now.' Elijah's heart went out to the young woman who had suffered so much heartache, only to have to go through the guilt-ridden misery of having her mother committed to jail.

'I know you're right, Elijah, thank you,' Mary said, then, drawing in a breath, she turned to their other visitor. 'My apologies, Mason. Welcome to our humble but happy home.'

'Thank you,' Mason muttered as he took the tea offered by Owl.

Lofty dug Carrot in the ribs and they grinned. Mason Covington-Smythe was almost drooling as he stared doe-eyed at Mary.

As the afternoon wore on, the adults happily passed the time while the children talked and played. They chatted about Elijah and Charity's forthcoming wedding. Mason was to be best man, but Charity would have to find someone to give her away.

'It's my guess she might ask you, Mary,' Elijah said.

'No, it should be a man,' Mary replied.

'Fingers could do it!' Skinny piped up.

'An excellent choice. Let me tell my wife-to-be that you'd be honoured to stand by her side,' Elijah agreed, before looking round the room at the children. 'We'll have to get you all new clothes for the big day.'

'I can do that now,' Mary said as she passed her new bank book to Elijah.

He whistled as he read the figure. 'You are a very wealthy young lady, now, Mary.'

Mary nodded, taking back the book the manager had given her before she had left the bank.

'You can afford to buy a new house big enough to fit you all in,' Elijah said.

'You're right, but funnily enough I've rather grown to like it here,' Mary said as she glanced at the children, sitting on the floor at her feet. 'I think we might have gas lighting fitted and maybe have an extension built onto each house.' The children cheered. 'We'll need furniture too; we can't do without chairs forever.'

'That sounds like a good plan. If I may be of service in any way, please feel free to call on me.' Mason took a small business card from his pocket and handed it to Mary.

The boys collected up the cups and saucers in a bid to hide their mirth at Mason's attempt to impress Mary.

'Thank you,' Mary said, a blush tinting her cheeks.

'What a lovely afternoon, but now I think it's time to leave these people in peace,' Elijah said.

'May I call again sometime? Just to assure myself that the workmen are not taking advantage of you, you understand,' Mason mumbled.

'You are most welcome to call whenever you please, Mason,' Mary answered, feeling for the moment they were the only two people in the room.

Everyone trooped outside to see their visitors off before returning indoors. And after a day that would change all their lives for the better, the children gathered around Mary, their arms stretching around each other.

'I do love you all,' Mary said.

'We love you too,' they chorused.

\* \* \*

Over the next week, the weather turned bitterly cold and woollens were donned beneath jackets and shawls.

Mary had been to town and ordered furniture for both houses: easy chairs and small chests of drawers for the bedrooms. There was no room for wardrobes until the extensions could be built. She had also instructed the gas company to fit gas lamps, and eager for her money, they had agreed to undertake the work straight away.

Elijah had sent Sam, the builder who had previously worked on the properties, to meet with Mary so they could hatch a plan for the extensions. Everyone contributed their ideas for the diagrams being drawn up by the builder.

'Mum, could we have an indoor privy?' Dora asked, and the girls sighed with pleasure at the thought of not having to go outside in the freezing cold.

'Will there be windows?' Skinny asked and when it was confirmed that there would be, he requested curtains to help keep the heat in.

'A big pantry would be most helpful,' Queenie put in quietly, feeling awkward about asking.

'Will there be bedrooms above the extra downstairs rooms, Mary?' Fingers asked.

'Yes indeed, Fingers, we have to try to give you all plenty of space.'

'This is all going to take time to do, we'll have to dig new foundations to start with. Unfortunately, we can't do that until after the winter,' Sam said.

'We'll help!' Lofty and Carrot said in unison.

'Sam, you've seen how we've been living, we are desperate for this work to be undertaken and completed as soon as possible. Anything you can do to get started, we'd all be very grateful.' Mary was almost begging.

'I'll get my lads around tomorra to make a start,' Sam relented, and he smiled as cheers went up. 'At least we can see if we can get the footings in place before the snow comes.'

Once Sam had left, Doe Bank had yet another visitor – the policeman who had arrested Edith. Over tea by the fire, he explained the reason for his calling. 'Mrs Pitt went up afore the Magistrate and he instructed she be held at Stafford Gaol until the quarter sessions.'

'When will that be?' Mary asked.

'I believe it is next week. After that it will be the Assizes in Birmingham. Theft of money or embezzlement is a serious crime, Mrs Parsons, so it is expected your mother will get a hefty sentence.'

Mary paled and part of her wished she had never involved the police in the first place. But another part of her knew it was inevitable that it should come to this, otherwise her mother would never have left them in peace.

'I'll let you know the outcome of the case as and when. It could be you'll be called as a witness, but with the testimony of the bank manager, it's unlikely you'll be needed. Thank you for the tea; I'll see myself out.' Stepping out into the cold wind, the bobby donned his helmet and marched swiftly away.

Next to call was the postman with wedding invitations for all – Elijah and Charity had clearly decided that there was no time like the present to get started with their new life together.

## 52

Excited chatter filled the house as the children opened and read their invitations, then Mary suggested they went to town for new outfits for the special occasion. They still had a few months to wait for the big day, but getting everyone kitted out could take a while. But firstly, as a treat, they found a café and had coffee served in china cups and saucers, an assortment of little sandwiches of cheese, salmon, and egg which were cut into triangles, followed by cream horns and doughnuts. The rest of the day was great fun, trying on dresses and suits, then it was off to buy new boots and winter coats and hats. Cabs brought them home, loaded down with parcels, and Queenie and Owl made a much-needed cup of tea before Mary began preparing a meal.

As evening drew in, there was a knock on the door and Mason Covington-Smythe was welcomed in. 'I do hope you don't mind my calling, but Uncle Eli said you had a builder coming and I thought...' Mason's nervousness was evident as he fumbled with his top hat.

'Please take a seat, would you care for tea?' Mary asked, doing her best to make him feel more relaxed and comfortable.

Seeing his nod, Dora spoke up. 'I'll do it, Mum.'

The boys were busy next door admiring their new clothes and whilst Mary chatted with their unexpected caller, Queenie and Owl joined Dora in the kitchen.

'Our wedding invitations arrived this morning, so a little shopping was in order. The children are very excited,' Mary said.

'I am too. I never expected Uncle Eli to marry after being alone all these years.'

'I'm delighted for them both,' Mary agreed.

'Do you know why he never wed?' Mason asked.

Mary shook her head.

'It's because his heart belonged to Miss Charity right from the outset. He has never loved anyone else,' Mason said.

'Oh, my! How very romantic, and how wonderful that they are able to come together at last.'

'Mary, may I ask you a personal question?' At Mary's nod Mason plunged in. 'Where is your husband?'

'Jim died a while ago,' Mary answered sadly.

'I'm so sorry, I shouldn't have pried,' Mason said. Feeling embarrassed, he cleared his throat in an effort to dispel the feeling.

Just then, Dora came through from the kitchen. 'Excuse me, Mum, but our meal is almost ready.'

'I should be going,' Mason said as he got to his feet.

'Will you join us? There's more than enough. You are most welcome, provided you don't mind having your plate on your knee. We haven't quite got round to having enough tables and chairs delivered!' Mary said with a little laugh.

The tantalising aroma persuaded him, and Mason readily agreed. It would also afford him more time with Mary, who had dominated his thoughts since they had first met.

'Dora, sound the gong for the boys, please,' Mary instructed.

Grabbing an old tin kettle and a spoon, Dora went outside and rattled the two together. A moment later, a host of hungry boys poured in and took their place in line after greeting Mason.

Mason joined the queue as steaming pans of potatoes and vegetables were laid on trivets on the table, as well as a large pan of faggots and a huge jug of gravy set alongside.

One by one, Mary served them, and everyone found a space on the floor. Skinny kindly fetched their one kitchen chair for Mason, and Mary occupied the other. Then all that could be heard was the scraping of cutlery on plates.

After they had eaten, Mason insisted he help with the washing up while Dora read by candlelight one of her stories to the others. There was silence as the tale of Marcus Decimus Drusus, a centurion in the Roman army, who went to fight in the Teutoburg forest in Germany, unfolded before them.

Mary and Mason joined them and sat quietly until Dora had finished. The applause was deafening, and Dora grinned.

And as all the children stood and stretched, the youngest yawning contentedly, Mason took his leave with thanks for the scrumptious dinner. The boys drifted back to their own house, tired and happy, and Queenie and Owl said goodnight and went to their beds.

'Mum, I think Mason likes you a lot,' Dora said.

'I like him too,' Mary said as she banked up the fire and set the guard in place.

'No, I mean – *a lot!*' Dora emphasised.

'You mustn't read anything into it, sweetheart, he's just being kind.'

'That's a shame.'

'Why?'

'Because I think he'd make a smashing dad.' With that, Dora tripped off upstairs, leaving Mary to stare after her with an open mouth.

* * *

The next day, Sam's workers arrived to begin digging out the foundations of the extensions. Sam mapped out the area and staked it off, and the boys grabbed shovels and got stuck in.

Over the course of the next few weeks, the two houses were buzzing with workers coming and going. Gas lighting was installed, much to everyone's delight, and the foundations were eventually ready for the concrete. The easy chairs and chests of drawers were delivered and before anyone realised, the time had passed, and Christmas would be upon them soon.

As for the wedding preparations, Fingers had been asked by Charity on one of her visits if he would give her away, and he had accepted gratefully.

During this time, Mason had been a regular visitor at Doe Bank and was getting on with the children famously. They played games together and the sound of laughter filled the girls' house often.

Mary found herself warming to Mason more on each of his visits, and eventually she agreed to walk out with him. Some days the children tagged along, and Mason enthused them all with his love of nature as they went. Trees, animal tracks and bird calls were all identified, and Mary marvelled at his knowledge.

They all spent a day at Mason's house in West Bromwich, the next town to Wednesbury, and the children were aghast at the size of it. They roamed from room to room, calling to each other to come look at this and that. They found the nursery with Mason's childhood rocking horse and chests full of lead toy soldiers still there waiting to be played with. A wooden fort stood in the corner and a bookcase full of books lined one of the walls. An old bicycle leaned against another wall and balls of every kind and size were stored in a large wicker basket.

There were a cook and maid in residence and lunch was

provided in the huge dining room where the conversation flowed freely. During the afternoon, they piled into a string of cabs which took them around the town so they might see the shops and businesses. Then they were transported back to Doe Bank, buzzing with the excitement of all they had experienced.

## 53

Early one morning, just before Christmas, snow began to fall in large lazy flakes. Wrapped up against the cold, the children raced outside to enjoy themselves by running around and trying to gather enough for a snowball fight.

Mary and the children had been invited to Charity's house for Christmas dinner, as had Elijah and Mason, and Mary had already been to town to buy gifts. She had requested they be wrapped in the shop so she could place them beneath the tree as soon as she got home. Mason had bought the tree and crammed it in the corner of the living room.

Queenie and Owl had baked little biscuits and wrapped them in paper to be hung on the branches, along with the candles the boys fixed in place to be lit later. In the evenings they sang carols and Dora read them *A Christmas Carol.*

Christmas day was full of excitement as presents were opened even before breakfast was ready. The children were elated at being given gifts after so many years of doing without.

Mary felt a warm glow when she heard the children laughing and talking as she stirred the porridge in the pan on the range.

Groans sounded when she called everyone to leave their games and come to eat. The food was hurriedly devoured before the children went back to their toys.

After washing the dishes, Mary joined in with the games she had bought. She and Dora played pick-up sticks while Owl and Queenie tackled tiddlywinks. Skinny wound up the clockwork train and set it on its rails, whooping with delight as it passed through a wooden tunnel. Lofty was trying his hand with the cup and ball, much to the amusement of Carrot, who guffawed loudly when the ball struck Lofty's fingers. Fingers and Whippet were enjoying a game of dominoes.

The morning fled past and then it was time to go to Charity's house. Mason and Elijah came to collect them in a string of cabs, the cabbies happy to work on Christmas day after being promised a handsome tip.

Lunch was a rowdy affair, with each of the children sharing what Mary had bought them and how much they loved their gifts.

After lunch, it was time to open more presents, which Charity had purchased. Wooden pop guns, tops which hummed gently as they spun rapidly, quoits with string hoops, Chinese chequers, a chess set, a whip and top, yo-yos, kaleidoscopes and a zoetrope with a box of extra cards were unwrapped with glee. Gasps of delight and profuse thanks were given.

Then Mason unveiled a large wooden toy box with all the children's names painted on the top, including Dora's.

The whole day was a resounding success, and everyone went home happy, including the cabbies who, having had lunch with their families, had returned to be richly rewarded.

With Christmas over, and in the old tradition, a dark-haired man, namely Mason, was asked to carry in a lump of coal, bringing with it the New Year. Life again settled into normality, and everyone began to look forward to Elijah and Charity's wedding at the beginning of March.

January and February were bitterly cold but no more snow fell. Mary kept the ranges and fires burning day and night to keep the houses warm and cosy.

Mason continued to be a regular visitor and Mary called in on Charity often for afternoon tea.

March came round quickly, and before anyone realised, the wedding was upon them.

On the morning of the wedding, once everyone was dressed in their finery, the constable came calling once more.

'You all look very smart; going out, are you?' he asked.

'We are attending a wedding,' Mary explained.

The constable nodded. 'I thought you might want to know, Mrs Pitt got ten years and will be spending them at Stafford.'

'Ten years! Isn't that a bit harsh?' Mary asked, shocked to her core.

'Not really. I did warn you that theft of finance is dealt with severely as it is considered one of the worst crimes. As I told you it might be, the bank manager's testimony was sufficient for the judge.'

'I see, well, thank you for taking the time to come and tell me.'

The constable nodded and left.

Mary sat and the children gathered around her. 'I feel so guilty for bringing this on my own mother.'

'Mary, you have to remember what she did to you and Dora,' Fingers said.

'I'm not sorry, Mum. As far as I'm concerned, Gran deserves everything coming to her,' Dora said firmly.

'The cabs are here!' Lofty said as he trundled in from next door, and Mary directed everyone to the waiting transport. Fingers' cab set off for Mesty Croft, where he would collect Charity, and the others travelled on to St Bartholomew's church.

Elijah and Mason were there to greet them, and Mary and her little family went inside to settle in the pews. The children buzzed with excitement as they waited for the bride to arrive and grinned when a large lady began pumping the bellows for the organ, then rushed back to her seat to play the music.

Friends of Charity, who she occasionally played Canasta with, were in attendance, dressed in their finery, and a sea of large hats filled the pews on one side of the church. The other side was crowded with businessmen and their wives, all colleagues of Elijah. The men were dressed in dark suits and the ladies were in an array of colours.

All heads turned as Fingers accompanied a radiant Charity down the aisle, he in a fine dark suit and she in an ivory organza dress. The flowers in her hair matched those in the posy she carried.

Elijah thought his heart would burst as he watched Charity glide towards him. She looked like an angel with the light through the stained-glass windows surrounding her.

They reached the end of the aisle just as the organ ran out of air and the large lady sighed with relief as she leaned on the instrument. Carrot and Lofty sniggered and Owl shot them a look which told them to behave.

The ceremony went off without a hitch and the guests congratulated the couple by showering them with rice before a stream of cabs ferried everyone back to Hady Moor House for a slap-up meal.

'Have you decided where you will live now you are married, Aunt Charity?' Mary asked later that evening as the party started to draw to an end.

'Yes, my dear, Elijah has agreed to move in here and rent out his house.'

'That makes sense,' Mason agreed as he joined them and surreptitiously squeezed Mary's hand as he walked past her.

'It's something you two will have to decide upon also,' Charity ventured.

Mary flushed as Mason cleared his throat, something he did when he was embarrassed.

'Have you proposed yet, Mason?' Elijah asked.

'Erm... no... I...'

'Then get on with it, lad,' Elijah said, whilst sidling up to his new wife, 'otherwise someone else will beat you to it.' Elijah was enjoying putting his nephew in the position he had been in himself not so long ago.

'Excuse me, I'll just see what the children are up to,' Mary said, feeling uncomfortable at the teasing. Mason was clearly not thinking about marriage, she thought, because otherwise he would not have been tongue-tied when asked about it. Maybe he just liked her as a companion. Mary couldn't help feeling disappointed at the thought; she had hoped he was feeling the same strong emotions as her, and that one day they might wed.

Gathering her brood, Mary said it was time to be heading for home and Skinny ran outside and whistled loudly for a cab or two.

With further congratulations and grateful thanks, Mary led her family out towards their transport, the children chatting loudly about the day's events.

'I ain't never been to a weddin' before,' Skinny said.

'It was a lovely service,' Queenie commented dreamily, and Owl agreed.

Lofty and Carrot dug each other in the ribs at the serene look on Queenie's face.

In the other cab, Dora and Fingers were discussing the merits of Elijah moving to Hady Moor House while Whippet listened in. Mary, however, was thinking about Mason and their future together. Questions floated through her mind as the cab rattled along. Did she want to be wed again? Would she be betraying Jim's memory? If she married Mason, where would *they* live? What would happen to the children? Would she and Dora have to move into Mason's house and leave the others behind? How would Dora feel about her mum marrying Mason? How did *she* feel about it? Was Mason the man for her? Should she remain single and continue to live at Doe Bank? Would Mason ever ask for her hand in marriage?

With no answers forthcoming, Mary sighed the questions into the air, just as they reached home.

## 54

Stafford Gaol was an imposing building with a gatehouse which stood on Gaol Road. A high brick wall surrounded the whole structure and yard, and it was against this wall that women, some with their children, leaned, waiting to be allowed entry to visit their menfolk. Dressed in rags, the women often walked many miles once every few months, only to be yelled at by incarcerated husbands for not bringing them food or money.

The prison comprised of a reception, a warm/cold bath house, a warders' room, laundry, dining room and small chapel. The cells ran either side of a long corridor or landing, three storeys high. Each of these landings had a large rectangular gap edged with a waist-high wrought iron barrier which allowed the warders to look right down to the ground floor.

The female inmates were all dressed the same, in grey cotton dresses and white cotton bonnets; the warders were in black dresses with a ring of keys hanging on their wide leather belts.

Edith Pitt stood in the governor's office with a female warder at her back.

'You have been brought here, inmate Pitt, to explain why you insist on constantly stirring up trouble. I'm informed that you have, yet again, incited a violent fracas between two other prisoners.'

Edith stood impassive and the governor sighed. Although the warders were women in the female section, the governor who oversaw the entire prison was a man. The men's section was kept quite separate at the other end of the massive structure.

'Have you nothing to say?' Governor Riley prompted.

'I'm innocent!' Edith snapped.

'Ah, as are all the others in here if you did but believe them.'

'Look, it's not my fault if these women can't get along. I mind my own business,' Edith replied.

'Really? So it was not you who informed inmate Giles that inmate Spencer had stolen her blanket?'

'I had nothing to do with it,' Edith lied.

'As I have no proof, on this occasion, I will let it go, although I fear inmate Spencer's hair will never grow back where it was ripped out at the roots.'

Edith shrugged her shoulders, making it clear that she didn't care one way or the other.

'Please ensure you are not brought before me again. Dismissed.'

Edith was taken back to her cell on the top landing which she shared with another woman. The warder pushed her inside, leaving the door open, and Edith grinned widely. She had caused trouble, her favourite pastime, and got away with it yet again. Dragging her cot away from the wall, she pulled out a brick and checked that all the objects she had stolen were still there. Satisfied they were, she returned the cell to its proper condition. Her cellmate was out on the landing with the other women, talking quietly amongst themselves.

Sitting on her cot bed, Edith began to formulate a plan to relieve another inmate of the few pennies she knew the woman had.

When all the cells were unlocked, the inmates gathered in small groups to gossip, and this was a perfect time to carry out her plan. Watching the woman with the pennies chatting, Edith slipped into her cell to make a quick search. Finding the pennies beneath the flock mattress, Edith palmed the coins before walking sedately back to her own cell. Stashing her booty in her hidey-hole, she wandered out to join the others.

It was just before the dinner gong sounded when all hell broke loose. The penny lady was screaming blue murder about her money having been stolen. Another inmate informed on Edith, saying she had seen her enter and leave the cell in question.

Before the warders could make their way along the landing to the angry crowd of women, Edith Pitt had been lifted from her feet and flung over the wrought iron railing.

The scream that came was from another inmate, as Edith landed with a sickening thump on the concrete of the ground floor, a pool of blood spreading around her head.

Chaos reigned as warders blew their whistles and the inmates were herded back to their cells and locked in.

The governor was informed and, with a sigh, he shook his head. At least there would be no more incidents concerning Mrs Pitt. Taking out paper, he began to pen a letter to the woman's relatives, informing them of Edith's unfortunate accident.

Back in Wednesbury, Mary was unaware of her mother's death, and had taken Dora to the market with her. The others were helping where they could with Sam and his building crew.

As they wandered along, Mary broached the subject that had been playing on her mind. 'Dora, what's your opinion of Mason?'

'I like him, Mum, he's funny and doesn't mind joining in games with us.'

'Sweetheart, how would you feel if Mason proposed to me?' Mary asked tentatively.

'I'd love it! I'd have a dad at last and I know you'd be happy again. Do you think he will?'

'I don't know, lovey, but I was rather hoping he might.'

Dora grinned with delight at the prospect. Then a thought struck her. 'Would he come to live with us? I mean, we're a bit cramped already and it will be a while before the extensions are finished.'

'That's a dilemma I've been thinking about. Should we wed, where to live? There's also the others to consider.'

'We could all move to Mason's house, and you could rent out our houses,' Dora said, as though it was the simplest remedy in the world.

'It's something to consider, I agree, but for now I just wanted to know if you would be happy if it came to pass.'

'I would, Mum, I definitely would.'

They walked on, both lost in their own thoughts of their future if Mason found the courage to ask Mary to marry him.

It was a few days later when Mary received the letter from Stafford Prison. Her tears fell as she read how Edith had fallen to her death. The governor had offered his condolences with heartfelt sadness and explained that Mrs Pitt would be interred at the prison's expense in the local graveyard.

Mary wept, surrounded by her family. None of this would have happened had she not walked out that day and left Edith to fend for herself. But they couldn't have carried on the way they were, with Dora Edith's constant victim. All that Mary could do now was try to forgive herself for leaving Edith alone.

Drying her eyes, Mary said, 'I should let Elijah and Charity know.'

'Would you like us to come with you?' Fingers asked.

'No, but thank you for the offer. This is something I have to do by myself.' Mary pulled on her coat, grabbed her bag in which she placed the letter and quietly left the house.

As she walked up the street, a cabbie called out to her, 'Need a cab, missus?'

With a nod, she gave the address and climbed aboard. As the carriage rolled along, she wondered how Charity would receive the news of her sister's death.

Elijah was at his work but Charity made Mary very welcome with coffee and cake as they sat together in the parlour.

'This came in the post today,' Mary said, passing over the letter.

A sadness crept over the older woman's face as she read. Passing the letter back, she said, 'I'm not surprised, Mary, and something tells me it wasn't an accident.' Seeing Mary's puzzled look, she explained her suspicion. 'Edith was ever out for a fight and it's my contention she may have upset someone very badly, in a place it's very unwise to be upsetting people. However, I suppose we shall never really know what actually happened.'

'I agree,' Mary said dolefully.

'It's done now, Mary, so you need to try to put it all behind you and move on. You have so much to look forward to,' Charity said gently.

'I know and I will try.'

They chatted for a while as Charity tried to cheer her niece up. She enquired about the building work and Mary wondered about how Charity was enjoying married life.

'I hope you don't mind, my dear, but I cancelled the food deliveries as you are now in a financial position to take care of yourself and the children.'

'Of course, Aunt Charity, thank you. Those hampers saved our lives and we are very grateful, but as you say, now is the time for me to stand on my own two feet.'

And with a hug for her aunt, Mary left for home.

Once she was alone again, Charity thought, *Edith, you were a tartar and hated by everyone you met. But you were my sister. Rest in peace, you miserable old sod!*

## 55

The building of the extensions was making progress, with the completion of the ground floor walls, but all work ceased as an unexpected and unseasonal snowfall turned the town into a white wonderland. Sledges were hauled out of storage and for those not fortunate enough to own one, a tin tray was made to suffice.

People were taken unawares and grumbled at Mother Nature for this cruelty before she allowed them to welcome spring proper. The smoke from countless chimneys spiralled towards the heavens as fires were kept lit night and day.

Women's long skirts weighed heavy as the hems became saturated by the thick white layer of wetness as they went about their business.

Carriages, cabs and carts were driven warily along the icy streets, the horses fighting to gain purchase with their iron shoes.

Mary shivered as she dressed quickly and went downstairs to poke the fire and feed the range. The kitchen and living room were soon feeling warmer and Mary stirred a huge pan of porridge on the hotplate. Bowls and spoons were already in situ on the table so, wrapping herself in a thick woollen shawl, Mary stepped outside to rattle the gong.

The girls came downstairs and were followed in by the boys, who banged the snow from their boots before coming inside.

After a hot breakfast, Mary set the children some lessons in arithmetic whilst she washed the dishes. She was surprised when a knock came to the door and in walked Mason.

'Come in out of the cold! I didn't expect to see you today, what with the snow and all.'

'A little inclement weather would not prevent me enjoying time with my lady,' Mason said with a grin. 'I thought as it's Sunday we might take a carriage ride around the park.'

Brunswick Park had opened two years previously to celebrate Queen Victoria's golden jubilee, and it was frequented by pedestrians and carriages alike.

'It's a little cold for that, don't you think?'

Lowering his voice to a whisper, Mason said, 'Mary, there's something I need to discuss with you and I can't in front of the children.'

Mary frowned, but she could see that whatever it was, she would only find out if she agreed to go.

'Very well, but we'll need to take a blanket, otherwise we'll freeze.'

'I have one in the cab already,' Mason grinned.

'I'll tell the children, then.'

Mary wondered what was so important that it would drag them out on a bitterly cold day. Was it Elijah – had he fallen ill? Donning her coat and pinning her hat in place, Mary suddenly stopped as the thought struck. Was Mason going to propose today? Her heart quickened its pace as she hoped this was what Mason had in mind. She began to feel nervous, so much so that she stabbed her finger with the hat pin.

*Pull yourself together, girl!* With a deep breath, Mary announced she was ready. Asking the boys to keep the fires burning, and warning them all to stay indoors for fear of them catching cold, Mary and Mason trudged towards the cab.

Jack Frost nipped her nose and Mary pulled up her scarf, leaving only her eyes exposed. She smiled inwardly, thinking she must look like one of those exotic veiled dancers from the east.

Inside the cab, Mason wrapped her in the blanket and banged his cane on the roof. The carriage lurched forward before settling into a slow and steady rhythm.

Pulling down her scarf, Mary asked, 'What is it that you wish to talk to me about?'

'Mary, we've been walking out for a while now and...'

*Here it comes!*

'Well... oh, damn it!'

Mary giggled at his nervousness.

Mason sighed with a smile. 'Mary Parsons, I love you with all my heart. Would you do me the honour of becoming my wife?'

*At last!*

'Before I give you my answer, Mason, there are a couple of things that we need to clear up.' Seeing his frown, she went on swiftly. 'If I were to say yes, then I need to know where we would live. Also, there are the children to consider. I couldn't possibly up and marry and leave them behind.'

'I have a house big enough for all of us, Mary, as you know, and of course the children would stay with us. I can't imagine life without them now. We could get them into school if they so wished, or into work if they decided that's what they wanted.'

'I have a lot of expense tied up in the houses at Doe Bank...'

'I know, but you could rent them out to families who are desperate for a roof over their heads. It would bring in a little revenue for the odd treat for the children.'

Mary considered his words. She didn't need the money, having been so well catered for by her father, but giving a home to families in need struck a chord.

'Please, Mary, say you will marry me and I'll be the happiest man alive – alongside Uncle Eli, that is.'

Mary burst out laughing and then, with a nod, she whispered, 'Yes, I'll marry you, Mason.'

Wrapping his arms around her, he laid his lips gently on hers and that kiss sealed a bond which would last a lifetime. Pulling away a mere inch, Mary whispered, 'I love you, Mason.'

His reply came in the same hushed tones. 'I adore you, Mary, and will until my dying day.'

Their lips met again, and Mary knew in that moment she would enjoy this pleasure every day of her life from now on.

Once they arrived back at Doe Bank, Mason helped Mary from the cab and grinned as she gave a loud whistle.

The children came running out of the house as Mason paid the cabbie. Then he yelled, 'Mary and I are going to be married!' Mason scooped up a handful of snow and threw it and he was bombarded in return. Whoops of joy could be heard all around and Mary laughed as a snowball fight broke out.

The cabbie sat and watched the pure innocent pleasure for a moment before he urged the horse to walk on. *Good luck to you all,* he thought as the cab rolled away.

Dora ran to her mother and threw her arms around Mary's waist. 'Thank you, Mum.'

'What for, sweetheart?'

'For giving me a dad! For making us a family.'

Mary kissed her daughter's hair. Watching the children and Mason lying in the snow making angel's wings with their arms and legs, she knew in her heart that everything would be all right from now on.

# REFERENCES

*Black Country Wit and Humour* by Brendan Hawthorne and Camilla Zajack

*Black Country Jokes and Humour* by Doug Parker

# MORE FROM LINDSEY HUTCHINSON

We hope you enjoyed reading *The Runaway Children*. If you did, please leave a review.

If you'd like to gift a copy, this book is also available as an ebook, digital audio download and audiobook CD.

Sign up to Lindsey Hutchinson's mailing list for news, competitions and updates on future books.

http://bit.ly/LindseyHutchinsonMailingList

*The Children From Gin Barrel Lane*, another gritty Black Country saga from Lindsey Hutchinson, is available now.

# ABOUT THE AUTHOR

**Lindsey Hutchinson** is a bestselling saga author whose novels include *The Children from Gin Barrel Lane*. She was born and raised in Wednesbury, and was always destined to follow in the footsteps of her mother, the multi-million selling Meg Hutchinson.

Follow Lindsey on social media:

- facebook.com/Lindsey-Hutchinson-1781901985422852
- twitter.com/LHutchAuthor
- bookbub.com/authors/lindsey-hutchinson

## ABOUT BOLDWOOD BOOKS

Boldwood Books is a fiction publishing company seeking out the best stories from around the world.

Find out more at www.boldwoodbooks.com

Sign up to the Book and Tonic newsletter for news, offers and competitions from Boldwood Books!

http://www.bit.ly/bookandtonic

We'd love to hear from you, follow us on social media:

facebook.com/BookandTonic

twitter.com/BoldwoodBooks

instagram.com/BookandTonic

Lightning Source UK Ltd.
Milton Keynes UK
UKHW041033200222
398924UK00002B/370